TOMORROW WHEN THE WAR BEGAN

John Marsden lives in an old country cottage at Sandon, Victoria, which he describes as the smallest town in Australia. He enjoys working in his wild, rambling garden, swimming in the creek and taking the dog for walks across the hills.

For some years, John Marsden taught English at secondary schools in Victoria and New South Wales, and in 1991 he spent six months in Paris as the visiting writer at the Keesing Studio.

John Marsden's books are published in fifteen countries and he has won several awards, including the CBC Australian Children's Book of the Year Award in 1988. *Letters from the Inside*, also published by Macmillan, was shortlisted for this award in 1992.

Tomorrow When the War Began is the first title in a series which has been published to wide acclaim in A

*Titles by John Marsden available from
Macmillan Children's Books*

TOMORROW WHEN THE WAR BEGAN

JOHN MARSDEN

MACMILLAN
CHILDREN'S BOOKS

This book was written while the author was in receipt of a writer's fellowship from the Literature Board of the Australia Council, whose help is gratefully acknowledged.

First published 1993 by Pan Macmillan Australia Pty Ltd

First published in Great Britain 1995 by Macmillan Children's Books
This edition reprinted 1998 by Macmillan Children's Books
a division of Macmillan Publishers Limited
25 Eccleston Place, London SW1W 9NF
Basingstoke and Oxford
Associated companies throughout the world
www.macmillan.co.uk

ISBN 0 330 33739 4

57986

A CIP catalogue record for this book is available
from the British Library.

Printed and bound in Great Britain by Mackays of Chatham plc, Kent

To my dear sister Robin Farran:
so much admired.

Acknowledgements

I'm grateful to Charlotte Austin, Frank Austin, Ross Matlock, Jeanne Marsden, Roos Marsden, Catherine Maxwell, Sarah Vickers-Willis and Scott Vickers-Willis for providing some of the ideas, information or stories used in this book.

Chapter One

It's only half an hour since someone – Robyn I think – said we should write everything down, and it's only twenty-nine minutes since I got chosen, and for those twenty-nine minutes I've had everyone crowded around me gazing at the blank page and yelling ideas and advice. Rack off guys! I'll never get this done. I haven't got a clue where to start and I can't concentrate with all this noise.

OK, that's better. I've told them to give me some peace, and Homer backed me up, so at last they've gone and I can think straight.

I don't know if I'll be able to do this. I might as well say so now. I know why they chose me, because I'm meant to be the best writer, but there's a bit more to it than just being able to write. There's a few little things can get in the way. Little things like feelings, emotions.

Well, we'll come to that later. Maybe. We'll have to wait and see.

I'm down at the creek now, sitting on a fallen tree. Nice tree. Not an old rotten one that's been eaten by witchetty grubs but a young one with a smooth

1

reddish trunk and the leaves still showing some green. It's hard to tell why it fell – it looks so healthy – but maybe it grew too close to the creek. It's good here. This pool's only about ten metres by three but it's surprisingly deep – up to your waist in the middle. There's constant little concentric ripples from insects touching it as they skim across the surface. I wonder where they sleep, and when. I wonder if they close their eyes when they sleep. I wonder what their names are. Busy, anonymous, sleepless insects.

To be honest I'm only writing about the pool to avoid doing what I'm meant to be doing. That's like Chris, finding ways to avoid doing things he doesn't want to do. See: I'm not holding back. I warned them I wouldn't.

I hope Chris doesn't mind my being chosen to do this instead of him, because he is a really good writer. He did look a bit hurt, a bit jealous even. But he hasn't been in this from the start, so it wouldn't have worked.

Well, I'd better stop biting my tongue and start biting the bullet. There's only one way to do this and that's to tell it in order, chronological order. I know writing it down is important to us. That's why we all got so excited when Robyn suggested it. It's terribly, terribly important. Recording what we've done, in words, on paper, it's got to be our way of telling ourselves that we mean something, that we matter. That the things we've done have made a difference. I don't know how big a difference, but a difference. Writing it down means we might be remembered. And by God that matters to us. None of us wants to end up as a pile of dead white bones, unnoticed, unknown, and worst of all, with no one knowing or appreciating the risks we've run.

That makes me think that I should be writing this like a history book, in very serious language, all formal. But I can't do that. Everyone's got their own way and this is mine. If they don't like my way they'll have to find someone else.

OK, better do it then.

It all began when… They're funny, those words. Everyone uses them, without thinking what they mean. When does anything begin? With everyone, it begins when you're born. Or before that, when your parents got married. Or before that, when your parents were born. Or when your ancestors colonised the place. Or when humans came squishing out of the mud and slime, dropped off their flippers and fins, and started to walk. But all the same, all that aside, for what's happened to us there was quite a definite beginning.

So: it all began when Corrie and I said we wanted to go bush, go feral for a few days over the Christmas holidays. It was just one of those stupid things: 'Oh wouldn't it be great if…' We'd camped out quite often, been doing it since we were kids, taking the motorbikes all loaded with gear and going down to the river, sleeping under the stars, or slinging a bit of canvas between two trees on cold nights. So we were used to that. Sometimes another friend would come along, Robyn or Fi usually. Never boys. At that age you think boys have as much personality as coat hangers and, you don't notice their looks.

Then you grow up.

Well there we were, only weeks ago, though I can hardly believe it, lying in front of the television watching some junk and talking about the holidays. Corrie said, 'We haven't been down to the river for ages. Let's do that.'

'OK. Hey, let's ask Dad if we can have the Landrover.'

'OK. Hey, let's see if Kevin and Homer want to come.'

'God yeah, boys! But we'd never be allowed.'

'I reckon we might. It's worth a try.'

'OK. Hey, if we get the Landrover, let's go further. Wouldn't it be great if we could go right up to Tailor's and into Hell.'

'Yeah OK, let's ask.'

Tailor's, Tailor's Stitch, is a long line, an arete, that goes dead straight from Mt Martin to Wombegonoo. It's rocky, and very narrow and steep in places, but you can walk along it, and there's a bit of cover. The views are fantastic. You can drive almost up on to it at one point, near Mt Martin, on an old logging track that's hard to find now, it's so overgrown. Hell is what's on the other side of Tailor's, a cauldron of boulders and trees and blackberries and feral dogs and wombats and undergrowth. It's a wild place, and I didn't know anyone who'd been there, though I'd stood on the edge and looked down at it quite often. For one thing I couldn't see how you'd get in there. The cliffs all around it are spectacular, hundreds of metres high in places. There's a series of small cliffs called Satan's Steps that drop into it, but believe me, if these are steps, the Great Wall of China is our back fence. If there was any access the cliffs had to be the way, and I'd always wanted to give it a go. The locals all told stories about the Hermit from Hell, an ex-murderer who was supposed to have lived up there for years. He was meant to have killed his own wife and child. I wanted to believe in his existence but I found it a bit difficult. My brain kept asking myself awkward questions like: 'How come he didn't get hung, like they did to murderers in those days?' Still, it was a good story and I hoped it was true; not the murders part but the hermit part at least.

Anyway, the whole thing, the trip, grew from there. We made this casual decision to do it, and we immediately let ourselves in for a lot of hard work. The first job was to persuade our mums and dads to let us go. It's not that they don't trust us, but as Dad said, 'It's a pretty big ask'. They spent a lot of time not saying no, but trying to talk us into other things instead. That's the way most parents operate I think. They don't like to start a fight so they suggest alternatives that they think they can say yes to and they hope you might say yes to. 'Why don't you go down the river again?' 'Why don't you ask Robyn and Meriam instead of the boys?' 'Why don't you just take bikes? Or even horses? Make it a real old-fashioned campout. That'd be fun.'

Mum's idea of fun was making jam for the Preserves section of the Wirrawee Show, so she was hardly an authority on the subject. I feel a bit odd, writing things like that, considering what we've all been through, but I'm going to be honest, not mushy.

Finally we came to an agreement, and it wasn't too bad, considering. We could take the Landrover but I was the only one allowed to drive it, even though Kevin had his P's and I didn't. But Dad knows I'm a good driver. We could go to the top of Tailor's Stitch. We could invite the boys but we had to have more people: at least six and up to eight. That was because Mum and Dad thought there was less chance of an orgy if there were more people. Not that they'd admit that was the reason – they said it was to do with safety – but I know them too well.

And yes, I've written that 'o' in 'know' carefully – I wouldn't want it to be confused with an 'e'.

We had to promise not to take grog and smokes, and we had to promise that the boys wouldn't. It made me wonder about the way adults turn growing up into such a complicated process. They expect you to be always on the lookout for a chance to do something wild. Sometimes they even put ideas in your head. I don't think we would have bothered to take any grog or smokes anyway. Too expensive, for one thing – we were all pretty broke after Christmas. But the funny thing is that when our parents thought we were doing something wild we never were, and when they thought we were being innocent we were usually up to something. They never gave me a hard time about the school play rehearsals for instance, but I spent all my time there with Steve, undoing each other's buttons and buckles, then frantically doing them up again when Mr Kassar started bellowing, 'Steve! Ellie! Are they at it again? Someone get me a crowbar!'

Very humorous guy, Mr Kassar.

We ended up with a list of eight, counting us. We didn't ask Elliot, because he's so lazy, or Meriam, because she was doing work experience with Fi's parents. But five minutes after we made the list, one of the boys on it, Chris Lang, turned up at my place with his dad. So we immediately put the question to them. Mr Lang's a big guy who always wears a tie, no matter where he is or what he's doing. He seems kind of heavy and serious to me. Chris says his father was born on the corner of Straight and Narrow, and that sums it up. When his dad's around, Chris stays pretty quiet. But we asked them as they sat at our kitchen table, pigging out on Mum's date scones, and we got knocked back in one sentence. It turned out that Mr and Mrs Lang were going overseas, and even though they had a worker, Chris had to stay home and keep an eye on the place. So that was a bad start to our plans.

Next day though, I took a bike and rode across the paddocks to Homer's. Normally I'd go by road, but Mum'd been getting a bit twitchy about the new cop in Wirrawee, who'd been booking people left, right and centre. His first week in town he booked the magistrate's wife for not wearing a seatbelt. Everyone was being careful till they'd broken this guy in.

I found Homer down at the creek testing a valve that he'd just cleaned out. As I arrived he was holding it high, watching optimistically to see if it was leaking. 'Look at that,' he said as I got off the Yamaha. 'Tight as a drum.'

'What was the problem?'

'I don't know. All I know is that three minutes ago it was losing water and now it isn't. That's good enough for me.' I picked up the pipe and held it for him as he started screwing the valve back on. 'I hate pumps,' he said. 'When Poppa pops off I'm going to put dams in every paddock.'

'Good. You can hire my earth-moving business to put them in.'

'Oh, is that your latest?' He squeezed the muscles on my right upper arm. 'You'll be able to dig dams by hand the way you're going.' I gave a sudden shove, to try to push him into the creek, but he was too strong. I watched him pump the pipe up and down, to force water into it, then helped him carry buckets up to the pump to finish the priming. On the way I told him our plans.

'Oh yeah, I'll have a go at that,' he said. 'I'd rather

we went to a tropical resort and drank cocktails with umbrellas in them, but this'll do in the meantime.'

We went back to his place for lunch, and he asked his parents for permission to come on the camp. 'Ellie and I are going bush for a few days,' he announced. That was Homer's way of asking permission. His mother didn't react at all; his father raised an eyebrow from above his cup of coffee; but his brother started firing the questions. When I gave the dates, his brother, George, said: 'What about the Show?'

'We can't go any earlier,' I said. 'The Mackenzies are shearing.'

'Yeah, but who's going to groom the bulls for the Show?'

'You're a class act with a hair dryer,' Homer said. 'I've seen you in front of the mirror Saturday nights. Just don't go woggy with the bulls and put oil through their coats.' He said to me, 'Poppa's got a forty-four-gallon drum of oil in the shed, especially for George on Saturday nights'.

As George was not known for his sense of humour, I kept my eyes down and had another mouthful of tabbouli.

So Homer was organised, and Corrie rang that night to say Kevin was coming too. 'He wasn't all that keen,' she said. 'I think he'd rather go to the Show. But he's doing it for me.'

'Er, yuk, vomit, spew,' I said. 'Tell him to go to the Show if that's what he wants. There's plenty of guys who'd kill to come with us.'

'Yeah, but they're all under twelve,' Corrie sighed. 'Kevin's little brothers are desperate to come. But they're too young, even for you.'

'And too old for you,' I replied rudely.

8

I rang Fiona after the call from Corrie, and told her our plans. 'Do you want to come?' I asked.

'Oh!' She sounded amazed, as if I'd told her all about the trip just to entertain her. 'Oh gosh. Do you want me to?'

I didn't even bother to answer that one.

'Oh gosh.' Fi was the only person I knew under sixty who said 'gosh'. 'Who else is coming?'

'Corrie and me. Homer and Kevin. And we thought we'd ask Robyn and Lee.'

'Well, I'd like to. Wait a sec, and I'll go and ask.'

It was a long wait. At last she came back with a series of questions. She relayed my answers to her mother or father, or both, in the background. After about ten minutes of this there was another long conversation; then Fi picked up the phone again.

'They're being difficult,' she sighed. 'I'm sure it'll be OK but my mum wants to ring your mum to make sure. Sorry.'

'That's cool. I'll put you down with a question mark and I'll talk to you at the weekend, OK?'

I hung up. It was getting hard to use the phone, because the TV was yelling at me. Mum had it turned up too loud, so she could hear the News in the kitchen. An angry face filled the screen. I stopped and watched for a moment. 'We've got a wimp for a Foreign Minister,' the face was shouting. 'He's weak, he's gutless, he's the new Neville Chamberlain. He doesn't understand the people he's dealing with. They respect strength, not weakness!'

'Do you think defence is high on the Government's agenda?' the interviewer asked.

'High? High? You must be joking! Do you know what they've cut from the defence budget?'

Thank goodness I'm getting away from this for a week, I thought.

I went into Dad's office and rang Lee. It took a while to explain to his mother that I wanted her son. Her English wasn't too crash hot. Lee was funny when he came to the phone, almost suspicious. He seemed to react slowly to everything I said, as though he was weighing it up. 'I'm meant to be playing at the Commemoration Day concert,' he said, when I told him the dates. There was a silence, which I finally broke.

'Well do you want to come?'

He laughed then. 'It sounds more fun than the concert.'

Corrie had been puzzled when I'd said I wanted to ask Lee. We didn't really hang round with him at school. He seemed a serious guy, very into his music, but I just thought he was interesting. I suddenly realised that we didn't have that much time left at school, and I didn't want to leave without getting to know people like Lee. There were people in our year who still didn't know the names of everyone else in the form! And we were such a small school. I had this intense curiosity about some kids, and the more different they were to the people I normally hung around with, the more curious I was.

'Well, what do you think?' I asked. There was another long pause. Silence makes me uncomfortable, so I kept talking. 'Do you want to ask your mum and dad?'

'No, no. I'll handle them. Yeah, I'll come.'

'You don't sound all that keen.'

'Hey, I'm keen! I was just thinking about the problems. But it's cool, I'll be there. What'll I bring?'

My last call was to Robyn.

'Oh Ellie,' she wailed. 'It'd be great! But I'd never be allowed.'

'Come on Robyn, you're tough. Put the pressure on them.'

She sighed. 'Oh Ellie, you don't know what my parents are like.'

'Well ask them, anyway. I'll wait on.'

'OK.'

After a few minutes I heard the bumping noises of the phone being picked up again, so I asked, 'Well? Did you con them into it?'

Unfortunately it was Mr Mathers who answered.

'No Ellie, she hasn't conned us into it.'

'Oh Mr Mathers!' I was embarrassed, but laughing too, cos I knew I could twist Mr Mathers round my pinkie.

'Now what's this all about, Ellie?'

'Well, we thought it was time we showed independence and initiative and all those other good things. We want to do a bushwalk along Tailor's Stitch for a few days. Get away from the sex and vice of Wirrawee into the clean wholesome air of the mountains.'

'Hmm. And no adults?'

'Oh Mr Mathers, you're invited, as long as you're under thirty, OK?'

'That's discrimination Ellie.'

We kidded around for five minutes till he started getting serious. 'You see Ellie, we just think you kids are a bit young to be careering around the bush on your own.'

'Mr Mathers, what were you doing when you were our age?'

11

He laughed. 'All right, one to you. I was jackaroo-ing at Callamatta Downs. That was before I got smart and put on a collar and tie.' Mr Mathers was an insurance agent.

'So, what we're doing's small time compared to jackarooing at Callamatta Downs!'

'Hmm.'

'After all, what's the worst thing that could happen? Hunters in four-wheel drives? They'd have to come through our place, and Dad'd stop them. Bushfires? There's so much rock up there we'd be safer than we would at home. Snakebite? We all know how to treat snakebite. We can't get lost, cos Tailor's Stitch is like a highway. I've been going up into that country since I could walk.'

'Hmm.'

'How about we take out insurance with you Mr Mathers? Would you say yes then? Is it a deal?'

Robyn rang back the next night to say it was a deal, even without the insurance. She was pleased and excited. She'd had a long conversation with her parents; the best one ever, she said. This was the biggest thing they'd ever trusted her on, so she was keen for it to work out. 'Oh Ellie, I hope there's no disasters,' she kept saying.

The funny thing about it was that if parents ever had a daughter they could trust it was the Mathers and Robyn, but they didn't seem to have worked it out yet. The biggest problem she was ever likely to give them was being late to church. And that'd probably be because she was helping a boy scout across the road.

Things kept going well. Mum and I were in town shopping, Saturday morning, and we ran into Fi and her mum. The two mums had a long serious conversation while Fi and I looked in Tozers' window and tried to eavesdrop. Mum was doing a lot of reassuring. 'Very sensible,' I heard her say. 'They're all very sensible.' Luckily she didn't mention Homer's latest trick: he'd just been caught pouring a line of solvent across the road and lighting it from his hiding place when a car got close. He'd done it half a dozen times before he got caught. I couldn't imagine the shock it must have given the drivers of the cars.

Anyway, whatever Mum said to Fi's mum worked, and I was able to cross off the question mark next to Fi's name. Our list of eight was down to seven, but they were all definite and we were happy with them. Well, we were happy with ourselves, and the other five were good. I'll try to describe them the way they were then – or the way I thought they were, because of course they've changed, and my knowledge of them has changed.

For instance, I always thought of Robyn as fairly quiet and serious. She got effort certificates at school every year, and she was heavily into church stuff, but I knew there was more to her than that. She liked to win. You could see it at sport. We were in the same netball team and honestly, I was embarrassed by some of the things she did. Talk about determined. The moment the game started she was like a helicopter on heat, swooping and darting around everywhere, bumping people aside if she had to. If you got weak umpires Robyn could do as much damage in one game as an aerial gunship. Then the game would end and Robyn would be quietly shaking everyone's hands, saying 'Well played', back to her normal self. Quite strange. She's small, Robyn, but strong, nuggety, and beautifully balanced. She skims lightly across the ground, where the rest of us trudge across it like it's made of mud.

I should exempt Fi from that though, because she's light and graceful too. Fi was always a bit of a hero to me, someone I looked up to as the perfect person. When she did something wrong I'd say, 'Fi! Don't do that! You're my role model!' I love her beautiful delicate skin. She has what my mother calls 'fine features'. She looked like she'd never done any hard work in her life, never been in the sun, never got her hands dirty, and that was all true, because unlike us rurals she lived in town and spent more time playing piano than drenching sheep or marking lambs. Her parents are both solicitors.

Kevin, now he was more your typical rural. He's older than the rest of us but he was Corrie's man, so he had to come or she would have lost interest straightaway.

The first thing you noticed about Kevin was his wide wide mouth. The second thing you noticed was the size of his hands. They were enormous, like trowels. He was known for having a big ego and he liked to take the credit for everything; he annoyed me quite often for that, but I still thought he was the best thing that ever happened in Corrie's life because before she started going round with him she was too quiet and unnoticed. They used to talk a lot at school, and then she'd tell me what a sensitive caring guy he was. Although I couldn't always see that myself, I could see the way she started getting so much more confident from going with him, and I liked that.

I always pictured Kevin in twenty years, when he'd be President of the Show Society and playing cricket for the club on Saturdays and talking about fat lamb prices and bringing up his three kids – with Corrie maybe. That was the kind of world we were used to. We never seriously thought it would change much.

Lee lived in town, like Fi. 'Lee and Fi, from Wirrawee,' we used to sing. That was all they had in common though. Lee was as dark as Fi was fair. He had a black crewcut and deep brown intelligent eyes, and a nice soft voice which clips the ends off some of his words. His father's Thai and his mother's Vietnamese, and they had a restaurant which served Asian food. Pretty good restaurant too; we went there a lot. Lee was good at Music and Art; in fact he was good at most things, but he could be very annoying when things went against him. He'd go into long sulks and not talk to anyone for days at a time.

The last one was Homer, who lived down the road from me. Homer was wild, outrageous. He didn't care what he did or what anyone thought. I always remember going there for lunch, when we were little kids. Mrs Yannos tried to make Homer eat Brussels sprouts; they had a massive argument which ended with Homer chucking the sprouts at his mum. One of them hit her in the forehead, pretty hard too. I watched goggle-eyed. I'd never seen anything like it. If I'd tried that at home I'd have been chained to the tractor and used as a clodbuster. When we were in Year 8 Homer organised some of his madder mates into daily games of what he called Greek Roulette. In Greek Roulette you'd go every lunchtime to a room that was away from teachers' eyes and then you'd take it in turns to walk up to a window and head-butt it. Each person kept doing it till the bell went for afternoon classes or the window broke, whichever came first. If it was your head that broke the window then you – or your parents – had to foot the bill for a new one. They broke a lot of windows playing Greek Roulette, before the school finally woke up to what was going on.

Homer always seemed to be in trouble. Another of his favourite little amusements was to watch for workmen going on the roof at school to fix leaks or get balls or replace guttering. Homer would wait till they were safely up there, working away hard at whatever they had to do, then he'd strike. Half an hour later you'd hear yells and cries from the roof: 'Help! Get us down from here! Some mongrel's pinched our bloody ladder!'

Homer had been quite short as a little kid but he'd filled out and grown a lot in the last few years, until he ended up one of the biggest guys in the school. They were always at him to play footy, but he hated most sports and wouldn't join a team for anything. He liked hunting and would often ring my parents to ask if he and his brother could come on to our place to wipe out a few more rabbits. And he liked swimming. And he liked music, some of it quite weird.

Homer and I had spent all our free time together when we were little, and we were still close.

So that was the Famous Five. I guess Corrie and I made it the Secret Seven. Hah! Those books don't have a lot of bearing on what's happened to us. I can't think of any books I've read – or films I've seen – that relate much to us. We've all had to rewrite the scripts of our lives the last few weeks. We've learnt a lot and we've had to figure out what's important, what matters – what really matters. It's been quite a time.

Chapter Two

The plan was to leave at eight o'clock, nice and early. By about ten o'clock we were nearly ready. By 10.30 we were about four k's from home, starting the ascent to Tailor's Stitch. It's a long slow grunt up a track that's become a real mess over the years; holes so big that I thought we'd lose the Landrover in them, mud slides, creek crossings. I don't know how many times we stopped for fallen trees. We'd brought the chain saw and after a while Homer suggested we keep it running and he'd nurse it as we drove along, to save having to start it when we came to another log. I don't think he was serious. I hope he wasn't serious.

It had been a long time since anyone had been up there. We always know, because they have to come through our paddocks to get to the spur. If Dad had known how bad the track was he'd never have let us take the Landrover. He trusts my driving, but not that much. Still, we bounced along, me wrestling with the wheel, doing a steady five k's, with occasional bursts up to ten. There was another unscheduled stop about half way when Fi decided she was going to be sick. I stopped fast, she exited through the rear door looking

17

white as a corpse, and donated a sticky mess in the bushes for the benefit of any passing feral dogs or cats.

It was not a pretty sight. Everything Fi did she did gracefully, but even Fi found it hard to be graceful while she was vomiting. After that she walked quite a while, but the rest of us continued to lurch on up the spur in the Landie. It was actually fun, in a strange sort of way. Like Lee said, it was better than the Cocktail Shaker ride at the Show, because it was longer – and it was free.

We were actually missing the Show to come on this trip. We'd left the day before Commemoration Day, when the whole country stops, but in our district people don't just stop. They stop and then they converge on Wirrawee, because Commemoration Day is traditionally the day of the Wirrawee Show. It's quite an occasion. Still, we didn't mind missing it. There's a limit to the number of balls you can roll down the clown's throat, and there's a limit to the number of times you can get excited over your mother winning Best Decorated Cake. A year's break from the Show wouldn't do us any harm.

That's what we thought.

It was about half past two when we got to the top. Fi had ridden the last couple of k's, but we were all relieved to get out of the Landie and stretch our bones. We came out on the south side of a knoll near Mt Martin. That was the end of the vehicle track: from then on it was shanks's pony. But for the time being we wandered around and admired the view. On one side you could see the ocean: beautiful Cobbler's Bay, one of my favourite places, and according to Dad one of the world's great natural harbours, used only by the occasional fishing boat or cruising yacht. It was too far from the city for anything else. We could see a couple of ships there this time though; one looked like a large trawler maybe. The water looked as blue as royal blood; deep and dark and still. In the opposite direction Tailor's Stitch seamed its way to the summit of Mt Martin, a sharp straight ridge, bare black rocks forming a thin line as though a surgeon had made a giant incision centuries ago. Another view faced back down the way we'd come; the track invisible under its canopy of trees and creepers. Way in the distance you got glimpses of the rich farmland of the Wirrawee district, dotted with houses and clumps of trees, the lazy Wirrawee River curving slowly through it.

And on the other side was Hell.

'Wow,' said Kevin, taking a long look into it. 'We're going to get into there?'

'We're going to try,' I said, having doubts already but trying to sound strong and sure.

'It's impressive,' said Lee. 'I'm impressed.'

'I've got two questions,' said Kevin, 'but I'll only ask one of them. How?'

'What's the other one?'

'The other one is "Why?". But I'm not going to ask that. Just tell me how and I'll be satisfied. I'm easily satisfied.'

'That's not what Corrie says,' said Homer, beating me to it.

A few rocks were thrown; there was some wrestling; Homer nearly took the fast route into Hell. That's two things guys are addicted to, throwing rocks and wrestling, but I've noticed these guys don't seem to do either any more. I wonder why.

'So how are we going to get in there?' Kevin asked again, at last.

I pointed to the right. 'There it is. That's our route.'

'That? That collection of cliffs?'

He was exaggerating a bit, but not much. Satan's Steps are huge granite blocks that look like they were chucked there in random descending order by some drunken giant, back in the Stone Age. There's no vegetation on them: they're uncompromisingly bare. The more I looked at them the more unlikely it all seemed, but that didn't stop me making my big motivational speech.

'Guys, I don't know if it's possible or not, but there's plenty of people round Wirrawee who say it is. If you believe the stories, there was an old ex-murderer lived in there for years – the Hermit from Hell. If some pensioner can do it, we sure can. I think we should give it our best shot. Let's make like dress-makers and get the tuck in there.'

'Gee Ellie,' said Lee with respect, 'now I understand why you're captain of the netball team.'

'How do you get to be an ex-murderer?' Robyn asked.

'Eh?'

'Well, what's the difference between an ex-murderer and a murderer?'

Robyn always did go straight to the point.

'I've got one more question,' Kevin said.

'Yeah?'

'Do you actually know anyone who's been down there?'

'Um, let's get the packs out of the Landie.'

We did that, then sat against them, admiring the views and the old blue sky, and munching on chicken and salad. Fi's pack was in direct line of vision from me, and the more I looked at it the more I began to realise how swollen it seemed.

'Fi,' I said at last; 'just what have you got in that pack?'

She sat up, looking startled. 'What do you mean? Just clothes and stuff. Same as everyone else.'

'What clothes exactly?'

'What Corrie told me. Shirts. Jumpers. Gloves, socks, undies, towel.'

'But what else? That can't be all.'

She started looking a bit embarrassed.

'Pyjamas.'

'Oh Fi.'

'Dressing gown.'

'Dressing gown? Fi!'

'Well, you never know who you'll meet.'

'What else?'

'I'm not telling you any more. You'll all laugh at me.'

'Fi, we've still got to get the food into these packs. And then carry them God knows how far.'

'Oh. Do you think I should take out the pillow then?'

We formed a committee of six to reorganise Fi's backpack for her. Fi was not a member of the committee. After that we distributed the food that Corrie and I had so carefully bought. There seemed to be a mountain of it, but there were seven of us and we planned to be away five days. But try as we might we couldn't get it all in. Some of the bulky items were a big problem. We ended up having to make some tough decisions, between the Vita Brits and the marshmallows, the pita bread and the jam doughnuts, the muesli and the chips. I'm ashamed to say what won in each case, but we rationalised everything by saying, 'Well, we mightn't get far from the

Landie anyway, so we can always come back for stuff'.

At about five o'clock we got moving, packs on our backs like giant growths, strange protuberances. We set off along the ridge, Robyn leading, Kevin and Corrie quite a way in the rear, talking softly, more absorbed in each other than in the scenery. The ground was hard and dry; although Tailor's Stitch was straight, the track wound around, on it and off it, but the footing was easy and the sun still high in the sky. We were each carrying three full water bottles, which added a lot to the weight of the packs, but which still wouldn't last us long. We were relying on finding water in Hell, assuming we could get in there. Otherwise we'd return to the Landie in the morning for more water. When the supply in the jerry cans there gave out we'd drive a couple of k's down the track to a spring where I'd often camped with Mum and Dad.

I walked along with Lee, and we talked about horror movies. He was an expert: he must have seen a thousand. That surprised me because I knew him mainly for his piano and violin, which didn't seem to go with horror movies. He said he watched them late at night, when he couldn't sleep. I got the feeling he was probably quite a lonely guy.

From the top, Satan's Steps looked as wild and forbidding as they had from a distance. We stood and looked, waiting for Kevin and Corrie to catch up.

'Hmm,' said Homer. 'Interesting.'

That was about the shortest sentence I'd ever heard from him.

'There must be a way,' Corrie said, arriving at that moment.

'When we were kids,' I said, 'we used to say that looked like a track, down to the left there. We always told ourselves that it was the Hermit's path. We used to scare ourselves by imagining that he'd appear at any moment.'

'He was probably just a nice, misunderstood old man,' Fi said.

'Don't think so,' I said. 'They say he murdered his wife and baby.'

'I don't think it's a path, anyway,' Corrie said, 'just a fault-line in the rock.'

We kept standing and looking for quite a while, as if staring at the tumbled rocks would cause a path to appear, as if this were Narnia or somewhere. Homer wandered along the escarpment a bit further. 'We could get over the first block I think,' he called back to us. 'That ledge on the other side, it looks like it drops pretty close to the ground at the far corner.'

We followed over to where he stood. It certainly looked possible.

'Suppose we get down there and can't go any further?' Fi asked.

'Then we climb back and try something else,' Robyn said.

'What if we can't get back?'

'What goes down must come up,' Homer said, making it clear how much attention he'd been paying in Science over the years.

'Let's do it,' Corrie said, with surprising firmness. I was glad. I didn't want to push people too much but I felt that the whole success or failure of this expedition reflected on me, or at least on Corrie and me. We'd talked them into coming, we'd promised them a good time, and it was our idea to take the plunge into

Hell. If we had a miserable failure I'd feel awful. It'd be like throwing a party, then playing Mum's 'Themes from Popular TV Shows' all evening.

At least they seemed willing to take a shot at the first of Satan's Steps. But even the first step was difficult. We had to drop into a tangle of old logs and blackberries, then scramble up the tilted scarred face of the rock. We got quite scarred ourselves. There was a fair bit of swearing and sweating and pulling other people up and hanging on to other people's packs before we were all standing on top, peering down at Homer's ledge.

'If they're all as difficult as this...' Fi panted, without needing to finish the sentence.

'Over here,' Homer said. He got on his hands and knees, turned to face us, then slid backwards over the edge.

'Oh yes?' Fi said.

'No worries,' we heard Homer say. There was a worry, and that was how we were going to get back up again, but no one else mentioned it so I didn't. I think we were too caught up in the thrill of the chase. Robyn followed Homer; then Kevin, with much scrabbling and grunting, lowered himself cautiously after them. I went next, scratching my hand a bit. It wasn't easy because the heavy packs kept wanting to overbalance us, to pull us backwards. By the time I got down, Homer and Robyn were already jumping off the end of the ledge and fighting their way through the scrub to inspect the second huge block of granite.

'The other side looks better,' Lee said. I followed him round there and we inspected the possibilities. It was very difficult. There was quite a sheer drop either side of the block, despite the bushes and grasses growing out of the cliff. And the rock itself was sheer and high. Our only hope was an old fallen log that disappeared into the shadows and undergrowth but at least seemed to be going in the right direction.

'That's our path,' I said.

'Hmmm,' Homer said, coming up beside us.

I straddled the log and started a slow slide down it.

'She loves it, doesn't she?' Kevin said. I grinned as I heard the slap of Corrie's hand hitting some part of Kevin's exposed flesh. The log was soft and damp but was holding together. It was surprisingly long, and I realised it was taking me under the front of the rock. Huge black beetles and slaters and earwigs started spilling out of the wood between my legs as I got towards the thin and more rotten end. I grinned again, hoping I'd scared them all away before Fi followed me down here.

When I stood up I found I was under an overhang, free of vegetation but facing a screen of trees that almost concealed the next giant block. We'd be able to force a way through the screen, no doubt getting torn and scratched a lot more, but there was no guarantee we could get around or over or under the granite. I sidestepped along, peering through the screen, looking for possibilities, as the others started joining me. Fi was the fourth, arriving a little breathless but without fuss; funnily enough it was Kevin who was unnerved by the insects. He slid the last few yards down the tree in a rush, yelling hysterically, 'God no, help, there's creepy-crawlies everywhere! Get them off me! Get them off me!' He spent the next three minutes brushing himself fiercely, spinning round and round in the narrow space we had, trying to catch glimpses of any more that might be on him, shaking his clothes frantically. I couldn't help wondering how he coped with fly-struck sheep.

Things calmed down with Kevin but we still couldn't see any way out of the overhang.

'Well,' said Robyn cheerfully, 'looks like we camp here for a week.'

There was a bit of a silence.

'Ellie,' Lee said kindly, 'I don't think we're going to find a way down. And the further we go, the harder it's going to be to get back.'

'Let's just try for one more step,' I asked, then added, a little wildly, 'Three's my lucky number.'

We poked around a bit more, but rather doubtfully. Finally Corrie said, 'There might be a chance if we wriggle through here. We might be able to get around the side somewhere.'

The gap she'd picked was so narrow we had to take our packs off to get through it, but I was game, so I took Corrie's pack while she wrestled her way into a prickly overgrown hole. Her head disappeared, then her back, then her legs. I heard Kevin say, 'This is crazy', then Corrie said, 'OK, now my pack', so I pushed that through after her. Then, leaving Robyn to look after my pack, I followed.

I soon realised that Corrie had the right idea, but it sure was difficult. If I wasn't such a stubborn pig-headed idiot I would have surrendered by this point. We ended up crawling along like myxo'd rabbits, me pushing Corrie's pack ahead of me. But I caught glimpses of a wall of rock on my left, and we were definitely going downhill, so I figured we were probably getting around the third of Satan's Steps. Then Corrie paused, in front of me, forcing me to stop too.

'Hey!' she said. 'Can you hear what I hear?'

There are some questions that really annoy me, like 'What do you know?', 'Are you working to your full capacity?' (our Form teacher's favourite), 'Guess what I'm thinking?', and 'What on earth do you think you're doing young lady?' (Dad, when he's annoyed). I don't like any of them. And 'Can you hear what I hear?' is in the same category. Plus I was tired, hot, frustrated. So I gave a bad-tempered answer. After a minute's pause Corrie, showing more patience than me, said, 'There's water ahead. Running water.'

I listened, and then realised I could hear it too. So I passed the word back to the others. It was only a small thing, but it kept us going that little bit longer. I crawled on grimly, listening to the sound get louder and closer. It had to be quite a busy stream, which at this altitude meant a spring. We could all do with a fresh cold drink of the water that came from these mountain springs. We'd need it for the struggle back up to the top of Hell. And it was time we started that struggle. It was getting late; time to set up a campsite.

Suddenly I was at the stream and there was Corrie, standing on a rock grinning at me.

'Well, we found something,' I said, grinning back.

It was a pretty little thing. The sun didn't reach it, so it was dark and cool and secret. The water bubbled over rocks that were green and slippery with moss. I knelt and soaked my face, then lapped like a dog as the others started to arrive. There wasn't much room but Robyn started exploring in one direction, stepping gingerly from rock to rock, as Lee did the same in the other direction. I admired their energy.

'It's a nice creek,' said Fi, 'but Ellie, we'd better start heading back up the top.'

27

'I know. Let's just have a relax first, for five minutes. We've earned it.'

'This is worse than the Outward Bound course,' Homer complained.

'I wish I'd gone on that now,' Fi said. 'You all went, didn't you?'

I'd gone on the course, and enjoyed it. I'd done a lot of camping with my parents but Outward Bound had given me a taste for something tougher. I'd just started thinking about it, remembering, when suddenly Robyn reappeared. The look on her face was almost frightening. In the dense overgrowth I couldn't stand, but I straightened up as far as I could, and quickly.

'What's happened?'

Robyn said, with the air of someone who is hearing her own voice but not believing her own words, 'I just found a bridge'.

Chapter Three

The path was covered with leaves and sticks, and was a bit overgrown in places, but compared to what we'd been down, it was like a freeway. We stood spread out along it, marvelling. I felt almost dizzy with relief and astonishment and gratification.

'Ellie,' Homer said solemnly, 'I'll never call you a stupid dumb obstinate slagheap again.'

'Thanks Homer.'

It was a sweet moment.

'Tell you what,' said Kevin, 'it's lucky I wouldn't let you pikers give up back there, when you all wanted to wimp out.'

I ignored him.

The bridge was old but had been beautifully built. It crossed the creek in a large clearing and was about a metre wide and five metres long. It even had a handrail. Its surface was made of round logs rather than planks but the logs were matched and cut with perfect uniformity. Joints cut in each end married the logs to crossbars and the first and last ones were then secured to the crossbars by wooden pegs.

'It's a lovely job,' said Kevin. 'Reminds me of my own early work.'

Suddenly we had so much energy it was as though we were on something. We nearly decided to camp in the clearing, which was cool and shadowy, but the urge to explore was too strong. We hoisted our packs on our backs again, and chattering like cockatoos we hustled down the path.

'It must be true about the hermit! No one else would have gone to all that trouble.'

'Wonder how long he was here for.'

'How do you know it was a he?'

'The locals always talked about him as a male.'

'Most hims are talked about as males.' That was Lee, being a smartarse.

'He must have been here years, to go to all that trouble with the bridge.'

'And the track's so well worn.'

'If he did live here years he'd have time to do the bridge and a lot more. Imagine how you'd fill your time!'

'Yeah, food'd be the big thing. Once you'd organised your meals, the rest of the day'd be yours.'

'I wonder what you'd live on.'

'Possums, rabbits maybe.'

'Wouldn't be many rabbits in this kind of country. There's wallabies. Plenty of possums. Feral cats.'

'Yuk.'

'You could grow vegetables.'

'Bush tucker.'

'Yeah, he probably watched that show on TV.'

'Wombats.'

'Yeah, what would wombats taste like?'

'They say most people eat too much anyway. If he

just ate when he was really hungry he wouldn't need much.'

'You can train yourself to eat a lot less.'

'You know Andy Farrar? He found a walking stick in the bush near Wombegonoo. It's beautifully made, handmade, all carved and everything. Everyone said it must be the Hermit's but I thought they were joking.'

The track was taking us downhill all the time. It wound around a bit, looking for the best route, but the trend was always downhill. It was going to be quite a sweat getting back up. We'd lost a lot of altitude. It was beautiful though, quiet, shady, cool and damp. There were no flowers, just more shades of green and brown than the English language knows about. The ground was deep in leaf litter: there were times when we lost the track beneath heaps of bark and leaves and twigs, but a search around under the trees always found it again. Every so often it brought us back to Satan's Steps, so that for a few metres we'd be brushing alongside the great granite walls. Once it cut between two of the steps and continued down the other side: the gap was only a couple of metres wide, so it was almost a tunnel through the massive hunks of rock.

'This is pretty nice for Hell,' Fi said to me as we paused in the cool stone gap.

'Mmm. Wonder how long since anyone's been down here.'

'More than that,' Robyn, who was in front of Fi, said. 'I wonder how many human beings have ever been down here, in the history of the Universe. I mean, why would the koories have bothered? Why would the early explorers, or settlers, have bothered?

31

And no one we know has. Maybe the Hermit and us are the only people ever to have seen it. Ever.'

By that stage it was getting obvious that we were close to the bottom. The ground was levelling out and the last of the sunlight was filtering through to warm our faces. The overgrowth and the undergrowth were both sparser, though still quite dense. The track rejoined the creek and ran alongside it for a few hundred metres. Then it opened out into our camp-site for the night.

We found ourselves in a clearing about the size of a hockey field, or a bit bigger. It would have been hard to play hockey on though, because it wasn't much of a clearing. It was studded with trees, three beautiful old eucalypts and quite a few suckers and saplings. The creek was at the western edge; you could hear it but not see it. The creek was flatter and wider here and cold, freezing cold, even on a summer day. In the early mornings it hurt and stung. But when you were hot it was a wonderful refreshing shock to splash your face into it.

That's where I am now of course.

For any little wild things living in the clearing we must have seemed like visitors from Hell, not visitors to it. We made a lot of noise. And Kevin – you can never cure Kevin of his bad habit of breaking branches off trees instead of walking a few extra metres to pick up dead wood. That's one reason I was never too convinced when Corrie talked about how caring and sensitive he was. But he was good with fires: he had the white smoke rising about five min-utes after we arrived, and flames burning like fury about two minutes after that.

We decided not to bother with tents – we'd only

brought two and a half anyway – but it was warm and no chance of rain, so we just strung up a couple of flies for protection against the dew. Then Lee and I got stuck into the cooking. Fi wandered over.

'What are we having?' she asked.

'Two-minute noodles for now. We'll cook some meat later, but I'm too hungry to wait.'

'What are two-minute noodles?' Fi asked.

Lee and I looked at each other and grinned.

'It's an awesome feeling,' Lee said, 'to realise you're about to change someone's life forever.'

'Haven't you ever had two-minute noodles?' I asked Fi.

'No. My parents are really into health foods.'

I'd never met anyone who hadn't had two-minute noodles before. Sometimes Fi seemed like an exotic butterfly.

I can't remember any hike or campout I'd been on where people sat around the fire telling stories or singing. It just never seemed to happen that way. But that night we did sit up late, and talk and talk. I think we were excited to be there, in that strange and beautiful place, where so few humans had ever been. There aren't many wild places left on Earth, yet we'd fluked it into the middle of this little wild kingdom. It was good. I knew I was really tired but I was too revved up to go to bed until the others started yawning and standing up and looking towards their sleeping bags. Five minutes later we were all in bed; five minutes after that I think I was asleep.

Chapter Four

We didn't do a lot the next day. No one got up till ten or eleven o'clock. First thing we found was a biscuit bag we'd overlooked when packing the food the night before. It was empty. Thanks to us some grateful animal was now a lot fatter.

Our breakfast merged into lunch and continued into the afternoon. Basically we just lay around and ate, in one long pigout. Kevin and Corrie got into a passionate little session on Kevin's sleeping bag; Fi and I sat with our feet in the cold stream, planning our lives after we left school and left Wirrawee. Lee was reading a book, *All Quiet on the Western Front*. Robyn had her Walkman on. Homer had a go at everything: climbed a tree, had a look in the creek for gold, got a pile of firewood, tried to flush out some snakes. When I got some energy going I went with him, to see if the path went any further. But we could find no trace of it. Thick bush met us in every direction. And strangely, we could see no sign of any hut or cave or shelter which the old guy must have had if he'd really lived down here. Finally, sick of trying to tear our way through unsympathetic scrub, we gave up and went back to the clearing. And when we got there Homer did find a snake. It was six o'clock and the ground was starting to cool off. Homer went to his sleeping bag and took off his boots, then stretched out comfortably with a packet of corn chips. 'This is a great place,' he said. 'This is perfect.' At that moment the snake, which had crawled into his sleeping bag, must have stirred under him, cos Homer leapt to his feet and ran about ten metres away. 'Jesus Christ!' he yelled. 'There's something in there! There's a snake in my sleeping bag!'

Even Kevin and Corrie stopped what they were doing and came racing over. There was a wild debate, first about whether Homer was imagining things, then, when we all saw the snake move, about how to get it out with as little loss of life as possible. Kevin wanted to weigh the sleeping bag down in the creek with rocks until the snake drowned; Homer wasn't keen on that. He liked his sleeping bag. We weren't too sure that the snake wouldn't be able to bite through the bag; as a kid I was told a terrifying story by a shearer about how his son had been bitten through a blanket as he lay asleep in his bed. I don't know if the story was true but I never forgot it.

We decided to trust all those experts who'd been telling us since we were kids that snakes are more scared of people than people are of snakes. We figured if we were at one end of the sleeping bag and the snake came out of the other end he'd probably do a big slither in the opposite direction, straight into the bush. So we got two strong sticks; Robyn held one while Kevin held the other; they pushed them under the bag and started slowly lifting. It was a captivating

scene; better than watching TV even. For a minute
nothing happened, though we could see the snake
clearly outlined as the material was stretched. He
sure was a big one. Robyn and Kevin were trying to
tip the bag so that the snake would virtually be
poured out of the mouth onto the ground. They were
doing it well too; perfect teamwork. The bag was at
shin height, then knee height, and still rising. Then
somehow the sticks got too far apart. Corrie called
out; they realised and started to correct, but Robyn
lost her grip for a moment. And a moment was all it
took. The sleeping bag slithered down to the ground
as though it had come to life itself, and one very mad
snake came bursting out. The only rational thought I
had at that moment was curiosity, that Kevin was
obviously as nervous of snakes as he was of insects.
He just stood there white in the face and trembling,
looking like he was going to cry. I think he was so.
paralysed that he would have waited and let the
snake crawl up his leg and bite him. It was funny,
considering how tough he'd been when he had the
stick and was lifting the bag, thinking he was safe. But
there wasn't really much time or space for rational
thoughts at that stage of my life; my irrational mind
was running the show. It told me to panic; I panicked.
It told me to run; I ran. It told me not to give a stuff
about anyone else; I didn't give a stuff. It was quite a
few moments before I looked around to see if they
were OK… and to see where the snake was.

Kevin was still standing at the same spot; Robyn
was a few metres in front of me and doing what I was
doing, standing and looking and puffing and trembling; Fi was in the creek, I've got no idea why; Lee
was up a tree, about six metres from the ground and

rising fast; Corrie was intelligently at the fire and using it as protection; Homer was nowhere to be seen. Neither was the snake.

'Where is it?' I yelled.

'It went that way,' said Corrie, pointing into the bush. 'It chased me, but when I got here I jumped over the fire and it veered away.'

For someone who'd just been chased by a frenzied snake she seemed the calmest of us all.

'Where's Homer?' I asked.

'He went that way,' said Corrie, pointing in the opposite direction to the snake. That sounded safe enough, even for Homer. I slowly stopped panicking and came in to the fire. Lee, looking a bit sheepish, began descending the tree. Even Homer appeared eventually, coming cautiously out of a dense patch of scrub.

'Why were you standing in the creek?' I asked Fi.

'To get away from the snake of course.'

'But Fi, snakes can swim.'

'No they can't... can they? Oh my God. Oh my God. I could have died. Thanks for telling me guys.'

That was the end of our major excitement for the day, unless you count the Sausage Surprise that Homer and Kevin produced for tea. It certainly was full of surprises, and like the snake it was the kind of excitement I could do without. We went to bed pretty early. It had been one of those days when everyone was exhausted from doing nothing. I climbed into the sleeping bag at about 9.30, after first checking carefully that it was empty. By that stage only Fi and Homer were still up, talking quietly at the fire.

I sleep pretty soundly, pretty heavily, and this night was typical. At one point I woke up but I've got no idea what time it was, maybe three or four o'clock. It was a cold night; I needed to go to the dunny but spent ten minutes trying to put it off. It just seemed too cruel to have to crawl out of that snug sleeping bag. I had to give myself a stern lecture: 'Come on, you know you have to go, you'll feel better when you do, stop being such a wimp, the quicker you do it the quicker you'll be back in this warm bag'. Eventually it worked; I struggled grimly out and staggered about ten metres to a convenient tree.

On my way back, a couple of minutes later, I paused. I thought I could hear a distant humming. I waited, still unsure, but it became louder and more distinct. It's funny how artificial noises sound so different to natural noises. For a start, artificial noises are more regular and even, I guess. This was definitely an artificial noise; I realised it had to be some kind of aircraft. I waited, looking up at the sky.

One thing that's different up here is the sky. This night was like any clear dark night in the mountains: the sky sprinkled with an impossible number of stars, some strong and bright, some like tiny weak pinpricks, some flickering, some surrounded by a hazy glow. Most views I get tired of eventually, but never the night sky in the mountains, never. I can lose myself in it.

Suddenly the loud buzzing became a roar. I couldn't believe how quickly it changed. It was probably because of the high walls of rock that surrounded our campsite. And like black bats screaming out of the sky, blotting out the stars, a V-shaped line of jets raced overhead, very low overhead. Then another, then another, till six lines in all had stormed through the sky above me. Their noise, their speed, their darkness frightened me. I realised that I was crouching, as though being beaten. I stood up. It seemed that they were gone. The noise faded quickly, till I could no longer hear it. But something remained. The air didn't seem as clear, as pure. There was a new atmosphere. The sweetness had gone; the sweet burning coldness had been replaced by a new humidity. I could smell the jet fuel. We'd thought that we were among the first humans to invade this basin, but humans had invaded everything, everywhere. They didn't have to walk into a place to invade it. Even Hell was not immune.

I got back to the sleeping bag and Fi said sleepily: 'What was that noise?' It seemed that she was the only one awake, though I could hardly believe it.

'Planes,' I said.

'Mmmm, I thought so,' she said. 'Coming back from Commem Day I suppose.'

'Of course,' I thought. 'That's what it'll be.'

I started to drift into a kind of sleep, restless and full of wild dreams. It still hadn't occurred to me that there was anything strange about dozens of aircraft flying fast and low at night without lights. It wasn't till much later that I even realised they'd had no lights.

In the morning, at breakfast, Robyn said, 'Did anyone else hear those planes last night?'

'Yes,' I said. 'I was up. I'd been to the toilet.'

'They just never stopped,' Robyn said. 'Must have been hundreds.'

'There were six lots,' I said. 'Close together and really low. But I thought you slept through it. Fi was the only one who said anything.'

Robyn stared at me. 'Six lots? There were dozens and dozens, all night long. And Fi was asleep. I thought you were too. Lee and I were counting them but everyone else just snored away.'

'God,' I said, starting to realise, 'I must have heard a different lot to you.'

'I didn't hear anything,' said Kevin, tearing the wrapper off his second Mars Bar. He claimed that he always had two Mars Bars for breakfast, and so far on this hike he was right on schedule.

'It's probably the start of World War Three,' said Lee. 'We've probably been invaded and don't even know.'

'Yes,' said Corrie from her sleeping bag. 'We're so cut off here. Anything could happen in the outside world and we'd never hear about it.'

'That's good I reckon,' said Kevin.

'Imagine if we came out in a few days and there'd been a nuclear war and there was nothing left and we were the only survivors,' Corrie said. 'Chuck us a muesli bar someone, will you please.'

'Apple, strawberry, apricot?' Kevin asked.

'Apple.'

'If there'd been a nuclear war we wouldn't survive,' Fi said. 'That fallout'd be dropping softly on us now. Like the gentle rain from Heaven above. We wouldn't even know about it.'

'Did you do that book last year in English?' Kevin asked. 'X or something?'

'Z? *Z for Zachariah*?'

'Yeah, that one. That was good I reckon. Only decent book we've ever done.'

'Seriously,' said Robyn, 'what do you think those planes were doing?'

'Coming back from Commem Day,' Fi said, as she had during the night. 'You know how they have all those flypasts and displays and stuff.'

'If you were going to invade that'd be a good day to do it,' Lee said. 'Everyone's out celebrating. The Army and Navy and Air Force are all parading around the cities, showing off. Who's running the country?'

'I'd do it Christmas Day,' Kevin said. 'Middle of the afternoon, when everyone's asleep.'

It was a pretty typical conversation I guess, but for some reason it was getting on my nerves. I got up and went down the creek, where I found Homer. He was sitting on a gravel spit, combing through the stones with a flat rock.

'What are you doing?' I asked.

'Looking for gold.'

'Do you know anything about it?'

'Nuh.'

'Found any?'

'Yeah, heaps. I'm putting it in piles behind the trees, so the others don't see it.'

'That's pretty selfish.'

'Yeah, well, that's the kind of guy I am. You know that.'

He was right about one thing, I did know him well. He was like a brother. Being neighbours, we'd grown up together. And although he had a lot of annoying habits he wasn't selfish.

'Hey El?' he said, after I'd sat there for a few minutes watching him scrutinising gravel.

'Yeah?'

'What do you think of Fi?'

I nearly fell into the creek. When someone asks you that question, in that tone of voice, it can only mean one thing. But coming from Homer! The only women Homer admired were the ones in magazines. Real women he treated like beanbags.

And Fi, of all people!

Still, I wanted to answer his question without putting him off.

'I love Fi. You know that. She seems so ... perfect sometimes.'

'Yeah, you know, I think you might be right.'

He got embarrassed at admitting even that much, and spent a few more minutes scratching for gold.

'Guess she thinks I'm just a big loudmouth, huh?' he said at last.

'I don't know. I haven't got a clue Homer. But I don't think she hates you. You were chatting on like old buddies last night.'

'Yeah, I know.' He cleared his throat. 'That's when I first ... when I realised ... Well, it's the first time I really took much notice of her. Since I was a little guy anyway. I always thought she was just a stuck-up snob. But she's not. She's really nice.'

'I could have told you that.'

'Yeah, but you know, she lives in that big house and she talks like Mrs Hamilton, and me and my family, I mean we're just Greek peasants to people like her.'

'Fi's not like that. You ought to give her a chance.'

'Gee I'll give her a chance. Trouble is I don't know if she'll give me one.'

He stared moodily into the gravel, sighed, and stood up. Suddenly his face changed. He went red and started wriggling his head around, like his neck had got uncomfortable after all these years of connecting his head to his body. I looked around to see what had set him off. It was Fi, coming down to the creek to brush her perfect teeth. It was hard not to smile. I'd seen people struck by the lightning of love before, but I'd never thought it would happen to Homer. And the fact that it was Fi took my breath away. I just couldn't imagine what she'd think or how she'd react. My best guess was that she'd think it was a big joke, let him down quickly and gently, then come and have a good giggle with me about it. Not that she'd laugh to be cruel; it was just that no one took Homer very seriously. He'd always encouraged people to believe he had no feelings – he used to say 'I've got a radium heart, takes five thousand years to melt down'. He'd sit in the back of the class encouraging the girls to criticise him. 'Yeah, I'm insensitive, what else? Sexist? Come on, is that all you can think of? You can do better than this. Oooh Sandra, get stirred up...' They'd get madder and madder and he'd keep leaning back on his chair, smiling and taunting them. They knew what he was doing but they couldn't help themselves.

So after a while we started believing him when he said he was too tough to have emotions. It seemed funny that Fi, the most delicately built girl in our year, looked like being the one to bring him undone, if that's the right way to put it.

I went for a walk back up the track, to the last of Satan's Steps. The sun had already warmed the great granite wall and I leaned against it with my eyes half shut, thinking about our hike, and the path and the man who'd built it, and this place called Hell. 'Why did people call it Hell?' I wondered. All those cliffs and rocks, and that vegetation, it did look wild. But wild wasn't Hell. Wild was fascinating, difficult, wonderful. No place was Hell, no place could be Hell. It's the people calling it Hell, that's the only thing that made it so. People just sticking names on places, so that no one could see those places properly any more. Every time they looked at them or thought about them the first thing they saw was a huge big sign saying 'Housing Commission' or 'private school' or 'church' or 'mosque' or 'synagogue'. They stopped looking once they saw those signs.

It was the same with Homer, the way for all those years he'd been hanging a big sign around his neck, and like a fool I'd kept reading it. Animals were smarter. They couldn't read. Dogs, horses, cats, they didn't bother reading any signs. They used their own brains, their own judgement.

No, Hell wasn't anything to do with places, Hell was all to do with people. Maybe Hell was people.

Chapter Five

We got fat and lazy, camping in the clearing. Every day someone would say 'OK, today we're definitely going up the top and doing a good long walk', and every day we'd all say 'Yeah, I'll come', 'Yeah, we're getting too slack', 'Yeah, good idea'.

Somehow though, we never got round to it. Lunchtime would creep up on us, then there'd be a bit of serious sleeping to do, a bit of reading or paddling in the creek, then it'd be mid-afternoon getting on to late afternoon. Corrie and I were probably the most energetic. We took a few walks, back to the bridge, or to different cliffs, so we could have long private conversations. We talked about boys and friends and school and parents, all the usual stuff. We decided that when we left school we'd earn some money for six months and then go overseas together. We got really excited about it.

'I want to stay away for years and years,' Corrie said dreamily.

'Corrie! You got homesick on the Year 8 camp, and that was only four days!'

'That wasn't real homesickness. That was because Ian and them were giving me such a hard time.'

'Weren't they such mongrels? I hated them.'

'Remember when they got caught bombing us with firelighters? They were crazy. At least they've improved since then.'

'Ian's still a dork.'

'I don't mind him now. He's all right.'

Corrie was much more forgiving than me. More tolerant.

'So will your parents let you go overseas?' I asked.

'I don't know. They might, if I work on them long enough. They let me apply for that exchange thing, remember.'

'Your parents are so easy to get on with.'

'So are yours.'

'Oh, most of the time I guess they are. It's only when Dad's in one of his moods. And he is awfully sexist. All the stuff I had to go through just to come on this trip. If I was a boy it'd be no problem.'

'Mmm. My dad's not bad. I've been educating him.'

I smiled. A lot of people underestimated Corrie. She just quietly worked away on people till she got what she wanted.

We figured out our itinerary. Indonesia, Thailand, China, India, then up to Egypt. Corrie wanted to go from there into Africa, but I wanted to go on to Europe. Corrie had this idea that she'd have a look at everything, come home, do nursing, then go back and work in the country that needed nurses most. I admired her for that. I was more interested in making money.

So the time drifted by. Even on our last full day, when food was getting short, no one could be bothered going all the way back to the Landrover to get more. Instead we improvised, and put together snacks that at any other time we would have chucked at the nearest rubbish tin. We ate meals that I wouldn't have fed to our chooks. There was no butter left, no powdered milk, no condensed milk because we'd sucked the tubes dry on our first day. No fruit, no tea, no cheese. No chocolate – that was serious. But not serious enough to motivate us to get off our butts. 'It's catch twenty-something,' Kevin explained. 'If we had chocolate it'd give me the energy to get up to the Landie to get some more. But without it I don't think I could make it to the first step.'

It was hot, that was our main excuse.

Homer was still rapt in Fi, always wanting to talk to me about her, trying to accidentally put himself wherever she happened to be going, turning red every time she spoke to him. But Fi was being very frustrating. She wouldn't discuss it with me at all, just pretended she didn't know what I was talking about, when it must have been obvious to anyone short of a coma.

The seven of us had got through five days without a serious argument, which was good going. Quite a few little arguments, I admit. There was the time Kevin had blown up at Fi for not doing any cooking or washing up. It was after the Great Snake Shemozzle; I think Kevin was embarrassed that he hadn't come out of that with much credit. Then his Sausage Surprise got such a poor response, so he probably was feeling a bit sensitive. Still, Fi was getting a reputation for disappearing when work appeared, so Kevin wasn't too far wrong.

There was Corrie's frequent cry of 'That's not funny Homer', heard when he tipped cold water on her in her sleeping bag, when he did cruel and disgusting things

47

to a black beetle, when he dropped a spider down her shirt, when he tore out the last page of her book and hid it so she didn't know whether the lovers made up or not. Corrie was one of Homer's favourite victims: he only had to give her a glimpse of the red cape and she charged straight at it every time. He was lucky she didn't hold grudges.

If I'm going to be honest I'd better admit that I managed to annoy one or two people once or twice. Kevin told me I was a know-all when I made a few suggestions about rearranging the fire. In fact the fire got me in trouble a few times. I guess I liked fiddling with it a bit too much. Whenever it died down a little, or the smoke started coming in the wrong direction, or the billy wasn't over the best coals, I'd be in there with a stick, 'fixing' it. Well, that's what I called it. The others called it 'being a bloody nuisance'.

My worst fight was really stupid. I don't know, maybe all fights are really stupid. We started talking about the colours of cars, which ones are the most conspicuous and which ones the least. Kevin said white was the most conspicuous and black the least; Lee said yellow and green; I said red and khaki; I forget what the others said. Suddenly it got quite heated. 'Why do you think they paint ambulances and police cars white?' Kevin yelled. 'Why do you think they paint fire engines red?' I yelled back. 'Why do you think they have so many yellow taxis?' Lee yelled a bit, although I don't think his heart was in it. It went on and on. I thought I was on safe ground with khaki for inconspicuous, because that's what the Army uses, but Kevin told some long story about how he nearly had a head-on with a black car a week after he got his P's. 'That doesn't prove black's hard to see,' I said, 'it just proves you shouldn't be allowed on the roads.' I can't even remember how it ended, which goes to show how stupid it was.

But on our last night, sitting around the fire playing True Confessions, Robyn unexpectedly said, 'I don't want to go back. This is the best place and this has been the best week.'

'Yeah,' Lee said. 'It's been great.'

'I'm looking forward to a hot shower though,' Fi said. 'And decent food.'

'Let's do this again,' Corrie said. 'Back here in the same place with the same people.'

'Yeah, OK,' Homer said, obviously thinking of another five days to spend adoring Fi.

'Let's keep this place a secret,' Robyn said. 'Otherwise everyone'll start using it and it'll be wrecked in no time.'

'It is a good campsite,' I said. 'Next time we should have a proper search for where the hermit lived.'

'He might have just had a shelter here and it's fallen down,' Lee said.

'But he built that bridge so well. You'd think he'd build his shelter even better.'

'Well maybe he just lived in a cave or something.'

True Confessions resumed, but I went to bed before they could make me confess to all the things I'd done with Steve. I figured I'd told enough already, so I got out while the going was good. But I still didn't sleep well. Like I said, normally I was a heavy sleeper, but the last few nights I just couldn't settle down to it. To my own surprise I realised I was quite anxious to get home, to see how things were, to make sure it was all OK. I did feel some kind of strange anxiety.

In the morning everyone got moving early, but it's

a funny thing, you can have ninety per cent of the work done in the first hour, but the other ten per cent takes at least two hours. That's Ellie's Law. So it was nearly eleven o'clock and starting to warm up before we were ready to go. A last check of the fire, a regretful farewell to our secret clearing, and we hit the track.

It was a steep climb, and we soon began to realise why we hadn't been too keen to do day trips back up onto Tailor's Stitch. Our biggest motivation, apart from Fi's enthusiasm for showers and food, was to see where the track started at the top. We couldn't figure out how we – and all those other people over the years – had missed it. So we kept plugging along, sweating and grunting up the hardest bits, sometimes pushing the person in front through a narrow gap in Satan's Steps. I noticed Homer stayed close to Fi, giving her helpful pushes whenever he got the chance, and she'd smile at him and he'd go red. Could she possibly like him, maybe? I wondered. Or was she enjoying stringing him along? It'd serve Homer right if a girl did that to him. One girl could get revenge for all of us.

Our packs were lighter, thanks to all the food we'd eaten, though after a short time they felt as heavy as ever. But soon enough we were close to the top, and looking ahead to see where we'd come out. The answer, when we got close enough to tell, was surprising. The track suddenly veered right away from Satan's Steps and struck out across a landslide of loose gravel and rocks. This was the first time we'd been out in the open since leaving the campsite. It took a few minutes to find it again on the other side, because it was much fainter and thinner. It was like going from a road onto a four-wheel-drive track. It was in public view, but it still would have been invisible to anyone standing on the arete. And anyone stumbling across it would have thought it was just an animal track.

It continued to wind upwards then, finishing at a big old gum tree near Wombegonoo. The last hundred metres were through scrub so thick that we had to bend double to get along the path. It was almost like a tunnel, but it was very clever because people looking down from Wombegonoo would see only impenetrable bush. The gum tree was at the base of a sheet of rock that stretched up to Wombegonoo's summit. It was an unusual tree, because it had multiple trunks, which must have parted from each other in its early days, so that now they grew out like petals on a poppy. The track actually started in the bowl in the middle of the tree: it brought us cunningly into the bowl by leading us under one of the trunks. The bowl was so big that the seven of us could squash into it. Either side of the tree and below it was the jungly scrub of Hell; above was the sheet of rock which, as Robyn said, would leave no tracks. It was a perfect setup.

We took a break on Wombegonoo, not for long because we had virtually no food left and we'd all been too lazy to carry any water up from the creek. It was about a forty minute walk to the faithful Landrover, which we found where we'd left it, backed in under the shady trees, patiently waiting. We fell upon it with cries of delight, getting into the water first, then pigging out on the food, even the healthy stuff that we'd rejected five days earlier. It's amazing how quickly your attitudes can change. I

51

remember hearing on the radio someone saying how prisoners of war had been so grateful for any little scrap of food when they were liberated at the end of World War Two, then two days later they were complaining because they got chicken noodle soup instead of tomato. That was just like us – and still is. That day at the Landie I was dreaming of an ice cream I'd chucked out from the fridge at home a week earlier, because it had too many little ice crystals sticking to it. I'd have given anything to have had it back in my hand. I couldn't believe how casually I'd thrown it away. But after an hour or two at home I guess I would have thrown it away again.

Once we got to the Landrover it seemed like the others lost any sense of urgency to get home. It was a hot day, humid, with quite a lot of low cloud drifting past. You couldn't see the coast at all. It was the kind of weather that sapped your energy. That wasn't really true for me though. I was still a bit uneasy, keen to get back, wanting to check that everything was OK. But I couldn't force the others to go at my pace. I was affected by Robyn telling me just that morning that I was bossy. I was a bit hurt by that, especially coming from Robyn, who didn't normally say unkind things. So I kept quiet while everyone lay around in the patchy sunlight, sleeping off the effects of all the food we'd just eaten.

After a while Kevin and Corrie disappeared down the road a way. Homer was lying as close as he dared get to Fi, but she didn't seem to be taking any notice of him. I talked to Lee a bit, about life in the restaurant. It was interesting. I didn't realise how hard it was. He said his parents wouldn't use microwaves or any modern inventions – they still did things in the traditional way –

so that meant a lot more work. His father went down to the markets twice a week, leaving at 3.30 in the morning. I didn't think running a restaurant would suit me, once I heard that.

Eventually, around midafternoon, we got going, picking up Kevin and Corrie down the road a kilometre or so. We lurched our way down at about the same speed as we'd lurched our way up. As we got a better view of the plains we were surprised to see six different fires in the distance, scattered across the countryside. Two looked quite big. It was really too early in the year for major bushfires, but too late for burning off. But that was the only unusual thing we noticed, and none of the fires was remotely close to our places.

At the river there was a majority vote for a swim, so we stopped again for a long time, more than an hour. I was getting quite edgy, but there was nothing I could do to hurry them up. I only swam for five minutes, and Lee didn't go in at all, so when I came out of the water I sat and talked to him again. After a while I said, 'I wish they'd get a move on. I'm really keen to get home.'

Lee looked at me and said, 'Why?'

'I don't know. I'm in a funny mood. A bad mood.'

'Yes, you seem a bit wound up.'

'Maybe it's those fires. I can't figure them out.'

'But you've been uptight most of this hike.'

'Have I? Yes, I suppose I have. I don't know why.'

'It's strange,' Lee said slowly, 'but I feel the same way.'

'Do you? You don't show it.'

'I try not to.'

'Yes, I believe that.'

'Maybe it's guilt,' I added, after a while. 'I feel bad about missing the Show. We exhibit there quite a lot. Dad thinks we should support it. It takes ages, grooming stock and getting them in there and brushing and feeding and walking them, and then presenting them. Dad was cool about it, and I did help groom them, but I left him with an awful lot of work.'

'Do you only take them in there to help keep the Show going?'

'No... It's quite an important show, especially for Charolais. It helps keep your name in front of people, so they realise you're a serious breeder. You've got to be so PR conscious nowadays.'

'That's one thing the same about restaurants... Here they come.'

Sure enough Robyn and Fi, the last two people left in the water, were coming out, dripping and laughing. Fi looked fantastic, flicking her long hair out of her eyes and moving with the grace of a heron. I sneaked a look at Homer. Kevin was talking to him and Homer was trying to act like he was listening, while he stared frantically at Fi out of the corner of his eye. But looking again at Fi, I was sure that she knew. There was something just a bit self-conscious about the way she was walking, and the way she stood there in the cooling sunlight, like a model doing a fashion shoot on a beach. I think she knew, and loved it.

It was about half an hour from the swimming hole to home. I don't know if I was happy that day – those tense and edgy feelings were getting stronger and stronger – but I do know I've never been happy since.

Chapter Six

The dogs were dead. That was my first thought. They didn't jump around and bark when we drove in, or moan with joy when I ran over to them, like they always had done. They lay beside their little galvanised iron humpies, flies all over them, oblivious to the last warmth of the sun. Their eyes were red and desperate and their snouts were covered with dried froth. I was used to them stretching their chains to their limits – they did that in their manic dancing whenever they saw me coming – but now their chains were stretched and still and there was blood around their necks, where their collars had held. Of the five dogs four were young. They shared a water bucket but somehow they had knocked it over and it lay on its side, dry and empty. I checked them quickly, in horror, one by one: all dead. I ran to Millie, their old mother, whom we'd separated from the young dogs because they irritated her. Her bucket was still standing and held a little water; as I came close to her she suddenly gave a feeble wag of her tail and tried to stand. I was shocked that she was still alive, after I'd made up my mind that she too must be dead.

The rational thing to do would have been to leave her and rush into the house, because I knew that nothing so awful could have happened to the dogs unless something more awful had happened to my parents. But I had already stopped thinking rationally. I slipped Millie's chain off and the old dog staggered to her feet, then collapsed forward onto her front knees. I decided, brutally, that I couldn't spend any more time with her. I'd helped her enough. I called to Corrie 'Do something for the dog', and started running for the house. Corrie was already moving that way; her mind was working faster than the others, who were still standing around looking shocked, starting to realise that something was wrong but not making the connections that I was making. I was making them too fast, and that was adding to my terror. Corrie hesitated, turned towards the dogs, then called to Kevin, 'Look after the dogs Kev'. Then she followed me.

In the house nothing was wrong, and that was what was wrong. There was no sign of life at all. Everything was neat and tidy. At that time of day there should have been food spread out on the kitchen table, there should have been dishes in the sink, the TV should have been chattering in the background. But all was silent. Corrie opened the door behind me and came in quietly. 'Jesus, what's happened,' she said, not as a question. The tone of her voice terrified me even more. I just stood there.

'What's wrong with the dogs?' she asked.

'They're all dead except Millie, and she's nearly dead.'

I was looking around for a note, a note to me, but there was nothing.

'Let's ring someone,' she said. 'Let's ring my parents.'

'No. Ring Homer's parents, they're nearest. They'll know.'

She picked up the phone and handed it to me. I turned it to 'Talk' and started pressing numbers, then realised that I'd heard no dial tone. I held it closer to my ear. There was nothing. I felt a new kind of fear now; a kind of fear I hadn't even known about before.

'There's nothing,' I said to Corrie.

'Oh Jesus,' she said again. Her eyes got very wide and she started going quite white.

Robyn and Fi came into the kitchen, with the others close behind them.

'What's happening?' they were asking. 'What's wrong?'

Kevin came in carrying Millie.

'Get her some food from the coolroom,' I said.

'I'll go,' Homer said.

I tried to explain everything, but I got confused trying to do it as quickly as possible, and ended up taking too long. So I stopped, and just said wildly, 'We've got to do something'.

At that moment Homer came in with a bowl of mince and a smell. 'The power's off in the coolroom,' he said. 'It stinks terrible.'

'Terribly,' I said, in absent-minded fear.

He just looked at me.

Robyn went to the TV as Homer and Kevin tried to persuade Millie to eat. We watched Robyn as she switched on the set, but it too was dead. 'This is weird,' she said.

'Did they say they were going away?' Fi asked.

I didn't bother to answer.

'If your grandmother got sick...' Corrie said.

'So they cut off the power?' I asked sarcastically.

'Some big electrical problem?' Kevin suggested. 'Maybe if the power was off for days they had to move.'

'They'd have left a note,' I snapped. 'They wouldn't let the dogs die.'

There was a moment's silence. No one knew what to say.

'There's just no explanation that fits all this,' Robyn said.

'It's like UFO stuff,' Kevin said. 'Like aliens have taken them away.' Then, seeing the expression on my face, he quickly added, 'I'm not trying to make a joke of it Ellie. I know something bad's happened. I just can't figure what it could possibly be.'

Lee whispered something to Robyn. I didn't bother to ask them what it was. When I saw the naked fear on Robyn's face, I didn't want to ask.

I made a big mental effort to get control of myself.

'Let's get back to the Landrover,' I said. 'Bring the dog. We'll go down to Homer's.'

'Wait a sec,' Lee said. 'Have you got a transistor radio? A battery one?'

'Um, yes, I don't know where,' I said, looking at him strangely. I still didn't know what he had in mind but I didn't like the look on his face, any more than I'd liked the look on Robyn's. 'Why?'

But I didn't want him to answer.

'I've got my Walkman in the Landrover,' Robyn said.

He turned to her. 'Have you heard any news bulletins since we've been away?'

'No. I tried a few times to pick up radio stations,

but I couldn't get any. I guess the cliffs around Hell cut them off.'

'Can you find your radio?' Lee said to me.

'I guess.' I ran to my bedroom. I didn't want to be wasting time like this; I desperately wanted to get to Homer's place and run to kind Mrs Yannos and have her hug me and hold me and explain everything away, so that it became just a simple little mistake. But there was something terrible in Lee's mind and I couldn't ignore it.

I came back with the radio, switching it on as I rushed along the corridor, spinning the tuner to find a station. By the time I got to the kitchen I'd already scanned the whole range once and got nothing but static. Must have gone too fast, I thought, like I always do. I never learn. I started the second search as the others watched anxiously, uncomprehending. This time I was slow and careful, but the result was the same: nothing.

Now we were all really frightened. We looked at Lee, as though we expected him magically to have the answer. He just shook his head. 'I don't know,' he said. 'Let's get to Homer's.'

As with the radio, so with the Landrover. I revved it so hard and dropped the clutch so roughly that Kevin, who was still sitting down, hit his head and hurt it, nearly dropping Millie, whom he was still nursing. The Landie kangaroo-hopped a few metres and stalled. I could hear Grandma's voice saying 'More haste, less speed'. I took a deep breath and tried again, more calmly. This time was better. We went out the gate and down the road, with me saying to Homer, 'I forgot to check the chooks'.

'OK Ellie,' he said, 'it'll be cool. We'll work it out.'

59

But he didn't look at me, just sat forward on the seat, peering anxiously through the windscreen.

Homer's place is about a k and a half from ours.

The one thing we wanted to see, the only thing, as we approached, was movement.

There was none. As we bumped over the cattle grid I was pressing the horn, making it roar, until Lee called out urgently from the back, 'Don't do that Ellie'. Again I was scared to ask why, but I stopped pressing the horn. We skidded hard to a halt near the front door and Homer hit the ground running. He flung the door open and ran in, calling 'Mum! Dad!'

But before I'd even left the driver's seat the hollowness of his voice gave me my answer.

I walked towards the door. As I did so I heard the Landrover start up behind me. I turned and looked. Lee was at the wheel. I watched. He was a terrible driver, but with much over-revving he got the vehicle into the shadows under the big old peppercorn tree, behind the tank stand. Memories of a light-hearted conversation in Hell suddenly came back to me. And suddenly I knew, and I hated and feared the memory. Lee climbed out of the car and came walking towards me, heading for the front door. I screamed at him, 'Lee! You're wrong! Stop doing these things! Stop thinking these things! You're wrong!'

Robyn came up behind me and grabbed my arm.

'He probably is,' she said. 'But the radio...' She paused. 'Hold yourself together Ellie. Just till we know.'

We walked into the house together. As we went through the front door into the bleak dead silence she added, 'Pray hard Ellie. Pray really hard. I am.'

I could hear a bellowing noise from out the back

60

of the house, so I walked straight through to the yard, and found Homer, grim-faced, trying to milk their cow. Milk was leaking from her teats, and she was shifting uncomfortably and bellowing whenever he tried to touch her.

'Can you milk, Ellie?' he asked quietly.

'No, sorry Homer. I never learned. I'll ask the others.'

As I went back in he called out, 'The budgie in the sunroom Ellie'.

'OK,' I called, and ran. But Corrie had already reached the budgie who was alive, but with just a little bit of mouldy water in its cage. We brought him fresh water, which he drank like Dad with his first beer after shearing.

'You've got a milker at home, haven't you?' I asked Corrie. 'Can you take over from Homer, out the back?'

'Sure,' she said, and went. We'd all started acting with unnatural calmness. I knew how frightened Corrie and the others must now be for their own families, but there was nothing we could do for them quite yet. I took the budgie into the kitchen, where Lee was putting down the phone. I raised my eyebrows at Lee; he shook his head. Homer came in a moment later.

'There's an RF radio in the office,' he said, without looking at anyone.

'What's an RF radio?' Fi asked. I hadn't noticed her, standing in the door of the pantry.

'Rural Firefighting,' Homer said briefly.

'Would it be safe?' Robyn asked.

'I don't know,' Homer said. 'Who knows anything?'

With desperate urgency, passionate to convince

them, I said, 'This is ridiculous. I know what you're thinking, and it is completely absolutely impossible. Absolutely not possible. These things just don't happen, not here, not in this country.' Then, with sudden hope, I remembered something. 'Those fires! They'll be out fighting those fires. There must have been some bad ones, so bad they couldn't get back.'

Homer said, 'Ellie, they weren't that kind of fire. You know that. You know what a bad fire looks like.'

Lee said, 'I don't know much about these things, but shouldn't your RF radio be alive with voices, while those fires are burning?'

'Yes!' said Homer, turning in a hurry.

'But there's no power,' Fi said.

'They have back-up batteries,' I said. We rushed after Homer and crowded into the little office. Homer was turning the volume knob on the radio up to full, but there was no need. Endless monotonous static filled the room. 'Did you check the frequency?' I asked quietly. Homer nodded, his face full of misery. I wanted to hug him, looked for Fi to see if she might be going to, then went ahead when I realised she'd left the room again.

After a minute Homer said, 'Do you think we should send out a call on the radio?'

'What do you think Ellie?' Lee asked me.

I knew I had to admit all the possibilities now. I remembered how tense things had been before we left, all those politicians shouting and carrying on. Trying to think calmly I said, 'The only reason for calling up would be if we can get help for our families. If they're in trouble, or danger. But if they are, everyone must be in the same boat. And the authorities must know about it. So we wouldn't be helping our families by transmitting the call...'

'The only other reason for calling is because we're so desperate to find out. But OK, I admit we may create danger for ourselves...' I tried to keep my voice steady, '...if there's something bad happened... if there's people out there...'

'So on balance?' Lee asked.

'I don't think we should call,' I said sadly.

'I agree,' Homer said.

'Me too,' Lee said.

'Then it's Corrie's turn,' Homer said. 'And Kevin's. I don't even know where Robyn lives.'

'Just outside town,' I said.

'Well, I guess geographically Corrie and Kevin come first.' He looked at Lee, who nodded without speaking. He'd already figured out who was last.

The seven of us came together in the kitchen, with almost perfect timing, Corrie carrying a bucket of milk. The milk stank. It looked like pale scrambled eggs. Kevin was with her. They were gripping each other's hands, hanging on tight. I poured some of the milk into a salad bowl and gave it to Millie, who at last started to show some enthusiasm. She sniffed it, then lapped it eagerly.

Kevin said to Homer, 'Do you mind if we go to our places? We'll go on our own if we can have a vehicle or...' he looked at me, '...the Landrover.'

'Dad said I was the only...' I started, then stopped, realising how weak it sounded. But I'd done enough logical thinking in the Yannos' office.

Robyn took over. 'We've got to think, guys. I know we all want to rush off, but this is one time we can't afford to give in to feelings. There could be a lot at stake here. Lives even. We've got to assume that something really bad is happening, something quite evil. If we're wrong, then we can laugh about it later, but we've got to assume that they're not down the pub or gone on a holiday.'

'Of course it's bad,' I yelled at her. 'Do you think my dad would leave his dogs to die like that? Do you think I'll be having a good laugh about that tomorrow?' I was screaming and crying at the same time. There was a pause, then suddenly everyone lost control. Robyn started crying, and yelling 'I didn't mean it that way Ellie, you know I didn't!'; Corrie was shouting 'Shut up! Everyone shut up!'; Kevin was rubbing his fingers through his hair, going 'Oh God, oh God, what's going on?'; Fi had her hand in her mouth and looked like she wanted to eat it. She was so white I thought she was about to faint. Suddenly Homer, madly, said, 'Fi, I've heard of biting your nails, but that's ridiculous'. We all looked at Fi and a moment later we were all laughing. Hysterical laughter, but it was laughter. Lee had had tears pouring down his face, but now he wiped them away and said quickly, 'Let's listen to Robyn. Come on everyone.'

'I'm sorry Robyn,' I said. 'I know you didn't mean…'

'I'm sorry too,' she said. 'It was a bad choice of words.' She took a deep breath and clenched her fists. You could see her calming herself, like she did at netball sometimes.

At last she continued. 'Look everyone, I didn't want to say much. Just that we've got to be careful. If we go rushing around the countryside, to seven different houses, well, it mightn't be such a bright thing to do, that's all. We should decide some things, like whether to stick together, or break into small groups, like Kevin and Corrie want to do. Whether we should

64

use the vehicles. Whether we should go any further in daylight. It's almost dark now. For a start I suggest no one goes on from here until it is dark, and that when they do go they don't use lights.'

'What do you think's happened?' I asked. 'Do you think the same as Lee?'

'Well,' said Robyn. 'There's no sign of anyone leaving in a hurry, like in an emergency. They left some days ago. And they expected to come back some days ago. Now, what's something that everyone would have gone off to some days ago, expecting to come back? We all know the answer to that.'

'Commemoration Day,' said Corrie. 'The Show.'

'Exactly.'

'Homer,' I said, 'is there some way you can tell if your parents came back from the Show? I mean, if I'd thought of it before, I could have looked for a couple of our bulls that I know Dad was showing, that he wouldn't have sold for any price. And he wouldn't have come back from the Show without them. I mean, he would have kept those bulls in the bedroom if Mum had let him.'

Homer thought for a minute.

'Oh yes,' he said. 'Mum's needlepoint. She enters a new piece every year, then win lose or draw she brings it back and hangs it on her Honour Wall. She gets a big thrill putting it up there. Hang on a sec.'

He ran out, and we waited in silence. He was back a moment later. 'Nothing,' he said. 'It's not there.'

'OK,' Robyn said. 'Let's assume that a lot of people went to the Show and didn't come back. And let's assume that since Commem Day all power and phones have been cut, all radio stations are off the air, and there have been a number of fires. And the people who went to the Show wanted to come back but couldn't. Where does that get us?'

'And there's the other thing,' Lee said.

Robyn looked at him. 'Yes,' she said.

Lee continued. 'The night of the Show those hundreds of aircraft, maybe even more than hundreds, that came in over the coast, flying low and at high speed.'

'And without lights,' I added, realising that critical point for the first time.

'Without lights?' Kevin said. 'You didn't tell us that.'

'It didn't strike me,' I said. 'You know how you notice something, but not consciously? That's what it was like.'

'Let's assume something else,' Fi said. She sounded, and looked, angry. 'Let's assume that what you're saying is absolutely ridiculous.' She sounded like me, in this same room, not very many minutes earlier. Hadn't I said 'absolutely ridiculous'? But now I was starting to come round to Lee and Robyn's way of thinking. That little point about the lights had made a difference to me. No legitimate aircraft, no aircraft on a legitimate mission, would have been flying without lights. I should have registered it at the time, and I was annoyed at myself that I hadn't.

But Fi continued, 'There are dozens more likely theories. Dozens! I don't know why you won't consider them.'

'OK Fi, fire away,' said Kevin. 'But fire quickly.' The strain was really showing in Kevin's face.

'All right,' said Fi. 'Number one. They're sick. They went to the Show and got food poisoning or something. They're in hospital.'

'Then the neighbours would have been here, looking after the place,' Homer said.

'They got sick too,' said Fi.

'That doesn't explain why all the radio stations are off the air,' said Corrie.

'Everyone's sick then,' said Fi. 'There's a national problem, with some illness or disease.'

'That doesn't explain the planes,' Robyn said.

'They were just coming back from Commem Day, like we said.'

'Without lights? And so many of them? Fi, I don't know if we even have that many planes. I don't know if our Air Force is that big.'

'OK,' said Fi. 'There is some national emergency, and everyone's had to go and help.'

'And the planes?'

'It's the Air Force, going to help. And maybe other countries' air forces too, all helping.'

'Then why would they have no lights?' Robyn was shouting now, getting mad, like she did on the netball court.

'We don't know that for sure.' Fi was shouting too. Fi shouting? First time for everything, I thought. Fi continued, 'Ellie might have been wrong. It was the middle of the night. She would have been half asleep. I mean she only just thought to mention it now. She couldn't be that certain.'

'I saw them Fi,' I said. 'I'm certain. It didn't strike me at the time. My eyes were working. It's just that my brain wasn't. Anyway, Robyn saw them, and Lee. Ask them.'

'We didn't see them,' Robyn snapped. 'We only heard them.'

'Everyone calm down,' Homer interrupted. 'Stay calm, or we'll get nowhere. Come on Fi, what else?'

'I don't know,' she said. 'I just think they've rushed

off somewhere to help. Maybe some whales got stranded.'

'So two lots of parents rush off without even leaving notes?' Kevin asked.

'But if you take out the planes,' said Fi, 'you haven't got nearly as much. Just some little local emergency.'

'Don't forget the radio stations,' Robyn said.

Lee spoke up. 'Fi, they're all valid theories. And I'm not saying you're wrong. You're probably right, and the planes are just a coincidence, and the radio can be explained away and so on. But the thing that scares the sweat out of me is there is one theory that does fit all the facts, and so bloody neatly it's perfect. Remember our conversation that morning in Hell? How Commemoration Day would be the ideal day to do it?'

Fi nodded dumbly, tears rolling down her face. We were all crying again now, even Lee, who kept talking as he wept.

'Maybe all my mother's stories made me think of it before you guys. And like Robyn said before, if we're wrong,' he was struggling to get the words out, his face twisting like someone having a stroke, 'if we're wrong you can laugh as long and loud as you want. But for now, for now, let's say it's true. Let's say we've been invaded. I think there might be a war.'

Chapter Seven

It was terrible waiting for it to get dark. We kept starting out, saying 'OK, that's enough, let's go', then someone would say 'No, wait, it's still too light'.

That's the trouble with summer, it's daylight for an awfully long time. But we'd made a decision to play it safe and we stuck to it.

The moon was thin and late to rise, so when we did get going it really was quite dark. We had a couple of torches that Homer had been able to find but we'd agreed not to use them unless absolutely necessary. We left Millie on a blanket in Homer's kitchen. She was too weak to move far. We walked along the road for about a k and a half, then branched across the last of the Yannos' paddocks, taking a short cut to the lane that led to Kevin's. I walked with Homer but we didn't talk much, except when I suddenly remembered I hadn't asked him about their dogs. 'We only had two left,' he said, 'and they weren't there. I'm not sure where they might have gone. I think Dad said something about taking them to the vet. They both had eczema badly. I can't remember if he said that or if I just imagined it.'

Once we were in the lane Kevin starting running. There were still about two k's to go but, without a word being exchanged, we all started running too, behind him. Kevin's a big guy, not built for sprinting, and he lumbered along like a draft horse, but for once we couldn't keep up with him. Except Robyn, who was always fit. After a while I couldn't see them ahead of us, but I could hear Kevin's heavy panting coming out of the darkness. As we grew closer to the house Lee called, 'Be careful when you get there Kev', but he got no reply.

He beat us there by two or three minutes I'd say, he and Robyn. But there wasn't much point. His house was the same as Homer's and mine. Three dead working dogs on chains, a dead cockatoo in a cage on the verandah, two dead poddy lambs by the verandah steps. But his old pet corgi had been locked in the house, with a bucket of food and a bucket of water in the laundry. She was alive but she'd chosen one of the bedrooms for a toilet, so the house smelt pretty foul. She was delirious with joy to see Kevin; when we got there she was still leaping at his face, crying pitifully, doing excited midair stunts and wetting herself with excitement.

Corrie, grim-faced, went past me with a mop and a handful of rags. I'd noticed when I'd stayed with Corrie that if things got too emotional she'd start cleaning up. It was a useful habit she had.

We had another quick conference. There seemed to be so many problems and so many choices. Robyn had the bright idea that bicycles were quick and silent – the perfect transport. Kevin had two little brothers, so we scored three bikes from their shed. Homer asked if we knew anyone who wouldn't have gone to the Show; he'd realised that finding someone who'd stayed home that day might be the solution to the whole mystery. Lee said he didn't think his parents would have gone: his sisters and brothers usually did, but not his parents. Kevin said he wanted to bring the corgi, Flip, along with us. He couldn't bear to leave her alone again after what she'd been through.

This was a tough one. We all felt sympathetic to the dog, who seemed to be attached to Kevin's heels by a metre of invisible lead, but we were starting to get more and more conscious of our own safety. We finally agreed to take her with us to Corrie's, and make another decision depending on what we found there.

'But Kevin,' warned Lee, 'we might have to make some ugly choices.'

Kevin just nodded. He knew.

Robyn, who'd thought of the bikes, ended up jogging most of the way to Corrie's. We could only get two on a bike, and she said she needed the exercise. Homer dinked Kevin, who nursed Flip in his arms. The little corgi spent the whole trip licking his face in an ecstasy of love and gratitude. It would have been funny, if we'd had any emotional energy left to laugh.

The image I'll always remember from Corrie's place is of Corrie standing alone in the middle of the sitting room, tears streaming down her face. Then Kevin came in from checking the bedrooms, saw her, and moving quickly to her took her in his arms and held her close. They just stood there for quite a few minutes. I liked Kevin a lot for that.

Under a lot of pressure from Robyn we agreed to try to eat before doing any more. She had been so logical all evening, and she was still being logical, even though it was her house that we would head for next. So she and I and Homer made sandwiches with stale bread and salami, and lettuce and tomatoes from Mrs Mackenzie's famous vegetable garden. We made tea and coffee too, using long-life milk and a little solid-fuel camping stove. It was hard to force the food down our dry and choked-up throats, but we nagged and nagged until everyone had eaten at least one sandwich, and it did make a difference to our energy and morale.

We decided as we ate that we would go to Robyn's, but we knew that we were heading into a whole new set of problems. Out here in the country, where most of us lived, where the air was free and the paddocks wide and empty, we had still been moving fairly confidently. Danger just didn't seem real. We knew that if there was trouble, if there was danger, it would be in town.

Robyn described, for the ones who hadn't been there, the layout of her house, and where it was in relation to Wirrawee. We figured that it should be safe to go in on Coachman's Lane, which was just a dirt track at the back of a few ten acre blocks, including Robyn's. From the hill behind Robyn's we could get a glimpse of the town, which might tell us something.

It was time to leave. Corrie was waiting for me at the front door. I'd been using the bathroom. I'd forgotten that the Mackenzies weren't on town water, and a pressure pump needs electricity to operate. So I'd had to go out to the bathtub in the vegetable garden, fill a bucket with water, and come back in to fill the cistern and flush the toilet. Corrie was getting impatient but I held her up a few moments longer. I was coming down the passageway, past their telephone, when I noticed a message on their fax. 'Corrie,' I called out, 'do you want to see this?' I held it out, adding as she came towards me, 'It's probably an old one but you never know'.

She took it and read it. As she went from line to line I saw her mouth slowly open. Her face seemed to become longer and thinner, with shock. She stared at me with big eyes, then pushed the message into my hands and stood there, shaking, as I read.

In a rough scrawl I saw these words, written by Mr Mackenzie:

Corrie, I'm in the Show Secretary's Office. Something's going on. People say it's just Army manoeuvres but I'm sending this anyway, then heading home to tear it up so no one'll know what an idiot I've been. But Corrie, if you do get this, go bush. Take great care. Don't come out till you know it's safe. Much love darling. Dad.

The last twenty or so words were heavily underlined, everything from 'go bush' onwards.

We looked at each other for a moment, then had a big hug. We both cried a bit, then ran outside to show the others.

I think I must have run out of tears after that day, because I haven't cried again since.

When we left the Mackenzies' we moved cautiously. For the first time we acted like people in a war, like soldiers, like guerillas. Corrie said to us, 'I've always laughed at Dad for being so cautious. The way he carries his spirit level everywhere. But his big motto is "Time spent in reconnaissance is seldom wasted". Maybe we'd better go with that for a while.'

73

We had another bike, Corrie's, so we worked out a way of travelling that we thought was a compromise between speed and safety. We fixed a landmark – the first one was the old Church of Christ – and the first pair, Robyn and Lee, were to ride to it and stop. If it was safe they'd go back and drop a tea towel on the road, two hundred metres before the church. The next pair would set out five minutes after Robyn and Lee and the last three five minutes later. We agreed on total silence, and we left Kevin's old corgi, Flip, chained up at the Mackenzies'. Our fear was making us think.

For all that, the trip to Robyn's was uneventful. Slow, but uneventful. We found her house in the same condition as the others, empty, smelling bad, cobwebs already. It made me wonder how quickly houses would fall apart if people weren't there to look after them. They'd always seemed so solid, so permanent. That poem Mum was always quoting, 'Look on my works ye mighty and despair'. That was all I could remember, but it was the first time I started to understand the truth of it.

It was 1.30 in the morning. We went up to the hill behind Robyn's house and looked at Wirrawee. Suddenly I was very tired. The town was in darkness, no street lights even. There must have been some power though, because there were quite strong lights at the Showground – the floodlights they used for the trotting track – and a couple of buildings in the centre of town were lit. As we sat there we talked softly about our next move. There was no question that we had to try to reach Fi's house, and Lee's. Not because we expected to find anyone, but because five of us had seen our homes, had seen the emptiness, had been given a chance to understand, and it was only fair that the last two should get the same right.

A truck drove slowly out of the Showground and to one of the lit buildings, in Barker Street I think. We stopped talking and watched. It was the first sign of human life, other than our own, that we'd seen since the planes.

Then Homer made an unpopular suggestion. 'I think we should split up.'

There was a whispered howl of protest, if you can have that. It was different to Kevin and Corrie offering to go on their own before. They just hadn't wanted to drag us away from Homer's. But now Homer wouldn't give in.

'We need to be out of town before dawn. A long way out of town. And we're running short of time. It's not going to be quick and easy, travelling around these streets. We're getting tired, and that alone will slow us down, not to mention the care that we'll have to take. Also, two people can move more quietly than seven. And finally, to tell you the truth, if there are soldiers here and anyone's caught... well, again, two's better than seven. I hate to mention the fact, but five people free and two people locked up is a better equation than no people free and seven locked up. You all know what a whiz I am at Maths.'

He'd talked us into silence. We knew he was right, except for the Maths part maybe.

'So what are you suggesting?' Kevin asked.

'I'll go with Fi. I've always wanted to see inside one of those rich houses on the hill. This is my big chance.' Fi aimed a tired kick at him which he allowed to hit his shin. 'Maybe if Robyn and Lee go to Lee's, what do you think? And you other three take a closer look at

75

the Showground. All those lights ... maybe that's their base. Or it could be where they're keeping people even.'

We digested all this, then Robyn said, 'Yes, it's the best way. How about anyone not wearing dark clothes come back to the house and help yourselves to some? And we meet back here on the hill at, say, three o'clock?'

'What if someone's missing?' Fi asked quietly. It was a terrible thought. After a silence Fi answered her own question. 'How about we wait till 3.30 if anyone's not back. Then move out fast, but come back tomorrow night – I mean tonight. And if you're the ones missing and you get back late, lie low for the day.'

'Yes,' said Homer. 'That's all we can do.'

Kevin and Corrie and I didn't need any darker clothing, so we were ready to go. We stood and hugged everyone and wished them luck. A minute later, when I looked back, I could no longer see them. We picked our way down the hill towards Warrigle Street, climbed through the Mathers' front fence and crept along the side of the road, keeping very close to the treeline. Kevin was leading. I just hoped he didn't come across any creepie-crawlies. It wouldn't be a good time for him to start yelling and screaming.

Although the Showground was on the edge of town, it was the opposite side to the edge we were on, so we had quite a walk ahead. But we could move fairly quickly, because we were well away from the main streets. Not that Wirrawee's got many main streets. I was glad that we were moving: it was the only thing keeping me sane. It was so hard concentrating on walking and watching and keeping quiet at the same time. Sometimes I forgot and made a noise, then the other two would turn and look angrily at me. I'd shrug, spread my arms, roll my eyes. I still couldn't comprehend that this might be a matter of life and death, that this was the most serious thing I'd ever been involved in. Of course I knew it; I just couldn't keep remembering it every single second. My mind wasn't that well disciplined. And besides, Kevin and Corrie weren't as quiet as they thought they were.

It was hard being so dark, too. Hard not to trip over stones, or tread on noisy sticks or, on one occasion, bump into a garbage can.

We got into Racecourse Road, and felt a little safer, as there are so few houses along there. Passing Mrs Alexander's I stopped for a moment to sniff at the big old roses that grew along her front fence. I loved her garden. She had a party there every year, a Christmas party. It had only been a few weeks since I'd been standing under one of her apple trees, holding a plate of biscuits and telling Steve I didn't want to go with him any more. Now it felt like it'd happened five years ago. It had been a hard thing to do, and Steve being so nice about it made me feel worse. Maybe that's why he was so nice about it. Or was I just being cynical?

I wondered where Steve was now, and Mrs Alexander, and the Mathers and Mum and Dad and everybody. Could we really have been attacked, invaded? I couldn't imagine how they would have felt, how they would have reacted. They must have been so shocked, so stunned. Some of them would have tried to fight, surely. Some of our friends were hardly the kind of people who would lie down and take it if a bunch of soldiers came marching in to take over their land and houses. Mr George for instance. A building inspector came onto his land last year, to tell him he couldn't extend his shearing shed, and Mr George had been summonsed for threatening him with a tyre lever. For that matter Dad was pretty stubborn too. I just hoped there hadn't been violence. I hoped they'd been sensible.

I stumbled along, thinking of Mum and Dad. Our lives had always been so unaffected by the outside world. Oh, we'd watched the News on TV and felt bad when they showed pictures of wars and famines and floods. Occasionally I'd tried to imagine being in the places of those people, but I couldn't. Imagination has its limits. But the only real impact the outside world had on us was in wool and cattle prices. A couple of countries would sign an agriculture treaty thousands of k's away, on another continent, and a year later we'd have to lay off a worker.

But in spite of our isolation, our unglamorous life, I loved being a rural. Other kids couldn't wait to get away to the city. It was like, the moment they finished school they'd be at the bus depot with their bags packed. They wanted crowds and noise and fast food stores and huge shopping centres. They wanted adrenalin pumping through their veins. I liked those things, in small doses, and I knew that in my life I'd like to spend good lengths of time in the city. But I also knew where I most liked to be, and that was out here, even if I did spend half my life headfirst in a tractor engine, or pulling a lamb out of a barbed-wire fence, or getting kicked black and blue by a heifer when I got between her and her calf.

At that stage I still hadn't come to terms with what had happened. That's not surprising. We knew so little. All we had were clues, guesses, surmises. For instance, I wouldn't allow myself to really consider the possibility that Mum or Dad – or anyone else – had been injured or killed. I mean, I knew in my logical mind that such things were logical outcomes of invasions and fights and wars, but my logical mind was in a little box. My imagination was in another box entirely and I wasn't letting one transmit to the other. I guess you can't really comprehend that your parents will ever die. It's like contemplating your own death.

My feelings were in another box again. During that walk I was desperate to keep them sealed up.

But I did let myself assume that my parents were being held somewhere, against their will. I pictured them, Dad, frustrated and angry, like a bull in a pen, refusing to accept what had happened, refusing to accept anyone else's authority. He wouldn't let himself begin to try to understand what was going on, why these people had come. He wouldn't want to know what their language was, or their ideas, or their culture. Even through my shock and horror I still wanted to understand; I still wanted answers to those questions.

Mum would be different. She'd be concentrating on keeping her mind clear, on not being taken over mentally. I pictured her staring out over the bare hills, through the fence of a prison camp maybe, ignoring the petty distractions, the background voices, the deliberate irritations.

Then I realised I was just thinking of both my parents as they were at home.

We'd reached the end of Racecourse Road. I'd fallen a little behind Kevin and Corrie, and they were waiting for me. We formed a little dark huddle between a tree and a fence. Anyone seeing us might have mistaken us for a strange black growth that had sprouted from the ground. It was getting quite cold and I felt the other two shivering as we crouched together.

'We'll have to be extra careful now that we're so close,' Kevin whispered. 'Try not to get so far behind, Ellie.'

'Sorry. I was thinking.'

'Well, what's the plan?' he asked.

'Just to get close enough to have a look,' Corrie said. 'We don't have all that much time. The main thing's to be careful. If we can't see anything then we just go back to Robyn's. If there's anyone there the dumbest thing we could do would be to have them see us and come after us.'

'OK, agreed,' Kevin said. He started standing. That annoyed me. It was typical Kevin not to ask me what I thought. I pulled him back down.

'What?' he said. 'We've got to get a move on El.'

'That doesn't mean rushing in like idiots. For example, what if we do get seen? Or if we get chased? We can't just run back to Robyn's place. That'd lead them there.'

'Well I guess, separate. It'd be harder for them to chase three different people than one group. Then, if we're sure we're not being followed, make our own way back to Robyn's.'

'OK.'

'Is that all?'

'No! If we're being strictly logical, like Homer was before, we shouldn't all sneak in close to the Showground. One of us should go and the other two stay here. Less chance of being seen, and less loss if one gets caught.'

Corrie gave a little cry. 'No! That's being too logical! You're my best friends! I don't want to be that logical!'

Neither did I, when I thought about it. 'OK then,' I said. 'All for one and one for all. Let's go. The three musketeers.'

We slipped across the road like shadows and moved around the corner. The light from the Showground reached even here, faintly, but enough to make a difference. We stopped at its edge, feeling nervous. It was as though a single step into that light would immediately make us visible to a whole army of hostile watchers. It was frightening.

That was the first moment at which I started to realise what true courage was. Up until then, everything had been unreal, like a night-stalking game at a school camp. To come out of the darkness now would be to show courage of a type that I'd never had to show before, never even known about. I had to search my own mind and body to find if there was a new part of me somewhere. I felt there was a spirit in me that could do this thing, but it was a spirit I hadn't known about. If I could only find it I could connect with it and then maybe, just maybe, I could start to defrost the fear that had frozen my body. Maybe I could do this dangerous and terrible thing.

A small single movement was my key to finding my spirit. There was a tree about four steps away, in front of me and to my left, well inside the zone of light from the Showground. I suddenly made myself leave the darkness and go to it, in four quick light steps, a dance that surprised me, but made me feel a little light-headed and proud. That's it! I thought. I've done it! It was a dance of courage. I felt then, and still feel

81

now, that I was transformed by those four steps. At that moment I stopped being an innocent rural teenager and started becoming someone else, a more complicated and capable person, a force to be reckoned with even, not just a polite obedient kid. There wasn't time then to explore this new and interesting me, but I promised myself I'd do it later.

I still felt light-headed when Kevin, then Corrie, joined me, moments later. We looked at each other and grinned, proud and excited and a little disbelieving. 'OK, what's next?' Kevin asked. Suddenly he was looking to me for directions. Maybe he recognised how I'd been changed in those few seconds. But then surely he had been too?

'Keep heading left, from tree to tree. We need to get to that big gum. That'll put us opposite the woodchop area. We'll get a bit of a view from there.'

I took off as soon as I'd finished speaking, so psyched up that I didn't realise I was doing to Kevin what I'd objected to his doing to me, moments earlier. From my new vantage point I could see human movement: three men in uniforms emerged slowly from the shadows behind the grandstand and walked steadily around the perimeter of the wire fence. They carried weapons of some kind, big rifles maybe, but it was too far to see them clearly. Despite all the evidence that we'd had already, this was the first confirmation that an enemy army was in our country, and in control. It was unbelievable, horrible. I felt my body fill with fear and anger. I wanted to yell at them to get out, and I wanted to run away and hide. I couldn't take my eyes off them.

After they'd faded out of sight again, behind the trotters' stables, I heard the quick rush of light feet as Kevin and Corrie reached me.

'Did you see the men?' I asked.

'Well, yes and no,' Corrie whispered. 'They weren't all men. At least one was a woman.'

'Really? Are you sure?'

She shrugged. 'You want to know the colour of their buttons?'

I took her point. Corrie does have good eyesight.

We kept going, making our little dashes from tree to tree, until at last we were gathered, panting, behind the big river gum. From there we peered out cautiously: Corrie, kneeling, looking around the base from the right; Kevin, crouching, looking through a low fork; and me, standing on the other side, peeping around the trunk. We were in quite a good spot, about sixty metres from the fence and able to see a third of the Showground. The first thing I noticed was a number of big tents on the oval. They were all different shapes and colours, but they were all big. The second thing was another couple of soldiers, with weapons, standing on the trotting track. They weren't doing anything, just standing, one facing the tents and one facing the pavilions. It was obvious that they were sentries, guarding whatever was in the tents probably. One was a woman, too; Corrie had been right.

The Showground was still set up for the Show, even though it should have been packed away four days ago. But the Ferris wheels and sideshows, the tractor displays and caravans, the logs for the woodchop and the trailers selling fast foods, all were still in position. Away to our left was a silent ocean of parked cars, most sitting like dark still animals, a few glinting in the artificial light. Our car would be in among them somewhere. Some cars would have had dogs in them too. I tried not to think about their horrible deaths, like the dogs back at our place. Maybe the soldiers had compassion and had rescued them when the fighting was over. Maybe there would have been time for that.

We watched for eight minutes – I was timing it – before anything happened. Just as Kevin leaned around the trunk and whispered to me, 'We'll have to go', and I nodded, a man came out of one of the tents. He walked out with his hands on his head and stood there. Immediately the sentries came to life, one of them going quickly to the man, the other straightening up and turning to look at him. The sentry and the man talked for a few moments, then the man, still with his hands on his head, walked to the toilet block and disappeared inside. It was only at the last second, as the light above the lavatory door shone on his face, that I recognised him. It was Mr Coles, my Year 4 teacher at Wirrawee Primary.

So, at last we knew. A coldness crept through me. I felt the goose bumps prickle on my skin. This was the new reality of our lives. I got the shakes a bit, but there was no time for that. We had to go. We slid backwards through the grass and began to retrace our tracks, from tree to tree. I remembered from a couple of years ago a big controversy when the Council had wanted to cut these trees down to make a bigger carpark. There'd been such an outcry that they'd had to give up on the idea. I grinned to myself in the darkness, but without humour. Thank God the good guys had won. But no one could ever have imagined how useful those trees were going to be to us.

I got to the last tree and patted its trunk gently. I felt a great affection for it. Corrie was right behind me, then Kevin snuck in. 'Nearly home free,' I said, and set off again. I should have touched wood once more before I did. The moment I showed my nose, a clatter of gunfire started up behind me. Bullets zinged past, chopping huge chunks of wood out of a tree to my left. I heard a gasp from Corrie and a cry from Kevin. It was as though I left the ground, with sheer fear. For a moment I lost contact with the earth. It was a strange feeling, like I had ceased to be. Then I was diving at the corner of the road, rolling through the grass and wriggling like an earwig into cover. At once I turned to yell to Kevin and Corrie, but as I did they landed on top of me, knocking the wind out of me.

'Go like stink,' Kevin said, pulling me up. 'They're coming.'

Somehow, with no air in my lungs, I started to run. For a hundred metres the only sounds I could hear were the rasping of my own lungs and the soft thuds of my feet on the roadway. Although we'd agreed, so logically, to split up if we were chased, I knew now I wasn't going to do that. At that moment only a bullet could have separated me from those two people. Suddenly they'd become my family.

Kevin was looking back all the time. 'Let's get off the road,' he gasped, just as I was starting to get some wind back. We turned into someone's driveway. As we did I heard a shout. A burst of bullets chopped through the branches with tremendous force, like a sudden short gale. I realised that it was Mrs Alexander's driveway we were sprinting along. 'I know this place,' I said to the others. 'Follow me.' It was not that I had any plan; I just didn't want to follow someone through the darkness if they didn't know where they were going. I was still operating on sheer panic. I led them across the tennis court, trying desperately to think. It wasn't enough just to run. These people were armed, they would be fast, they could summon help easily. The only thing we had going for us was that they couldn't be sure if we were armed or not. They might even think we were leading them into an ambush. I hoped they'd think that. I wished we were leading them into an ambush.

We got round to the back of the house, where it was darker. It was only then that I realised that while thinking about ambushes I'd actually led Kevin and Corrie into a trap. There was no back fence or back gate, just a row of old buildings. Last century they'd been the servants' quarters, and a kitchen and laundry. Now they were used as garages, gardening sheds, store rooms. I stopped the other two. I was horrified by how utterly terror-stricken they looked; horrified because I knew I must look the same way. Their teeth and eyes gleamed at me and their uncontrolled panting seemed to fill the night, like a demonic wind. My mind was falling apart. All I could think of was how my arrogance in taking the lead, in being so sure I knew my way, might cost us our lives. I wasn't yet sure if the others realised how ignorant I'd been. I forced myself to speak, through rattling teeth. I wasn't even sure what I was going to say, and my fury at myself seemed to come out as anger directed at them. I'm not very proud of how I was that night. 'Shut up! Shut up and listen,' I said. 'For Christ's sake. We've got a couple of minutes. This is a big garden. They won't go rushing around in it, in the darkness. They'll be a bit unsure of us.'

'I've hurt my leg,' Corrie moaned.

'What, you didn't get shot?'

'No, I ran into something, just back there.'

'It's a ride-on mower,' Kevin said. 'I nearly hit it too.'

A volley of gunfire interrupted us. It was frighteningly loud. We could see the flashes of fire from the guns. As we watched, trembling, we began to recognise their tactics. They were keeping together, moving through the garden, firing into anything that could have concealed a person: a bush, a barbecue pit, a compost heap. They'd probably seen enough of us to have an idea that we were empty handed, but they were still moving cautiously.

I was struggling to get some air, to breathe. At last I was starting to think. But my brain was operating like my lungs, in great gasping bursts. 'Yes, petrol... we could roll it ... no, that'd give them time... but if it sat there... matches... and a chisel or something...'

'Ellie, what the hell are you on about?'

'Find some matches, or a cigarette lighter. And a chisel. And a hammer. Quick. Very quick. Try these sheds.'

We spread out, rushing to the dark buildings, Corrie limping. I found myself in a garage. I felt around with my hands, locating the smooth cold lines of a car, then quickly going to its passenger door. The door was unlocked; like most of us who lived around Wirrawee, Mrs Alexander didn't bother to lock her cars. Everyone trusted people. That was one thing that was going to change forever. When the door opened, the interior light, to my horror, came on. I found the switch and turned it off, then stood there trembling waiting for the bullets to come tearing through the walls of the building. Nothing happened.

I opened the glove box, which had its own light, but it was small, and anyway I needed it. And there it was, a blessed box of matches. Thank God Mrs Alexander was a chain smoker. I grabbed the matches, slammed the glovebox shut and ran from the garage, forgetting in my excitement that the soldiers could be out there. But they weren't, just Kevin.

'Did you get them?'

'I got the hammer and chisel.'

'Oh Kevin, I love you.'

'I heard that,' came Corrie's whisper from the darkness.

'Take me to the ride-on,' I said.

Before, two people had found it when they didn't want to. Now, when three of us wanted to find it, none of us could. Two agonising minutes passed. I felt my skin go colder and colder. It was like icy insects were crawling over it. At last I thought, 'This is hopeless. We'll have to give up.'

But stubbornly, like an idiot, I kept looking.

Then another whisper from Corrie: 'Over here'.

Kevin and I converged on it at the same time. Just as we did I saw a torch flash for a moment, somewhere near the front verandah. 'They're coming,' I said. 'Quick. Help me push it. But quietly.'

We got it on one side of the driveway, near the brick wall of Mrs Alexander's studio.

'What are the hammer and chisel for?' Kevin whispered urgently.

'To make a hole in the petrol tank,' I said. 'But now I think it'll make too much noise, doing it.'

'Why do you need a hole?' he asked. 'Why not just unscrew the lid?'

I just kept right on feeling stupid. Later I realised I

was even more stupid again, because a hammer and chisel would have caused a spark that would have blown us all up.

Kevin had worked out what I wanted and he unscrewed the cap.

'We'll need to be behind the wall,' I whispered. 'And we need a trail of petrol to it.' He nodded and pulled off his T-shirt, pushing it into the tank to soak it. Then he sat the cap back on the tank and used his shirt to lay the trail of liquid to the wall. We only had seconds left. We could hear the crunch of gravel under soft menacing feet, and an occasional muttered comment. I heard one male voice and one female. The torch flashed again, right at the corner of the drive.

Kevin's voice breathed in my ear. 'We need to make sure they're all together.'

I nodded. I'd just realised the same problem. I could see two dark figures but I assumed we were being hunted by the three patrolling sentries we'd seen before. Kevin confirmed it, breathing in my ear again, 'I saw three of them in the road'.

I nodded again, then took a deep breath and let out a short weak moan of pain. The effect on the two soldiers was dramatic. They turned towards us like they had antennae. I gave a little gasp and a sob. One of the soldiers, the male, called out, urgently, in a language I didn't recognise, and a moment later the third soldier came through the line of trees and joined the first two. They talked for a moment, gesturing in our direction. They must have known by then that we weren't armed: we would have surely let off a few shots by now if we had been. They spread out a little though, and came walking slowly towards us. I waited and waited, till they were about three metres from the mower. The small squat dark shape sat there, as if demanding that they notice it. For the first time I saw their faces; then I struck the match.

It didn't light.

My hand, which had been very steady till then, got the shakes. I thought, 'We're about to die, just because I couldn't light a match'. It seemed unfair, almost ridiculous. I tried again, but was shaking too much. The soldiers were almost past the mower. Kevin grabbed my wrist. 'Do it' he mouthed fiercely in my ear. The soldiers seemed to have heard Kevin, from the way their eager faces turned in our direction again. I struck the match for the third time, almost sure that there wouldn't be enough sulphur left to ignite. But it lit, making a harsh little noise, and I threw it to the ground. I threw it too fast; I don't know how it didn't go out. It should have, and it almost did. For a moment it died to a small dot of light and again I thought 'We're dead, and it's all my fault'. Then the petrol caught, with a quiet quick whoosh.

The flames ran along the line of petrol in fits and starts, like a stuttering snake, but very fast. The soldiers saw it, of course. They turned, looked, seemed to flinch. But in their surprise they were too slow to move, just as I would have been. One lifted an arm, as if to point. Another leaned backwards, almost in slow motion. That's the last image I have of them, because then Kevin pulled me back, behind the brick wall, and an instant later the mower became an exploding bomb. The night seemed to erupt. The wall swayed and shook, and then settled again. A small orange fireball ripped up into the darkness, with little tracer bullets of fire shooting away from it. The noise was shrill and loud and frightening. It hurt my ears. I could see bits of shrapnel hurtling into the trees and I heard and felt a number of bits thud into the wall behind which we were hiding. Then Kevin was tugging at me, saying, 'Run, run'.

At the same time the screams began from the other side of the wall.

We ran through the fruit trees and down the slope at an angle, past the chook shed, reaching Mrs Alexander's front fence at the corner where it met the next property. The screams behind us were ripping the night apart. I hoped that the faster and further we ran the quicker the screams would fade, but that didn't seem to be happening. I didn't know if I was hearing them only with my ears or in my mind as well.

'There's just time,' Corrie panted, from behind me. It took me a minute to realise what she meant: time to meet the others.

'We can go straight there,' Kevin called.

'How's your leg Corrie?' I asked, trying unsuccessfully to return to the normal world.

'OK,' she answered.

We saw headlights coming and ducked into a garden as a truck went past at high speed. It was a tray truck from Wirrawee Hardware, but with soldiers in the back instead of garden tools. Only two soldiers though.

We ran on, reaching Warrigle Street, then racing up the Mathers' steep drive, taking no precautions at all. We were struggling for breath now. My legs felt old and slow. They were really hurting. I stopped and waited for Corrie, then we walked on together, holding hands. We couldn't do any more, go any faster, or fight anyone else.

Homer and Fi were there, surrounded by bikes, a full set of seven now. Our dinking days were over, but ironically, just when we had enough bikes, there were only five of us to ride them. There was no sign of Lee and Robyn. It was 3.35, and from the hill we could see other vehicles leaving the Showground, all heading for Racecourse Road. One of them was the Wirrawee ambulance. We couldn't wait any longer. With only a few tired mumbled words between us – mainly to find out that Fi's house too had been empty – we mounted the cold bikes and pedalled down the hill. I don't know about the others but I felt as though I was going round and round on the spot. I stood and made my legs go harder and faster. As we warmed up we all started to accelerate. It seemed incredible that we could find any more energy but for me the simple need to keep up with the others, not to be left behind, forced me to increase my rate. By the time we passed the 'Welcome to Wirrawee' sign we were going like bats out of Hell.

Chapter Eight

We arrived at Corrie's place a few minutes before dawn. The sky was just starting to lighten. It had been a horrible ride. At every tree I promised myself that we were nearly at the turnoff, but I doubt if we were even half way there when I started promising that. I had pain in every part of me, first in the legs, but then in the chest, then the back, the arms, the throat, the mouth. I burned, I felt sick, I ached. My head got lower and lower, until I was following the back wheel of whoever was in front of me, Corrie I think. My mind was singing a tired chorus of a meaningless song:

'I look at your picture and what do I see?
The face of an angel looking back at me…'

I must have sung that a thousand times. It went round and round in my head like the wheels of the bicycle until I could have screamed in frustration, but nothing would make it go away. I didn't want to think about what had happened at Mrs Alexander's, or the fate of the three soldiers who had chased us, or what might have happened to

Lee and Robyn, so it seemed I had no choice but to sing to myself:

'The face of an angel, come from Heaven above,
You're my sweet angel, the one that I love.'

I tried to remember more of it than just the chorus, but I couldn't.

At one point someone said to me, 'What did you say Ellie?' and I realised I must be singing out loud, but I was too tired to answer whoever was asking the question – I don't even know who it was. Maybe I imagined it anyway. I don't recall anyone else speaking. Even the decision to go to Corrie's seemed to have been taken by osmosis.

We were half way down her driveway before I let myself believe that we'd arrived, that we'd made it. I guess everyone was in the same state. I stopped in front of the Mackenzies' porch and stood there, trying to find the energy to lift my foot and get off the bike. I stood there a long time. I knew eventually I'd have to raise that leg but I didn't know when I'd be able to do it. Finally Homer said kindly, 'Come on Ellie', and I was ashamed of my weakness and managed to stumble off the bike and even wheel it into a shed.

Inside the house Flip was bounding around Kevin like she was a puppy in love, Corrie was making coffee on the camp stove, Fi was sitting at the kitchen table with her head in her hands, and Homer was getting out plates and cutlery. I couldn't believe what a difference it made not having Lee and Robyn; it was like the kitchen was almost empty. 'What do you want me to do?' I said, kind of stupidly, no longer able to think for myself.

'Just sit down and eat,' Homer said. He'd found

cereal and sugar and more long-life milk. I nearly choked on the first few mouthfuls, but after a while I got into the habit of eating again, and the food started to stay down.

Gradually we got talking, and then we couldn't stop. As well as being tired we were so wound up that the conversation became a battle of babbling voices, no one listening to each other, till we were all shouting. Finally Homer stood up, grabbed an empty coffee mug and threw it hard at the back of the fireplace, where it smashed into large white pieces. 'Greek custom,' he explained to our astonished faces, and sat down again. 'Now,' he said, 'let's take it in turns. Ellie, you go first. What happened with you guys?'

I took a deep breath, and fuelled by the mixture of muesli and Rice Bubbles that I'd just eaten, launched into a description of what we'd seen at the Showground. Kevin and Corrie chimed in occasionally when I forgot a detail, but it was only when I got to the part in Mrs Alexander's back garden that I began to have trouble. I couldn't look at anyone, just down at the table, at the piece of muesli box that I was screwing up and twisting and spinning around in my fingers. It was hard for me to believe that I, plain old Ellie, nothing special about me, middle of the road in every way, had probably just killed three people. It was too big a thing for me to get my mind around. When I thought of it baldly like that: killed three people, I was so filled with horror. I felt that my life was permanently damaged, that I could never be normal again, that the rest of my life would just be a shell. Ellie might walk and talk and eat and drink but the inside Ellie, her feelings, was condemned to wither and die. I didn't think much about the three

95

soldiers as people: I couldn't, because I had no real sense of them. I hadn't even seen their faces properly. I didn't know their names or ages or families or backgrounds, the way they thought about life. I still didn't know what country they were from. Because I didn't know any of the things you need to know before you truly know a person, the soldiers hardly existed for me as real people.

So I tried to describe it all as though I were an outsider, a spectator, someone reading it from a book. A history book about other people, not about me. I felt guilty and ashamed about what had happened.

Another thing I was afraid of was almost the opposite: that if I told the story of the mower with any drama at all, the others, especially the boys, would get all macho about it, and start acting like it was a big heroic thing.

I didn't want to be Rambo, just me: just Ellie.

Their reactions weren't what I expected though. Half way through, Homer put one of his big brown hands over mine, which made it harder to shred the muesli box, and Corrie moved up closer and put an arm around me. Fi listened with her eyes fixed on my face and her mouth open, like she couldn't believe what she was hearing. Kevin sat there grim-faced. I don't know what he was thinking but he sure wasn't doing war cries or carving notches on his belt, like I'd half-feared he might.

There was a silence after I finished, then Homer said, 'You guys did well. Don't feel so bad. This is war now, and normal rules don't apply. These people have invaded our land, locked up our families. They caused your dogs to die, Ellie, and they tried to kill you three. The Greek side of me understands these things. The moment they left their country to come here they knew what they were doing. They're the ones who tore up the rule book, not us.'

'Thanks Homer,' I said.

He really had helped me.

'So what happened to you two?' Kevin asked.

'Well,' Homer began. 'We had a good run at first, along Honey Street. But the further into town we got, the more careful we had to be, and the slower we went. There wasn't any excitement till the corner of Maldon and West. There'd been some kind of action there. Must have been a bit of a battle I think – there were two police cars, both on their sides, and a truck just down the road that had crashed into a tree. And there were spent cartridges everywhere, hundreds of them. But no bodies or anything.'

'But blood,' said Fi. 'A lot of blood.'

'Yes, well we think it was blood. A lot of dark stains. But there was oil and stuff everywhere – it was just a big mess. So we went through that pretty carefully, then cut through Jubilee Park. Our idea was to go down Barker Street, but honestly, it was a disaster area. Looked like those American riots on TV. Every shop's had its windows smashed, and there's stuff all over the road and footpaths. I'd say these guys have had themselves a big party.'

'They must think it's Christmas.'

'I don't know if they're heavily into Christmas. We had to laugh though: straight opposite us was a big sign in Tozers' window, saying "Shoplifters will be prosecuted". Well, they've had themselves some shoplifters. The whole shop's been lifted.

'Anyway, we decided to go down that little lane

97

beside Tozers'. It was all dark and shadowy, which suited us. Funny how quickly you adapt to being a night creature. So we moseyed along there, across the carpark, and into Glover Street. Then Fi, who's got hearing like a bat, thought she heard voices, so we ducked into the public dunnies. Into the men's of course: I wasn't going to risk being caught in a ladies' toilet. Actually it wasn't that smart a move. You guys seem to have got into the right kind of thinking pretty quickly, but we've still got to retrain our minds. If anyone had seen us going in there, or if they'd caught us inside it, we'd have been dead meat – the place was a perfect trap. And there was someone coming – I could hear the voices by then too. I'd been thinking of taking a leak, but when you're scared – well, I don't know what it's like for girls but a guy can stand there for half an hour, and not a drip...'

'Come on Homer, get on with it. I want to go to bed soon.'

'OK, OK. Well, we waited and waited. Whoever they were, they were sure taking their time.'

'Homer kept himself busy graffitiing the walls,' Fi interrupted.

'Yes, that's true,' Homer admitted shamelessly. 'I figured it was one time in my life when I could get away with it. When this is all over they'll have more important things to worry about than my messages on the lavatory walls. And they were patriotic messages that I wrote.'

'I don't see what's patriotic about "Wogs Rule",' Fi interrupted again.

'But I wrote other things too.'

'You're an idiot Homer,' Kevin grumbled. 'You never take anything seriously.'

But I remembered Homer's hand on mine when I talked about the screams of the three soldiers who'd been hit by my home-made shrapnel. And I remembered what he'd said to comfort me. I smiled at him, and winked. I knew what he was trying to do.

'Anyway, these guys kept getting closer. And when I say guys, I mean a mixture. Like your patrol, there were men and women. About six or seven altogether, we thought. Our biggest worry was that they would decide to use the toilets. I wanted to go into a cubicle and lock the door, so the "Occupied" sign was showing, and I'm sure they would have respected that. But Fi wasn't so keen, so we got in the cleaner's cubicle instead, by wriggling under the door. That was one place they still hadn't looted. There was no room in there and the smell was terrible, but we felt more secure, although really, like I said before, we were crazy. The whole place was a deathtrap. And sure enough, two minutes later these boots came crunching in: three guys, we thought. Two of them used the urinal and the other one headed for the throne. So it was lucky we did hide, because I wouldn't have liked Fi to be seeing things like that. The guy in the cubicle was right next to us, and geez, if the smell had been bad before, it was shocking now. I think they were trying to save ammunition by gassing us to death. And as for the sound effects...'

Homer gave an imitation. The little dog, Flip, sitting on Kevin's lap, pricked up her ears and barked. Even Fi laughed.

'Lucky we didn't have Flip with us,' Homer commented. He continued his story. 'We didn't learn much, except that they eat a lot of eggs and cheese. They talked a lot, but no language that I recognised.

Not that that means much. All I can say is that they weren't Greek. But Fi's the language student – she does about six, don't you Fi? – and she couldn't tell who they were.'

I reflected that the night they'd spent together had given Homer more confidence with Fi. He'd found the style, the tone, to use with her. And she seemed to enjoy it. She laughed at his jokes and there was more life and colour in her face when she looked at him. She was losing the coolness she'd had before.

'Well,' Homer continued. 'At last they finished whatever it was they were doing, and we heard them shuffle off. We gave them five minutes and then slithered back out under the cleaner's door. We could see the soldiers though, from the door, as they disappeared down Glover Street. They were a funny looking bunch. There were eight altogether, and I think three were women. But of the men, two looked pretty old, and two looked quite young, about our age or even younger. And they were dressed in rough old uniforms.'

'I guess,' said Corrie, 'that to invade a country this size they would have had to call up everyone with four limbs.'

'We didn't have any ride-on mowers lying around,' Homer went on, 'so we tiptoed off in the opposite direction. Nothing much else happened till we got to Fi's...'

'Yes it did,' Fi cut in. 'Remember the shadows?'

'Oh yes,' Homer said. 'You tell them. I didn't see them.'

'About two blocks from my place,' Fi began, 'there's a milk bar, with a little park behind it. The milk bar had been looted, like all the other shops. We were sneaking across the park when I thought I saw a couple of shadows coming out of the milk bar. Shadows of people, I mean. I don't mean shadows either; that's just what I called them, because it was so dark it's what they looked like. At first I thought they would be soldiers, and I grabbed Homer and we hid behind a tree. When I looked out they were disappearing towards Sherlock Road, but I could see they weren't soldiers, just from the way they were acting. I called out to them, and they stopped and looked around, then they talked to each other for a minute, then they ran off. That's all.'

'I never saw them,' Homer explained. 'I nearly died when Fi started yelling out. I thought she must have inhaled too much Dettol in the cleaner's cupboard. But when you think about it, it's logical that there'd still be people running around loose. They can't have caught everyone in the district in this short a time.

'Anyway, we kept plugging up the hill. We got to Fi's place. It was locked but Fi knew where there was a spare key. And now I know too, which could be handy one day. Fi sent me inside with my orders: to open the curtains and pull up the blinds. The main windows are about a hundred metres from the front door, across this enormous hall, so Fi sat on the steps outside while I crept through this pitch-black room. I tell you, it was pretty spooky. You know how psychic I am, and I could feel a presence in there, a being. I knew I was not alone. I got about half way across and suddenly there was this unearthly scream from above, and the next thing, I was being attacked. Devilish claws were tearing at me and a ghostly voice was howling in my ear. And that's how we found that Fi's cat was alive and well and living in the rafters. Fi's folks have been having the ceiling renovated.'

'God you're hopeless Homer.' Kevin yawned. 'Get on with it.'

'Well, I won't go into the depressing details. Like we told you back at Robyn's there was no one home. But everything was in good nick. I'm sure they're OK, that everyone's folks are going to be OK. It sounds like they're all bailed up at the Showground, and once these people have got themselves organised they might start letting them out again. Plenty of food there, anyway. They've got my mum's decorated cake for a start, and that was a prize-winner if ever I saw one.'

There was a bit of a pause, then Corrie asked, 'Did you have any trouble on the trip back to Robyn's?'

Homer became serious, and his voice softened. 'Do you know the Andersens?'

'Is that Mr Andersen who coaches the footy team?'

'Yes. You know their house? Well, we came back a different way, to avoid the shopping centre, and we passed the Andersens' place. Or what's left of it. My mum always says my room looks like a bomb hit it. I know what she means now. I think a bomb did hit the Andersens' place. And two more houses between there and the railway. There's been a bit of damage done round that part of town.' He sat gazing at the table, as though he could still see the wrecked houses. Then he lifted his head and shoulders and kept talking. 'That's about it really. We got back to Robyn's about a quarter to three. We'd been hoping we might see Lee and Robyn on the way, but there was no sign of them. That wait at Robyn's sure seemed a long time. We were terrified that none of you would turn up, that you'd all been caught. Then we heard the shots from the Showground. Scared the buttons off my shirt. Then more shooting, and finally this explosion, in Racecourse Road. My God, it was like fire and brimstone shooting up in the sky. Would have cracked a five on the Richter scale. It was dramatic. You guys sure know how to put on a fireworks show. But of course, standing there and watching it, but not knowing, that wasn't so good. I wouldn't like to do that again.'

He yawned too. 'I think we should have a sleep. It's no use sitting here trying to guess what's happened to Lee and Robyn. We'll only depress the hell out of ourselves. And we can work out our tactics later. What we need is to keep our energy levels high. If we take it in turns to be on watch, we should be OK here for today. I don't think these people would have the manpower to search the whole district in a day.'

'That's fair enough,' I said. 'But we should have an escape route, in case they do come. What you realised when you and Fi were in the cleaner's cupboard applies here too.'

'Those little yellow balls,' Fi said, wrinkling her nose. 'There must have been a thousand of them in there. Why do boys' toilets always have those little yellow balls?'

'How do you know what boys' toilets always have?' Homer asked.

Corrie said, 'Suppose we sleep in the shearers' quarters? Whoever's keeping watch can sit up in the treehouse. If we have a vehicle behind the shearers' quarters we could be away and across the paddock into the bush before anyone gets too close.'

'Would they see or hear the vehicle?' Homer asked.

Corrie considered. 'They might. They shouldn't, if

the sentry picks them up early enough, and if every-one moves fast.'

'Well let's take the bikes up there too, so we've got the silent option if we need it. And let's clean up this kitchen, so there's no sign that we've been here.'

Homer was becoming more surprising with every passing hour. It was getting hard to remember that this fast-thinking guy, who'd just spent fifteen min-utes getting us laughing and talking and feeling good again, wasn't even trusted to hand out the books at school.

Chapter Nine

Fi woke me at around eleven o'clock. That's what we'd agreed, but it was a lot easier to make the agreement than to keep it. I felt heavy and stupid and slow. Climbing the tree was an ordeal. I stood at the trunk and looked up at it for five minutes before I could find the energy.

Some people wake up fast and some people wake up slow. I wake up dead. But I know from experience that if I sit it out for half an hour the energy gradually comes. So I sat lethargically in the treehouse, watching the distant road, waiting patiently for my body to begin to function again.

Once I got used to it, sitting there was OK though. I realised to my disbelief that it had been only about twenty hours since we'd emerged from the bush into this new world. Lives can be changed that quickly. In some ways we should have been used to change. We'd seen a bit of it ourselves. This treehouse, for instance. Corrie and I had spent many hours under its shady roof, holding tea parties, organising our dolls' social lives, playing school, spying on the shearers, pretending we were prisoners trapped there. All our games were imitations of adult rituals and adult lives, although we didn't realise it then of course. Then the day came when we stopped playing. We'd gone a couple of months without our usual games, but a few days into the school holidays I got my dolls out and tried to start up again. And it had all gone. The magic didn't work any more. I could barely even remember how we'd done it, but I tried to recapture the mood, the storylines, the way the dolls had moved and thought and spoken. But now it was like reading a meaningless book. I was shocked that it could have all gone so quickly, sad at how much I'd lost, and a little frightened about what had happened to me and how I'd fill the future hours.

There was a sudden sound from below, and looking down I saw Corrie's red head as she started to climb the tree. I moved to the left to make room for her, and she swung up beside me a moment later.

'I couldn't sleep,' she explained. 'Too much to think about.'

'I slept, but I don't know how.'

'Did you have awful dreams?'

'I don't know. I never remember my dreams.'

'Not like that Theo what's-his-name at school. Every morning in Home Group he'd tell us his full dreams from the night before, in detail. It was so boring.'

'He's just boring full stop.'

'I wonder where they all are now,' Corrie said. 'I hope they are at the Showground. I hope they're OK. It's all I can think about. I keep remembering all the stories we read in History about World War Two and Kampuchea and stuff like that, and my brain just overloads on terror. And then I think about the way those soldiers were shooting at us, and the way they screamed when the mower blew up.'

She picked unhappily at a piece of bark. 'Ellie, I just can't believe this is happening. Invasions only happen in other countries, and on TV. Even if we survive this I know I'll never feel safe again.'

'I was thinking about the games we used to play here.'

'Yes. Yes. The tea parties. And dressing the dolls up. Remember when we put lipstick on them all?'

'Then we lost interest.'

'Mmm, it just faded away, didn't it? We grew up, I guess. Other things came along, like boys.'

'They seemed such innocent days. You know, when we got to high school and stuff, I used to look back and smile and think "God, was I ever innocent!" Santa Claus and tooth fairies and thinking that Mum stuck your paintings on the fridge because they were masterpieces. But I've learnt something now. Corrie, we were still innocent. Right up to yesterday. We didn't believe in Santa Claus but we believed in other fantasies. You said it. You said the big one. We believed we were safe. That was the big fantasy. Now we know we're not, and like you said, we'll never feel safe again, and so it's bye-bye innocence. It's been nice knowing you, but you're gone now.'

We sat there, looking out across the paddocks to the dark fragment of road in the distance, lying across the countryside like a thin black snake. That's where people would appear, if they came in search of us. But there was no movement, just the birds going about their unchanging routines.

'Do you think they'll come?' Corrie asked presently.

'Who? The soldiers? I don't know, but there's something Homer said . . . about them not having the manpower to search the whole district. There's a lot of truth in that, I think. See, my theory is that they're using this valley as a corridor to the big towns and the cities. I reckon they've landed at Cobbler's Bay, and their main interest in Wirrawee is to keep it quiet so they can get free access to the rest of the country. Cobbler's Bay is such a great harbour, and remember, we couldn't see it when we came out of Hell, because of the cloud cover. I bet it's full of ships and there's traffic pouring down the highway right now. But it's not as though Wirrawee's going to be a major target for anyone. We don't have any secret missile bases or nuclear power plants. Or at least we didn't, the last time I looked.'

'I don't know,' said Corrie doubtfully. 'You never know what Mrs Norris was getting up to in the Science Lab at school.'

'You children come down from that tree right now!' said a voice from below. We didn't need to look to know who it was. 'Great bloody sentries you are,' Homer said, climbing to join us. 'And I heard what you said about Mrs Norris, my favourite teacher. I'm going to tell her when we go back to school.'

'Yeah, in twenty years.'

'Wasn't it Mrs Norris's class when you went out the window and down the drainpipe?' I asked.

'It could have been,' Homer admitted.

'What?' said Corrie, laughing.

'Well it got a bit boring,' Homer explained. 'Even more boring than usual. So I thought I'd leave. The window was closer than the door, so when she turned to write on the whiteboard I went over the windowsill and down the drainpipe.'

'And then Ms Maxwell came along,' I chipped in.

'And said, "What are you doing?".'

'Quite a fair question really,' I said.

'So I told her I was inspecting the plumbing,' Homer finished, hanging his head as if he remembered the storm that followed. We were laughing so much we had trouble keeping our grip on the branches.

'I've heard of people being out of their trees,' Corrie said, 'and you nearly are.'

A familiar sound interrupted us. We stopped talking and craned our necks, searching the sky. 'There it is,' said Corrie, pointing. A jet screamed across the hills, so low that we could see the markings. 'One of ours!' Homer yelled excitedly. 'We're still in business!' The jet lifted a little to clear the range and turned to the left, belting away into the distance towards Stratton. 'Look!' Corrie called. Three more jets, dark and ominous, were in hot pursuit. They were flying a little higher but following the same course. The noise was piercing, splitting the peaceful sky and land, like a long Velcro tear. Homer sank back to his position in the bole of the tree. 'Three against one,' he said. 'I hope he makes it.'

'He or she,' I muttered, absent-mindedly.

The long day wore on. When everyone was awake we had a late lunch and talked endlessly of Lee and Robyn, of where they might be, of what could have happened. After a while we realised we were going round in tired circles. Homer had been silent for ten minutes or so, and as our voices trailed off we found ourselves looking at him. Maybe that always happens when someone's been quiet for a while. Maybe it happened because we were starting to recognise

Homer's leadership. He didn't seem to notice, just began talking naturally, as though he had it all worked out.

'How about this?' he said. 'You know how I feel about everyone sticking together. It might be nice for our feelings but it's ultimately stupid. We've got to toughen up, and fast. Just because we like being together, that's not important any more. You know what I'm saying? So, what I suggest is two of us go into Wirrawee to look for Lee and Robyn. If no one's turned up by midnight say, they make their way to Lee's place, and see if they're holed up there, injured maybe.'

'I thought you didn't believe in friendship any more,' Kevin said. 'Seems a hell of a risk to go to Lee's, if we're so worried about saving ourselves.'

Homer looked at him coldly and even Corrie rolled her eyes.

'I'm not doing it just for friendship,' Homer said. 'It's a calculated risk. Seven people are better than five, so we take a risk to try to build up our numbers to seven again.'

'And we could end up with three.'

'We could end up with none. Everything's a risk from now on Kev. We're not going to be safe anywhere, any time, until this thing is over. All we can do is to keep calculating the odds. And if it goes on long enough we'll be caught. But if we do nothing we'll get caught even sooner. The biggest risk is to take no risk. Or to take crazy risks. We've got to be somewhere between one and the other. Obviously whoever goes looking for Lee and Robyn has to be incredibly careful. But I'm sure they can work that out for themselves.'

'So what do the other three do?' Kevin asked. 'Sit back here and eat and sleep? Shame there's nothing on TV.'

'No,' said Homer. He leaned forward. 'Here's what I suggest. They load Corrie's Toyota with everything useful they can find. Then they go to Kevin's and do the same. And to my place and Ellie's if there's time. They pick up the Landrover at Kevin's and fill it too. I'm talking food, clothes, petrol, rifles, tools, everything. By dawn we want to have two vehicles fuelled up, packed to their roofs, and ready to go.'

'To go where?' Kevin asked.

'To Hell,' Homer answered.

That was Homer's genius. He combined action with thought, and he planned ahead. He sensed, I think, that inaction was our enemy. Anyone seeing us at that moment wouldn't have thought that we were in the most desperate positions of our lives. We were all sitting up excitedly, faces flushed and eyes gleaming. We had things to do, positive definite things. It suddenly seemed so obvious that if we had a future, it would be in Hell. And we began to realise that there might still be a life for us.

'We'll make lists,' Fi said. 'We need pens and paper, Corrie.'

Our lists took nearly an hour to compile. They included all kinds of things, such as where the keys to petrol tanks were kept, how to find a foot pump for car tyres, what grade oil to put in the Landrover, and which of my teddies I wanted to have – Alvin. For food we went mainly for rice, noodles, cans, plus tea, coffee, jams, Vegemite, biscuits and cheese. Kevin looked a bit depressed when he realised what a vegetarian he was about to become. But there were sure

111

to be heaps of eggs, in kitchens and chook sheds. Clothing was just all the obvious stuff, but with an emphasis on warmth, in case the weather broke or we were in the bush for a long time – and with an emphasis on dull colours, too, that would camouflage successfully. But it was the extras that took the time. A lot of the stuff was still in the Landrover from our five days in Hell, but it would need to be checked. And we kept thinking of new things, or things that needed topping up. Soap, dishwashing brushes and liquid, shampoo, toothpaste and toothbrushes, firestarters, pens, paper, maps of the district, compasses, books to read, transistor radio – in case a station came back on the air – and batteries, torches, insect repellent, first-aid kits, razors, tampons, packs of cards, chess set, matches, candles, sun cream, binoculars, Kevin's guitar, toilet paper, alarm clock, cameras and film, family photos. Homer didn't comment on the family photos but when that encouraged other family treasures being added to the list he spoke up.

'We can't take things like that,' he said, when Corrie nominated her mother's diaries.

'Why not? They're so important to her. She's always said that if the house was burning they'd be the first things she'd save.'

'Corrie, this isn't a picnic we're going on. We've got to start thinking of ourselves as guerillas. We're already taking teddy bears and guitars. I think that's enough.'

'If we can take family photos we can take my mother's diaries,' Corrie said obstinately.

'That's exactly what'll end up happening,' Homer said. 'You'll say, "Well if the photos can go, the diaries can", and then someone else'll say, "Well if her diaries

112

can go then my father's football trophies can go", and before we know it we'll need a couple of trailers.'

It was just one of many arguments we seemed to have that afternoon. We were tired and nervous and scared for Lee and Robyn and our families. That particular fight was resolved by Fi, who made one of those suggestions that immediately seem so obvious you wonder why it took so long for anyone to think of it.

'Why don't you pack up all the valuables in the house,' she said to Corrie. 'Your mother's jewellery and everything. Then hide them somewhere. Bury them in the vegetable garden.'

It was such a good idea that I hoped there would be time later for me to do the same thing.

Meanwhile Kevin kept trying to sneak extra things onto the list, the most important of which seemed to be condoms. As fast as he wrote them down Corrie crossed them off, till the paper had as many erasures as items. But when we came to firearms he got serious. 'We've got a couple of rifles and a shotgun. One rifle's only a .22 but the other's a .222. The shotgun's a beauty, a twelve-gauge. Plenty of ammo for the rifles, not so much for the shotgun. Unless Dad got some more while we were away, which I doubt. He was talking about it, but I don't think he was going into town except for Commem Day, when the sports store'd be shut.'

Between the rest of us we had only a .22 hornet and a .410. My father had a .303, but ammunition for it had become so expensive that I didn't think he still had any.

I was in the middle of explaining to the others where we kept our ammo. I'd already figured out I'd be one of the people going to town. Suddenly we heard a distant disturbing noise. It sounded like a plane, but louder and rougher, and it was getting closer very quickly. 'It's a helicopter,' Corrie said, looking scared. We ran for the windows. 'Get away from the bloody windows,' Homer yelled, then to me, 'We forgot to have a sentry.' He rattled out a string of orders. 'Kevin, go to the sitting room; Fi, the bathroom; Corrie, your bedroom; Ellie the sunroom. Look carefully out of the windows to see if there's anyone coming by road or across the paddocks. Report to me in the office. I'll be getting the .22.'

We did what he said. He'd chosen four rooms that together gave us a 360 degree view of the countryside. I scuttled across the floor of the sunroom like a big startled cockroach, then stood behind the curtains, wrapped myself in them and peeped out. I couldn't see the helicopter but I could hear it, loud and coarse and threatening. I scrutinised the countryside carefully but could see nothing. Then something did move into my view. It was the little corgi, Flip, waddling across the courtyard. I felt sick. They would have to see her from the air, and what would they make of that? A healthy dog wandering happily around a house that was meant to have been deserted for a week? Should I call her, I wondered, in case they haven't seen her yet? But if she responded too enthusiastically to my call it might make them even more suspicious. I made a decision, to do nothing, and at that moment the helicopter itself came swooping around to my side of the house. It was a great big ugly dark thing, like a powerful wasp, buzzing and staring and hungry to kill. I shrank back into the curtains, afraid to look into the faces of the people in the machine. I felt that they could see through the walls of the house. I squatted, then retreated along the wall of the room, around the next wall, fled through the door and down to the office, where the others were waiting.

'Well?' Homer asked.

'No soldiers,' I said, 'but Flip's out there, wandering around. They must have seen her from the helicopter.'

'That might be enough to make them suspicious,' Homer said. 'They'd be trained to notice anything out of the ordinary.' He swore. 'We've got a lot to learn, assuming we even come out of this. How many soldiers in the chopper?'

He got various answers: 'Hard to say', 'Maybe three', 'I didn't see', 'Three or four, maybe more sitting up the back'.

'If they do land they'll probably spread out.' Homer was thinking aloud. 'A .22 won't be much use. The Toyota's still up at the shearing shed. I can't believe we've been so stupid. It'd be no use trying for that. Go back to the same rooms, and see what they're doing. And try to count the number of soldiers. But don't give them the slightest chance to see you.'

I ran back to the sunroom but the helicopter was not in sight. Its ugly angry sound seemed to fill my head though, to fill the house. It was in every room. I hurried back to the office. 'It's on the west side,' Kevin said. 'Just hovering there, not landing.'

'Look guys,' Homer said. 'If it lands I think we've only got two options. We can sneak out on the opposite side to where it's landed, and use the trees to try to get away into the bush. The bikes are no use and the Toyota's out of reach. So we'd be on foot and relying on our brains and our fitness. The second option would be to surrender.'

There was a grim and frightened silence. We had only one option really, as Homer knew.

'I don't want to be a dead hero,' I said. 'I think we'd have to take our chances and surrender.'

'I agree,' Homer said quickly, as though anxious to get in before someone disagreed.

The only one likely to disagree was Kevin. The four of us looked at him. He hesitated, then swallowed and nodded: 'All right.'

'Let's go back to the sitting room,' Homer said. 'We'll see if it's still there.'

We ran down the corridor, then Kevin eased himself into the room and sidled to the window. 'Still there,' he reported. 'Not doing anything, just watching. No, wait… it's on the move… coming down a little…' Fi gave a cry. I glanced at her. She'd been very quiet all afternoon. She looked like she was about to pass out. I grabbed her hand, and she squeezed mine so hard I thought maybe I'd be the one to pass out. Kevin kept up his commentary. 'They're staring right at me,' he said. 'But I can't believe they could see me.'

'Don't move,' Homer said. 'It's movement that's the giveaway.'

'I know,' Kevin complained. 'What do you think, I'm going to start tap dancing?'

For another two minutes we all stood like mannequins in a shop window. The room seemed to grow darker and darker. When Kevin did speak again it was in a whisper, as though there were soldiers in the corridor.

'It's moving… can't tell… sideways a little, up a bit, up some more. Maybe going over the house, to have a look at the other side.'

'This'll be the big move, one way or the other,' Homer said. 'They won't hang round much longer.' Fi gripped my hand even tighter, something I wouldn't have thought possible. It was worse than carrying a lot of plastic shopping bags loaded with dog food. Kevin kept talking as though he hadn't heard Homer.

'Still going sideways... up a bit more... no, backing off a bit. Come on, back off beautiful. Yes, backing off now, and accelerating too. Oh yes. Make like a hockey player sweetheart; get the puck out of here. Yes! Yes! Fly away, fly away home.' He turned to us with a casual shrug. 'See! All I had to do was use my charm.' Corrie picked up the nearest object and threw it at him, as the helicopter began to sound more like a distant chain saw. The object was a little statue of Mary, which luckily for Corrie, Kevin caught. Fi burst into tears. Homer gave a shaky smile, then swung into action again.

'Let's get cracking,' he said. 'We've been lucky. We can't afford to make that many mistakes again. He herded us all into the sitting room and out the front door. 'We'll have this conference out here, where we can see the road,' he said. 'Now look, I'll tell you what I think. If there's any major holes in it, tell me. Otherwise, let's just do it, OK? We haven't got time for long debates.

'All right. Starting with the dogs. Flip and the other one, at my place, whatsitsname.'

'Millie,' I offered.

'Yes,' said Homer. 'Millie. Guys, we have to abandon them. Leave out all the dry dog food you want for them, but that's all you can do. Second, the milkers. I've had a look at yours Corrie. She's not only got mastitis, it's gone gangrenous as well. We're going to have to shoot her. It'd be too cruel to leave her here to suffer.' I glanced at Corrie. She was absorbing this dry-eyed. Homer continued. 'Third, the Toyota. We can't take it now. They will have seen it from the air, so if it goes missing they might notice that. The three people packing the vehicles will have to take everything they can on bikes, and ride to Kev's and pick up another four-wheel drive there, to go with the Landie.' He glanced at Kevin, to check if that were possible.

Kevin nodded. 'The Ford's still there.'

'Good. One thing I was hoping we could get from here is lots of vegetables from Corrie's mum's garden. But I don't think there'll be time, unless it's done in darkness. For now, I think we should go bush till tonight. Take the bikes and anything else that's absolutely vital, and get going, in case they send troops out from town. I'm sure they won't come out after dark, but till then there's a risk.

'Finally, about tonight.' He was talking very fast, but we weren't missing a word. 'I think Ellie and I should go into town. We need a driver to stay here, and Kevin and Ellie are our best drivers. And it wouldn't be fair to have an all girls group and an all guys group. Then if you three aim to get to Ellie's by dawn, we'll meet you there. If we're not there tomorrow, give us till midnight tomorrow night, then leave for Hell. Leave one car hidden at Ellie's and hide the other one at the top somewhere, near Tailor's Stitch, and go down to the campsite. We'll find our own way there when we can.'

As he talked, Homer had been nervously scanning the road. Now he stood. 'I'm really spooked about that helicopter. Let's get out right now, and save the looting till tonight. I'll meet you at the shearing shed. We'll have to take all the bikes. We need them.'

He picked up the rifle and glanced at Corrie, raising his thick brown eyebrows. She hesitated, then murmured 'You do it'. She came with us as Homer went off alone, to the trees at the end of the house paddock, where the cow was standing restlessly. The shot came a few minutes later, as we jogged up to the shearers' quarters. Corrie wiped her eyes with her left hand. The other one was holding Kevin's hand. I patted her back, feeling inadequate. I knew how she felt. You do get attached to your milkers. I'd seen Dad shoot working dogs that were too old, kangaroos that were trapped in fences and too weak to get up, sheep that were a glut on the market. I knew Millie's days were numbered. But we'd never shot a milker.

'I hope Mum and Dad don't mind us doing these things,' Corrie sniffed.

'They'd have minded if you'd broken that statue,' I said, trying to cheer her up.

'Lucky I play first base,' Kevin said.

We got to the shearers' quarters, where Homer joined us a couple of minutes later. He was just in time. It was maybe ninety seconds after that when a black jet, fast and lethal, came in low from the west. It sounded like every dentist's drill I'd ever heard, magnified a thousand times. We watched from the little windows of a shearer's bedroom, too fascinated and afraid to move. There was something sinister about it, something diabolical. It flew with a sense of purpose, deliberate and cold-blooded. As it crossed the road it seemed to pause a little, give a slight shudder. From under each wing flew two little darts, two horrible black things that grew as they approached us. They were coming terribly fast. Corrie gave a cry that I'll never forget, like a wounded bird. One rocket hit the

119

house, and one was all it took. The house came apart in slow motion. It seemed to hang there in the air, as though it were the kit of a house, a Lego set, about to be assembled. Then a huge orange flower began to bloom within the house. It grew very quickly, until there was no more room for it and it had to push the pieces of house out of the way, to give it room to flower. And suddenly everything exploded. Bricks, wood, galvanised iron, glass, furniture, the sharp orange petals of the flower, all erupting in every direction, till the house was spread all over the paddock, hanging from trees, clinging to fences, lying on the ground. Where the house had stood was now black: no flames, just smoke rising slowly from the foundations. The noise of it rolled across the paddocks like thunder, echoing away into the hills. Bits of debris rattled on the shearers' roof like hail. I couldn't believe how long they kept falling, and after that, after the rattling of the heavy fragments was starting to fade, how long the soft snowflakes took to float down: the pieces of paper, the bits of material, the fragments of fibro, gently and peacefully scattering across the countryside.

The second rocket slammed into the hillside behind the house. I'm not sure if it was meant for the shearing sheds or not. It didn't miss us by much. It hit the hill so hard the whole range seemed to quiver; there was a pause, then the explosion, and a moment later a whole section of the hill just fell away.

The jet turned steeply and did a circuit above the river paddock, so they could watch and enjoy the show I suppose. Then it turned again and accelerated into the distance, back to its foul lair.

Corrie was on the floor, hiccupping, and thrashing

around like a fish on a line. Her pupils had rolled back so far into her head that you couldn't see them any more. Nothing would calm her. We became frightened. Homer ran and got a bucket of water. We splashed some in her face. It seemed to calm her a bit. I picked up the whole bucket and tipped the water over her head. She stopped hiccupping and just sobbed, her head on her knees, her hands clasped around her ankles, water dripping off her. We dried her and hugged her, but it was hours before she calmed enough even to look at us. We just had to stay there and wait, hoping the planes would not come back, hoping they would not send soldiers in trucks. Corrie would not move, and we could not move until she did.

Chapter Ten

With the coming of night Corrie seemed to regather some reason, to be able to understand and to whisper back to us. Her voice was lifeless though, and when we got her up and walking she moved like an old lady. We had her wrapped in blankets from the shearers' beds and we knew that we would never get her on a bike. So at dusk Homer and Kevin took the Toyota and drove to Kevin's, bringing back the Ford and the Toyota. Homer still thought it important to leave the Toyota at Corrie's, to make it look as though we hadn't used it. He was hoping that they'd think we were blown up in the house. 'After all, they may not even be sure that anyone was here,' he argued. 'They may have just seen a movement in the house, or Flip might have made them suspicious.'

Homer had an ability to put himself into the minds of the soldiers, to think their thoughts and to see through their eyes. Imagination, I suppose it's called.

I went looking for Flip, but there was no trace of her. If she'd survived the explosion she was probably still running. 'Be at Stratton by now,' I thought. Still, I'd promised Kevin I'd look, while he was getting the Ford.

The two boys came back at about ten. We'd been nervous while they were away; we'd come to depend on each other so much already. But at last the cars came lurching slowly up the driveway, dodging around pieces of wreckage. It was easy to tell that Homer was driving the Toyota. He wasn't much of a driver.

We had another argument then though, when Homer said that we had to go through with the original plans, including separating into two groups. Corrie had been bad enough when the boys had gone to get the cars. But now, at the thought of Homer and me going into Wirrawee, into what she feared was dangerous territory, she sobbed and clung to me and pleaded with Homer. But he wouldn't back down.

'We can't just crawl under the bed and stay there till this is over,' he said to her. 'We've made a lot of mistakes today, and we've paid a hell of a price. But we'll learn. And we've got to get Lee and Robyn back. You want them back, don't you?'

That was the only argument that seemed to work, a little. While she was thinking about it, Kevin got her into the Ford. Then he and Fi hopped in either side of her; we said quick goodbyes and mounted our bikes, for the ride to Wirrawee.

I can't pretend I was keen to go. But I knew we were the right ones to do it. And I wanted to spend more time with this new Homer, this interesting and clever boy whom I'd known but not known for so many years. Since our trip to Hell I'd been getting quite interested in Lee, but a few hours away from him, and in Homer's company instead, were making a difference.

I remember going to the meatworks once with

Dad for some reason, and while he talked business with the manager I watched the animals being driven up the ramp to the killing floor. What I'd never forgotten was the sight of two steers half way up the ramp, just a couple of minutes away from death, but one still trying to mount the other. I know it's a crude comparison, but that's a bit the way we were. 'In the midst of death we are in life.' We were in the middle of a desperate struggle to stay alive, but here was I, still thinking about boys and love.

After we'd been riding silently for a few minutes Homer came up beside me to ride two abreast. 'Hold my hand Ellie,' he said. 'Can you ride one-handed?'

'Sure.'

We went like that for a k or two, nearly colliding half a dozen times, then had to let go so we could make more speed. But we talked a bit, not about bombs and death and destruction, but about stupid little things. Then we played Categories, to pass the time.

'Name four countries starting with B, by the time we get to the turn-off.'

'Oh help. Brazil, Belgium. Britain, I suppose. Um. Bali? Oh! Bolivia! OK, your turn, five green vegetables, before we pass that telegraph pole.'

'Cabbage, broccoli, spinach. Slow down. Oh, peas and beans of course. Now, five breeds of dog, by the signpost.'

'Easy. Corgis, Labradors, German shepherds, border collies, heelers. Right, here's a Greek one. Name three types of olives.'

'Olives! I wouldn't know one type!'

'Well there are three. You can get green ones, you can get black ones, or you can get stuffed.' He laughed so much he nearly ran off the road.

At the five k sign we started getting serious again, keeping to the edge, staying quiet, Homer riding two hundred metres behind me. I like taking charge – that's no secret – and I think Homer had had enough for a while. Approaching each curve I'd get off and walk to it, then wave Homer up if the road was clear. We passed the 'Welcome' sign, then the old church, and were into what Homer called the suburbs of Wirrawee. As the population of Wirrawee would barely fill a block of flats in the city, the idea of suburbs was another Homer joke. The closer we got to Robyn's, the more tense I became. I was so worried about her and Lee, had been missing them so much, was so scared at the prospect of any more confrontations with soldiers. So much had happened during the day that there'd hardly been time to think of Robyn and Lee, except to say to myself the trite and obvious things, 'I wonder where they are. I hope they're there tonight. I hope they're OK.'

They were true thoughts though, for all that they were trite and obvious.

The last k to Robyn's we moved very very carefully, walking the bikes and ready to jump at anything, the movement of a branch in the breeze, the clatter of a falling strip of bark from a gum, the cry of a night bird. We got to the front gate and looked up the drive. The house was silent and dark.

'I can't remember,' Homer whispered. 'Did we say we'd meet at the house or on the hill at the back?'

'On the hill, I think.'

'I think so too. Let's check there first.'

We left the bikes hidden behind a berry bush near the front gate, and detoured around the house, through the long grass. I was still in front, moving as quietly as I could, except for a couple of surprises – like bumping into a wheelbarrow and falling painfully over a tall sprinkler. After the ride-on mower at Mrs Alexander's that had got Corrie I began to wonder if anyone ever put anything away. But I couldn't see any hope of converting the wheelbarrow or the sprinkler into weapons. Maybe we could turn the sprinkler on and wet the enemy? I giggled at the idea, and got a startled look from Homer.

'Enjoying this are you?' he whispered.

I shook my head, but truth to tell I was feeling more confident and relaxed. I always prefer action; I'm happier when I'm doing things. I've always found TV boring for instance; I prefer stock work or cooking, or even fencing.

At the top of the hill nothing had changed. The view over Wirrawee was the same, the lights were still on at the Showground, and in a few other places. One of those places, as Homer pointed out, was the Hospital. It looked like they had it functioning. But there was no sign of Robyn or Lee. We waited about twenty minutes; then, as we were both yawning and getting cold, we decided to try Plan B, the house.

We stood, and started down the hill. We were fifty metres from the house when Homer grabbed my arm. 'There's someone in there,' he said.

'How do you know?'

'I saw a movement in one of the windows.'

We kept watching for quite a time, but saw nothing.

'Could have been a cat?' I suggested.

'Could have been a platypus but I don't think so.'

I began to inch forward, not for any particular reason, just because I felt we couldn't stand there forever. Homer followed. I didn't stop till I was almost at the back door, so close I could have reached out and touched it. I still wasn't sure why we were doing this. My biggest fear was that we were about to be ambushed. But there was a chance Robyn and Lee were in the house, and we could hardly walk away while there was that possibility. I wanted to open the door, but couldn't figure out how to do it without making a sound. I tried to recall some scenes in movies where the heroes had been in this situation, but couldn't think of any. In the movies they always seemed to kick the door down and burst through with guns drawn. There were at least two reasons we couldn't do that. One, it was noisy; two, we didn't have guns.

I sidled closer to the door and stood in an awkward position, pressed backwards against the wall and trying to open the door with my left hand. I couldn't get enough leverage however, so instead turned and crouched, reaching up with my right hand to grip the knob. It turned silently and smoothly but my nerve failed me for a moment and I paused, holding the knob in that cocked position. Then I pulled it towards me, a little too hard, because I had half expected it to be locked. It came about thirty centimetres, with the screech of a tortured soul. Homer was behind me, so I could no longer see him, but I heard, and could feel, his breath hang in the air and his body rise a little. How I wished for an oilcan. I waited, then decided there was no point in waiting, so pulled the door open another metre. It rasped every centimetre of the way. I was feeling sick but I stood and took three slow careful steps into the darkness. I waited there, hoping my eyes would adjust and I'd be able to make some sense of the dull shapes I could see in front of me. There was a movement of air behind me as Homer came in too: at least, I hoped it was Homer. At the thought that it might be anyone else I felt such a violent moment of panic that I had to give myself a serious talk about self-control. But my nerves sent me forward another couple of steps, till my knee bumped into some kind of soft chair. At that moment I heard a scrape from the next room, as though someone had pushed back a wooden chair on a wooden floor. I tried desperately to think what was in the next room and what it looked like, but my mind was too tired for that kind of work. So instead I tried to tell myself that it hadn't been the scrape of a chair, that no one was there, that I was imagining things. But then came the dreadful confirmation, the sound of a creaking board and the soft tread of a foot.

I instinctively went for the floor, quietly slipping down to the right, then wriggling around the soft chair that I'd just been touching. Behind me I felt Homer doing the same. I lay on the carpet. It smelt like straw, clean dry straw. I could hear Homer shuffling around, sounding like an old dog trying to get comfortable. I was shocked at how much noise he was making. Didn't he realise? But in front of me came another noise: the unmistakable sound of a bolt being drawn back in a breech, then slid forward to cock the rifle.

'Robyn!' I screamed.

Afterwards Homer said I was mad. And even when I explained, he said it wasn't possible I could have worked all that out in a split second. But I could and I did. I knew that the soldiers who'd chased us had modern automatic weapons. And the weapon I'd heard being cocked was just a typical single-shot rifle. Also, I remembered that Mr Mathers had gone hunting with Dad quite often, and he did have his own rifle, a .243. So I knew it had to be Robyn or Lee, and I thought I'd better say something before the bullets started flying.

Later I realised it could have been someone else entirely, a looter, deserter or squatter, or someone on the run from the soldiers. Luckily it wasn't, but I don't know what I would have done if I'd thought of that at the time.

'Ellie,' Robyn said, and fainted. She'd always been a bit prone to fainting. I remember when the School Medical Service came around and in Home Room Mr Kassar had announced the girls would be having rubella injections. As soon as he'd mentioned the word injections, Robyn had been on the floor. And in Geography, while we were watching a film on face carving in the Solomon Islands, we'd lost her again that time.

Homer had a torch and we got some water from the bathroom and splashed it in her face till she came around. We seemed to be giving a few facewashes that day. I was interested to see that the town water supply was still working. There was no electricity at Robyn's, even though we'd seen the power on in other parts of Wirrawee.

I was still pretty calm through all this but one of our worst moments was about to come. When Robyn sat up, the first thing I asked her was 'Where's Lee?'

'He's been shot,' she said, and I felt as though I'd been shot and everything in the world had died.

Homer gave a terrible deep groan; in the torchlight

I saw his face distort, and he suddenly looked old and awful. He grabbed Robyn; at first I thought it was to get more information from her, but I think it was just that he needed to hold on to someone. He was desperate.

'He's not dead,' Robyn said. 'It's a clean wound, but it was quite big. In the calf.'

Robyn looked ghastly too; the torchlight didn't help, but her face was more like a skull than a face, high cheekbones and gaunt cheeks and sunken eyes. And we all smelt so bad. It seemed a long time since our swim in the river, and we'd sweated a lot in the meantime.

'How do we find him?' Homer asked urgently. 'Is he free? Where is he?'

'Take it easy,' Robyn said. 'He's in the restaurant. But it's too early to go back there. Barker Street's like rush hour in the city. I took the worst risks to get here.'

She told us what had happened. They'd had trouble at every street corner, nearly running into a patrol, having to hide from a truck, hearing footsteps behind them. Lee's parents' restaurant was in the middle of the shopping centre, and their house was above the restaurant. As Homer and Fi had found, Barker Street, the main shopping drag, was a mess. Robyn and Lee had come in from the opposite end to Homer and Fiona, but their problems were the same. They'd taken an hour to travel one block, because there were two groups of soldiers looting; one group in the chemists and one in Ernie's Milk Bar.

As they waited, hiding in the staircase of City and Country Insurance, they'd heard a noise at the top of the stairs. They'd turned around and found themselves

130

looking at Mr Clement, the dentist, crouching there furtively, peering down at them.

Lee and Robyn had been wildly excited to see him, just as Homer and I were to hear about it. But he hadn't been so excited to see them. It turned out that he'd been there the whole time, watching them without saying anything. It was only when he got a cramp that he made a noise. When they asked why, he just said something about 'least said, soonest mended'.

He did give them some valuable information, however grudgingly and impatiently. He said everyone who'd been caught was held at the Showground. He said that there were two types of soldiers: professionals and the ones who were just there to make up the numbers. Conscripts probably. The professionals were super efficient but the conscripts were badly trained and poorly equipped, and some of them were really vicious. Oddly enough, it was the professionals who treated people better.

He said that the soldiers hadn't got the numbers to search the town thoroughly, house by house. Their policy was to preserve their own lives at any cost. If they suspected danger in a house they'd set up a rocket launcher and destroy the house, rather than go in to a possible ambush. He said he thought there were a few dozen people like himself hiding out, but after they'd seen what happened to people who, in his words, 'tried to be heroes', they were all keeping well out of sight. Robyn got the impression that Mr Clement had his family hidden somewhere close by but he wouldn't answer any personal questions, so they gave up asking. Then a patrol went past the building, and Mr Clement got really agitated and told them to go.

131

They crept along the street, but there was little cover and not enough darkness, as the lights were on in several shops. They were dodging towards the door of the newsagency when shots started pouring down the street. Robyn said they sounded so loud it was like they were from ten metres behind, but in reality they didn't know who was firing or where the shots were coming from. But Robyn and Lee were definitely the targets.

'We were two steps from the glassed-in bit that takes you to the door of the newsagents,' Robyn explained. 'That was the only thing that saved us. It was like we already had the momentum up to go those two steps. Even if we'd been hit by a dozen bullets we'd still have gone the two steps.'

They got into that little bit of cover and went straight on, through the smashed door of the newsagency itself. Robyn took the lead, not realising that Lee had been shot. The newsagency was dark but there was enough light from the street for them to see their way. The trouble was there was enough light to make them good targets, too.

Both of them knew of course that the newsagency goes right through to the carpark and Glover Street. Their idea was to get out the back and then go in whatever direction seemed better at the time. But when Robyn was nearly at the back door she realised two things: that the door was locked, and that Lee was a long way behind her. 'I thought he'd stopped to look at the pornos,' she said. But when she turned around she could see by the paleness of his face that he was hurt. He was limping heavily, staring at her but biting his lip, determined not to cry out. She hoped he'd just pulled a muscle but she said 'Were you hit?' and he nodded.

Robyn skipped over the next bit pretty quickly but it's one of the reasons for writing all this down, because I want people to know about stuff like this, how brave Robyn was that night. I don't want medals for her, and neither would she – well I don't know, I haven't asked her, she'd probably love it – but I think she was a bloody hero. She picked up the photocopier that sits on a stand near the lottery desk and chucked the whole thing through the door. Then she ran to Lee, heaved him onto her back, across her shoulders, and carried him through the shattered door, kicking out bits of glass as she went. Now I know Robyn's fit, and strong, but she's not that strong. Don't ask me to explain it. I reckon it's like those stories of mothers lifting cars to get trapped babies out from underneath, then you ask them the next day to do it again and they can't even move it, because the urgency's gone. Robyn, being religious, has got a different explanation, and who knows? I'm not stupid enough to say she's wrong.

Well, carrying Lee, she staggered along the five buildings to get to the restaurant. The old door at the back, facing the carpark, had been broken open, so she got in there OK. She dropped Lee onto the loading dock and pulled up the roller door and dragged him into the darkness. Then she raced out to the front to have a look into Barker Street. There were three soldiers looking into the newsagency. After a couple of minutes two more came out and joined the other three, then the five of them came walking past the restaurant, lighting cigarettes and talking and laughing. They seemed to just walk off into the distance without showing much interest, so she figured there wouldn't be any more problems from them for a while.

'They probably thought you were looters,' Homer said. 'Like Mr Clement said, there must be a few around, so the patrols'd see them quite often. They wouldn't bother mounting a big operation just for that. And they wouldn't want to blow up Barker Street unnecessarily.'

'But they blew up Corrie's,' I said.

'Mmm,' Homer agreed. 'But the shops in Barker Street are still full of stuff. And maybe they found some way of connecting Corrie's with the lawn-mower bomb. Or maybe it was just an easy low-risk target for them. Maybe they're wiping out all the farm houses.'

Robyn looked horrified and we had to explain what had happened at Corrie's. Eventually, though, she finished her story. She'd cut Lee's trousers off while he lay there making rude jokes, but he was cold and pale and she thought he was in shock. She'd stopped the bleeding with a pressure bandage, wrapped him up warmly, then somehow found the courage to go back to City and Country Insurance and wait there nearly an hour, for Mr Clement. When he arrived, with a couple of bags of food, she bullied him into coming to look at Lee.

'He wasn't keen,' she admitted, 'but in the end he was good. He went into his surgery and came back with all kinds of bits and pieces, including painkiller injections. He gave Lee a needle, then inspected the wound. He said it was clean, and the bullet had gone right through, and if we kept it clean he'd probably be OK, but it'd take a while to heal. He stitched it up, then he taught me how to give injections, and on condition I didn't bother him again he left some stuff with me – painkillers and disinfectant and a syringe and needles. I've given him two injections today. It was cool fun.'

'Robyn!' I nearly passed out myself, in amazement. 'You faint when people even mention injections!'

'Yes, I know,' she said, with her head on one side as though she were a botanist studying herself. 'It's funny, isn't it?'

'What's he like now?' Homer asked. 'Can he walk?'

'Not too much. Mr Clement said he's got to rest it till the stitches come out, in a week minimum. He showed me how to take them out.'

I just rolled my eyes. Robyn taking out stitches! There was no point even commenting.

'Was there any sign of Lee's family?'

'No. And the place was a mess. Windows broken, tables and chairs smashed. And the flat upstairs had been ransacked. It's hard to know whether there'd been a fight, or whether the soldiers did it for fun.'

'How's Lee reacting to all this?'

'He couldn't get upstairs, because of his leg, so I had to describe it to him. Then he'd think of something else that he wanted to know about, and I'd have to run up the stairs to look for it. I went up and down those stairs a lot of times. He was pretty upset though, about everything: his family, the flat, the restaurant, his leg. But he was a bit better tonight. Getting some colour in his face. That was about three hours ago. I've been sitting here a long time, waiting for you guys. I was getting slightly worried.'

'You were meant to wait on the hill behind the house,' I said.

'No I wasn't! It was here! That's what we said!"

'No! It was the hill!'

135

'Listen, we agreed we'd…'

It was crazy. We were having an argument. Homer said, in a tired voice, 'Belt up. We'll just have to make better arrangements next time. Anyway Ellie, when we were talking about it before, you couldn't remember whether it was the house or the hill.'

There was a pause. Then Homer continued. 'We're going to have to get him out. They'll find him pretty quickly there. The more settled these people get, the more they'll organise themselves, and the more they'll start getting tighter control of everything. They might be tolerating guys like Mr Clement for now, but he won't last long. These people showed at Corrie's how serious they are.'

We sat there, in silent agreement, three minds working on one topic: how to get Lee away from Barker Street despite his wounded leg.

'One of the biggest problems is that Barker Street seems to crawl with soldiers, compared to the rest of town, anyway,' Homer added.

'We need a vehicle,' Robyn said helpfully.

'Well whoopiedoo,' I said, unhelpfully.

'What about a silent vehicle?' said Homer. 'It'd be hard to drive a car in there without us all getting shot up.'

'Let's brainstorm,' Robyn said.

'Great,' I said. 'I'll get the textas and butcher's paper.'

'Ellie!' Robyn said.

'Strike two,' Homer said to me. 'Three strikes and you're out.'

I don't know what was wrong with me. Just tired I guess. And I tend to get a bit sarcastic when I'm tired.

'Sorry,' I said. 'I'll get serious. What was the last

nomination? Silent vehicles. OK. Golf carts. Shopping trollies. Wheelbarrows.'

I was quite impressed with myself, and the others were definitely impressed.

'Ellie!' Robyn said again, but in quite a different tone to the last time.

'Prams. Pushers,' said Homer.

The ideas started flying.

'Furniture on wheels.'

'Pedicabs.'

'Horse-drawn vehicles.'

'Toboggans. Skis. Sleighs. Forklift trucks.'

'Those things, what are they called, on wheels, that people served afternoon tea from in the old days.'

'Yeah, I know what you mean.'

'Billy carts.'

'Beds on wheels. Hospital beds.'

'Stretchers.'

'Wheelchairs.'

Like with the cap of the petrol tank on the ride-on mower we'd been ignoring the obvious all this time. Homer and I looked at Robyn. 'Could he ride in a wheelchair?'

She considered. 'I guess so. I think it'd hurt him, but if we could elevate his leg and make certain we didn't bump it... And,' she added with eyes gleaming, 'I could give him another shot.'

'Robyn! You're dangerous!'

'What else was possible, from the things we said?'

'A wheelbarrow's possible, but again it'd have to hurt him. From our point of view it's easier than a lot of things. A stretcher would be good for Lee, but we're all pretty tired. I don't know how far we could carry him.'

'A forklift would be the most fun. I think they're easy to drive. And the bullets would just bounce off it.'

Something in Homer's last sentence flicked a switch in my brain.

'Maybe we're going about this the wrong way.'

'Yes?'

'Well, we're thinking of little quiet sneaky things. We could go to the other extreme. Rock up in something so indestructible that we didn't give a damn who saw or heard us.'

Robyn sat up. 'Such as?'

'I don't know, a bulldozer.'

'Oh!' Robyn said. 'One of those trucks with the shovel in front. We could use the shovel as a shield.'

Suddenly the three of us got very excited.

'All right,' said Homer. 'Let's look at this carefully. Problem one, driver. Ellie?'

'Yes, I think so. We've got the old Dodge at home, for taking hay round the paddocks and stuff. Driving that's just like driving a big car. It's got a two-speed diff but that's cool. I couldn't say for certain until I saw it, but it should be OK.'

'Problem two then. Where would we get it?'

Robyn interrupted. I'd forgotten she hadn't seen Homer in action at Corrie's.

'Homer, are you on something?'

'Sorry?'

'You keep going like this, you'll lose your reputation. Aren't you meant to be just a wild and crazy guy?'

He laughed, but then went straight back to being serious. Robyn made a face at me and I winked back.

'So, problem two?'

'Well, the Council Depot's the obvious place. It's what, three blocks from the restaurant. It's probably been broken open, but we should take bolt cutters in case. The keys to the vehicles would be in an office there somewhere, again assuming they haven't been looted.'

'All right. Sounds logical. Problem three. Suppose we pick Lee up. We can't drive to Ellie's in the truck, obviously. And Lee can't use a bike. How do we get him to Ellie's?'

This was the toughest one. No one had any easy answers. We sat staring at each other, turning ideas over in our minds. Finally Homer spoke up.

'OK, let's come back to that one. Let's look at other details. The plan's basically a good one. It's got the big advantage of surprise, plus it puts us in a position of strength. If we had Lee in a wheelchair or a wheelbarrow and we were pushing him down the street and a patrol appeared, what could we do? Push harder? Dump Lee? We'd be in such a weak position. But if Robyn goes back to the restaurant, gets Lee ready, gets him close to the street, gives him acupuncture and whips his appendix out and anything else she feels like to fill in time, Ellie and I could get the truck, burn down the street, stop, throw you guys in, accelerate and go like hell. If we do it between three and four am, that should be when they're at their weakest.'

'That's when humans are always at their weakest,' I contributed. 'We did that in Human Dev. Three to four am, that's when most deaths occur in hospitals.'

'Well, thanks for that comforting thought,' Robyn said.

'We'll have to be at our strongest,' Homer said.

'Where do we actually put Lee?' I asked. 'It'll need to be such a quick pick-up. There won't be room in the cab, so we'll have to get him into the tray part somehow.'

Homer looked at me, eyes shining with joy. I realised the wild and crazy guy wasn't so far away. 'We pick him up in the shovel,' he said, and waited for our reactions.

Our first reactions didn't disappoint him, but the more I thought about it, the more it made sense. It all depended on us being able to operate the shovel part quickly and accurately. If we could do that, it was the best solution. If we couldn't, we had a disaster.

After we tossed the options around Robyn suggested some more of the plan. 'If we have a car waiting,' she said, 'in a place where it'd be hard for them to follow, or hard for them to use their guns, then we transfer to that... And either head out to Ellie's, or hole up in town another night...'

I tried to think of some unusual place where we could swap vehicles. Somewhere special... somewhere different... my eyes closed and I had to sit up with a jerk and shake myself awake.

'The cemetery?' I said hopefully. 'Maybe they're superstitious?'

I don't think the other two knew what I was talking about.

Homer looked at his watch. 'We have to make some quick decisions,' he said.

'OK,' said Robyn, 'how about this? Ellie mentioned the cemetery. You know Three Pigs Lane? Past the Cemetery? That long narrow track across to Meldon Marsh Road? Here's what I think we should do.'

Ten minutes later she'd finished. It sounded OK to me. Not great, but OK.

Chapter Eleven

The time was 3.05 am. I had the shivers; not the shakes but the shivers. It was getting hard to tell the difference though. It was also getting hard to tell when one shiver ended and the next began.

Cold, fear, excitement. They were all contributing generously. But the greatest of these was fear. That rang a bell – a quote from somewhere. Yes, the Bible: 'and the greatest of these was love'. My fear came from love. Love for my friends. I didn't want to let them down. If I did, they would die.

I looked at my watch again. 3.08. We really had coordinated our watches, just like in the movies. I pulled my chinstrap a little tighter. I must have looked pretty silly, but the only useful things I'd found in the Council Depot, apart from ignition keys, were these safety helmets. I'd put one on and chucked six more in the truck. They probably wouldn't stop a bullet, but they might make the difference between death and just permanent brain damage. The shiver became a shudder. It was 3.10. I turned the ignition key.

The truck rumbled and shook. I reversed carefully, trying not to see soldiers under every tree, behind every vehicle. 'Never reverse an inch more than you have to.' That was Dad's voice. With him it applied to going forward too. And I wasn't just talking about driving. I grinned, put in the clutch again, and chose low second. Out with the clutch – and I stalled. Suddenly I was hot and sweaty instead of cold and lonely. That was one of the weaknesses of this plan: I had no time to get used to the vehicle, to practise.

Coming out of the gates I put the lights on as I turned into Sherlock Road. This was one of the things we'd argued most about. I still didn't think Homer and Robyn were right, but we'd agreed to do it, so I did it. Homer had said, 'It'll confuse them. They'll have to think it's one of their own. It might just give us another few seconds.' I'd said, 'It'll attract them. They might hear the noise a block or two away but they'll see the lights a k away.' So the argument had gone, backwards and forwards.

I came to Barker Street and began the turn. It was so awkward manoeuvring this big heavy slothful thing around a corner. I'd started working at it a hundred metres before the corner but even that wasn't enough and I went far too wide, nearly hitting the gutter on the opposite side of Barker Street. By the time I got it straightened and on the right side of the road I was nearly on top of Robyn and Lee.

And there they were. Lee, white-faced, leaning on a telegraph pole, staring at me like I was a ghost. Or was he the ghost? He had a big white bandage wrapped around his calf and the wounded leg was resting on a rubbish tin. And Robyn, standing beside him, not looking at me but peering with sharp eyes in every direction.

I'd already brought the shovel down as low as I

could, as I drove along. Now I brought it down further and hit the brakes. I should have done it the other way round, the brakes then the shovel, because the shovel hit the ground with a burst of sparks, ploughing up bitumen for about twenty metres, till the truck came to a rocking halt and stalled again. I hadn't really needed to bring the shovel down any further, because Lee could have easily hopped into it, but I was trying to be smart, show off my skill and finesse. Now I had to start the engine, slam the truck into reverse and, as Lee came hopping painfully forward, bring the shovel up a bit and come in again.

Robyn helped him into the shovel. She was being so calm. I watched through the windscreen, too intent on their silent struggle to look anywhere else. A whistle was the first I realised anything was wrong. I looked up, startled. Lee had just got into the shovel and was lying down. Robyn, hearing the whistle and without even looking to see where it was from, came pelting round to the passenger door. I could see some soldiers at the end of the street, pointing and staring. Some were dropping to one knee and lifting their rifles. Perhaps the headlights had bought us a moment, for they hadn't fired yet. Although we'd worked out a route and agreed on it I decided I was no longer bound by majority vote: circumstances had changed. I tilted the shovel up then grabbed the gearstick. The truck rasped reluctantly into reverse again. 'Don't drop the clutch,' I begged myself. 'Don't stall,' I begged the truck. We started going backwards. 'Put a helmet on,' I yelled at Robyn. She actually laughed but she took a helmet. The first bullets hit. They rang on the steel of the truck like a giant with a sledgehammer was attacking it. Some of

143

them hummed away again, out into the darkness, violent blind mosquitos, ricochets. I hoped they wouldn't hit anyone innocent. The windscreen collapsed in a waterfall of glass. 'Never reverse an inch more than you have to.' We're using metrics now Dad, in case you hadn't noticed. Inches went out with paddle steamers and black and white TV. Anyway, sometimes you have to go backwards before you can go forwards. Before you go anywhere. We were going backwards way too fast though. I wanted to take the corner in reverse, as there wouldn't be time to stop, change gears and go around it the right way. I started spinning the wheel, hoping that Lee was holding on tight. My poor driving was at least making it hard for the soldiers – we were an erratic target. We lurched over something, then I instinctively ducked as something else whipped over the top of the truck. It was a tree. I spun the wheel even more sharply and the wheels on the left hand side left the ground. Robyn lost her composure and screamed, then said 'Sorry'. I couldn't believe she'd said it. Somehow the truck didn't turn over; the wheels came down again and we rocked our way along a footpath, knocking down fences and shrubs. I was using the wing mirrors mostly; the tray and its sides blocked the view through the back window or in the rear vision mirror. I dragged hard on the wheel again, as hard as I dared. We'd either roll now or make the corner. One more bullet hit us as we went around; it flew so close to me that it made a breeze against my skin, then shattered the side window. We thumped back on to the road, out of sight of the patrol. In the wing mirror on my side I caught one glimpse of a small vehicle with lights on high beam. It was a jeep I think. There was no way we could miss it, and we didn't. We smashed into it bloody hard and ran right over the top of it. Both Robyn and I hit our heads on the roof of the truck, justifying the safety helmets. I gave a savage grin at that thought.

Running over the jeep was like running over a small hill at high speed. I wrenched on the wheel and the truck made a sharp 180-degree turn. Now at last we were facing in the right direction. Ahead of us was the car we'd hit. I could see bodies in it, but the car looked like a huge boulder had been dropped on top of it. Two or three soldiers were crawling away into the darkness, like slaters. I gunned the engine and we charged. We swerved around the jeep but still hit it a glancing blow, first with the shovel, then with the left-hand front side of the truck. I felt sorry for Lee: I'd forgotten to raise the shovel. We raced down Sherlock Road. It was hard to see a lot. I tried the lights on high beam but nothing happened: it seemed that we only had parking lights left. Then Robyn said 'There's blood absolutely pouring down your face', and I realised another reason I couldn't see too well. I'd thought it was sweat. 'Put your safety belt on,' I said. She laughed again but she buckled it on.

'Do you think Lee's all right?'

'I'm praying my ass off.'

At that moment came the happiest sight I'd ever seen. A thin hand appeared out of the shovel, made a V sign or a peace sign – it was hard to tell in the dimness – and disappeared again. We both laughed this time.

'Are you all right?' Robyn asked anxiously. 'Your face?'

'I think so. I don't even know what it is. It doesn't hurt, just stings.'

Cold wind was rushing into our faces as I accelerated. We got another block, past the High School, before Robyn, looking out of her side window, said 'They're coming'.

I glanced in the wing mirror, and saw the headlights. There seemed to be two vehicles.

'How far to go?'

'Two k's. Maybe three.'

'Start praying again.'

'Did you think I'd stopped?'

I had my foot pressed so hard to the floor my arch was hurting. But they were gaining so fast we might as well have been standing still. Within another block they were fifty metres behind us.

'They're firing,' said Robyn. 'I can see the flashes.'

We roared through a stop sign, doing 95 k's. One of the cars was now right on our tail, the headlights glaring into my mirror. Then the mirror disappeared. Even though I was looking right at it I didn't see it go. But it definitely went.

The stop sign didn't give me the idea; I'd already vaguely thought of it as a possible tactic. But the sign seemed like an omen, appearing when it did. I decided to follow its advice. I just hoped Lee would survive.

'Hold on real tight!' I yelled at Robyn, then hit the brakes with everything I had. I used the handbrake as well as the foot brake. The truck skidded, went sideways, nearly rolled. It was still skidding when I heard the satisfying crump of the car behind hitting us on our rear right side, then saw it spinning out of control away into the darkness. Then it rolled. We came to a stop and sat there, rocking heavily. The engine stalled again and for a minute we were a perfect target. I furiously wrenched at the key, so hard that the soft metal actually twisted in my grip. The second car was braking and almost stationary, but about a hundred metres away. The truck started. I rammed it into gear. More flashes of gunfire came from the second car, and suddenly there were two bangs from underneath me. I swung the truck onto the road and hit the accelerator, but the truck was tilting and sluggish, wallowing all over the road and bumping badly. 'What's wrong?' Robyn said. She looked scared, unusual for Robyn.

'They've shot some tyres out.' Robyn's mirror was still there and I glanced at that. The second car had started again and was coming on fast. Robyn was looking through the little rear window.

'What's in the back here?'

'I don't know. I didn't look.'

'Well there's something there. How do you operate the tipper?'

'That blue lever I think.' Robyn grabbed it and heaved it down. The second car was now trying to pass us. I was swerving all over the road to prevent him, a process made easier by the punctured tyres. Then something did start pouring out of the back, with a slow sliding noise. I still don't know what it was, gravel or mud or something. In Robyn's mirror I saw the car brake so hard it nearly stood on its head. A minute later we were at Three Pigs Lane.

I slewed the wheel around and blocked the lane with the truck as we'd agreed. For a moment I couldn't see Homer. I felt sick. All I wanted to do was fall on my knees in the dirt of the lane and vomit. Robyn had total faith though. She was out of the truck and running to the shovel, helping Lee to stand. Then I saw Homer, backing dangerously fast, without lights, towards us. I jumped out of the truck and ran at him as he brought the car to a wobbling halt, just a few metres away from me and in the gutter. Everyone seemed to be reversing tonight, and not very efficiently. I heard a bang, and another bullet whirred past me, somewhere in the darkness. Homer was out of the car. It was a station wagon, a BMW, and he was opening the tailgate and helping Lee in. Robyn left him to it and ran to the front passenger door, opening it, and the back one for Homer. A bullet hit the car, smashing a hole in the rear passenger door. Only one person seemed to be firing at us, using a handgun. It was quite possible that there'd only been one person in that second car. Homer had left the driver's door open and the engine running. I clambered in, out of the gutter, and looked around. Lee was in, Homer was getting in, Robyn was in. Close enough. I pushed it in gear, not adjusting well after the truck, and using too much force on the clutch and the gearstick. We kangaroo-hopped out of the gutter. There was a cry of pain from the back of the BMW. I put the clutch back in and tried again, this time getting a smoother takeoff, then lost yet another side window and windscreen, to a bullet that must have angled past me.

We'd been lucky, but when anyone's shooting at a wildly moving target in the dark the luck should favour the target. I knew that from hunting trips. Sometimes I'd have a shot at a hare or rabbit that the dogs were chasing. It was a waste of ammunition, and dangerous for the dogs, but fun. I only ever got one, and that was a fluke. These guys had actually done pretty well in their attempts at us. They weren't to be underestimated. Some of them might be undertrained, like Mr Clement had said, but they'd given us a hard time.

The BMW was flying. It was a dirt road, but straight, and smoother than most. 'Nice car,' I said to Homer, glancing at him in the rear vision mirror.

He gave an evil grin. 'Thought I might as well get a good one.'

'Whose is it?'

'I don't know. One of those big houses by the golf course.'

Robyn, beside me, turned and looked to the rear of the car.

'You OK, Lee?'

There was a pause, then Lee's quiet voice, which I felt like I hadn't heard in a year. 'Better than I was in that bloody truck.' We all laughed, loudly, like we had a lot of nervous energy.

Robyn turned to me, took my helmet off and started inspecting my forehead as I drove. 'Don't,' I said. 'Too distracting.'

'But there's blood all over your face and shoulders.'

'I don't think it's anything.' I certainly hadn't felt a thing. 'It's probably just a bit of glass. Head wounds always bleed a lot.'

Already we were approaching Meldon Marsh Road. I slowed down and turned the lights off, leaning forward to concentrate. Driving at night without lights is horribly hard and dangerous, but I figured we'd lost the element of surprise that we'd had with the trucks. These guys would have radios. We had to rely on concealment now.

To drive directly to my place would have taken about forty or fifty minutes. But we still had a couple of hours of darkness left, and we'd agreed when making our plans, back at Robyn's, to use that time. It

149

was a choice of two evils. To go straight home would make it too easy for them to track us. To stay on the roads would expose us to enemy patrols. We could have hidden up somewhere and gone to my place the next night, but we figured that with every passing day, the grip these people had on the district would tighten. And after the damage we'd just done to them they might well bring in more troops by the next night.

Besides, we all wanted so desperately to get back to Fi and Corrie and Kevin, and to the sanctuary of Hell. We couldn't bear the thought of another day so far away from it. We wanted to get as close as we could. It took all our self-control to take a roundabout route now.

Homer'd had the time, as he sat silently waiting in the BMW, parked in the shadows of Three Pigs Lane, to work out a rough route, and now he started calling out instructions from pencil marks he'd made on a map. 'This takes us past Chris Lang's place,' he said, as we drove as fast as I dared along Meldon Marsh Road. 'We'll change cars there. If the keys aren't in the cars, I know where they'll be.'

'Why are we changing cars?' asked Lee's tired voice from the back. I think he was dreading another painful move.

Homer explained. 'Our plan is to go up to Hell in four-wheel drives and hide out there for a while. The Landrover'll be packed and ready, at Ellie's. That means we'll be dumping whatever car we've used to get there. Now if, a day or two later, a patrol arrives at Ellie's and finds a shot up BMW, that they've been searching the district for... well, some very nasty things could happen to Ellie's parents.'

There was a pause, then Lee said, 'Chris's parents have got a Merc.'

'That did cross my mind,' Homer admitted. 'And they're overseas, so the Merc's probably in the garage, not at the Showground. I don't think Chris has got his licence yet. If we're going to have a war we may as well have it in style. Next left, El.'

We arrived at Chris's ten minutes later, racing straight past the house to the garage and sheds, about a hundred metres away. We were getting tired, not just with physical exhaustion but with the emotional intensity of the last few hours. We climbed stiffly out of the car. The others went looking for the Merc while I went to the back of the BMW to talk to Lee. I was shocked by how pale he looked; his hair was blacker and his eyes bigger than ever. He smelt even worse than we did, and there was a new dark red stain on his bandage.

'You're bleeding,' I said.

'Only a little. I'd say a couple of stitches probably came apart.'

'You look awful.'

'And smell it too. Lying there sweating for twenty-four hours, I wouldn't recommend it.' There was a pause, then, self-consciously, he said, 'Listen, Ellie, thanks for getting me out of there. Every minute of the twenty-four hours I could hear the footsteps of soldiers coming to get me.'

'Sorry about the wild trip in the truck.'

He grinned. 'I couldn't believe it. Towards the end there, when you hit the brakes, I actually got thrown out, but I did a sort of roll and landed back in. That's when I bust a few stitches I think.'

'Yeah, I'm sorry. We needed to get rid of a car

behind us.' I wiped my face. 'God, I can't believe the things we've done.'

'A couple of bullets hit the shovel. They didn't go through it, but the noise they made! I thought I was dead. But I don't think they knew I was in there, or they would have sprayed it with bullets.' Homer came backing out of the garage in a large olive-green Mercedes. Lee laughed. 'Homer hasn't changed.'

'Yes he has.'

'Has he? I'll be interested to see that. He's a pretty smart guy, Homer. Listen Ellie, there's one problem here. If we leave the BMW sitting where it is, and a patrol finds it, they'll think there's a connection between us and Chris's family. They might burn his house, or if they've got Chris as one of their prisoners, they might do something to him.'

'You're right.' I turned to the others, who were getting out of the Merc, and repeated what Lee had said. Homer listened, nodded, and pointed to the dam.

'Can we do that?' I asked. 'To a nice new BMW with only a couple of bullet holes?'

It seemed that we could. I drove it to the upper side of the dam, put it in neutral, got out and gave it a good push. It was a light car and moved easily. It ran down the slope, holding almost a perfect line, and went straight into the water. It floated out for a few metres, getting lower and lower, then stopped floating, leaned to one side and began sinking. With a sudden gurgle and a lot of bubbles, it disappeared. There was a small cheer from Robyn and Homer and me.

And it was the noise of that small cheer which brought Chris out from his hiding place.

He looked funny, dressed in pyjamas, standing there, rubbing his eyes and staring at us. But we probably looked funny to him, like scarecrows in shock, staring back at him in astonishment. He'd come out of their old piggery, which these days was just a row of old sheds, so obviously abandoned and derelict that it was a good choice for a hiding place.

Time was getting short. We had to make some quick decisions. It didn't take Chris long to decide he wanted to come with us. For a week he'd had no contact with anyone, just watched from a tree, and later the piggery, as patrol after patrol came through the property. The first group had taken all the cash and jewellery; Chris had buried the other small valuables after that, but had spent the rest of the week in hiding, emerging only to check animals and pick up supplies from the house.

His story, told from the back seat of his family Merc as we cruised the side roads, made us realise how lucky we'd been to avoid ground patrols. His house was closer to town than ours, and much grander and more conspicuous, and he'd had daily visits from soldiers.

'They seem nervous,' he said. 'They're not into being heroes. They stick close together. The first few days they were really jumpy, but they're more confident now.'

'How did it start?' I asked. 'Like, when did you first realise something funny was happening?'

Chris was normally quiet but he hadn't talked for so long that now he was the life of the party.

'Well, it was the day after Mum and Dad left for their trip. You remember? That's why I couldn't come on the hike with you. Murray, he's our worker, was taking his family into the Show and he offered me a lift, but I didn't want to go. I didn't think it'd be much fun without you guys, and I'm not heavily into that kind of stuff anyway.' Chris was a lightly built boy with intense eyes and a lot of nervous habits, like coughing in the middle of every sentence. He wouldn't be into Commem Day or woodchopping competitions; he was more into the Grateful Dead, Hieronymus Bosch, and computers. He was also known for writing poetry and using more illegal substances than you'd find in the average police laboratory. His motto was 'If it grows, smoke it'. Ninety per cent of the school thought he was weird, ten per cent thought he was a legend, everybody thought he was a genius.

'Well, Murray never came back that night, but I didn't realise, because their house is quite a way from ours. I didn't really notice anything unusual. There were Air Force jets racing around, but I just thought it was Commem Day stuff. Then, about nine o'clock, the power went off. That's so common I didn't get excited, just waited for it to come back on again. But an hour later it was still off, so I thought I'd better ring up and see what was happening. Then I found the phone was off too, which is unusual – we often lose one or the other, but not both. So I walked over to Murray's place, found they weren't home, thought "They must have gone out to tea", came home, went to bed with a candle – if you know what I mean – woke up in the morning, found everything was still off. "Now this is serious," I thought, went back to Murray's, still no one there. I walked along the road till I got to the Ramsays' – they're our neighbours – went in there, it was empty, kept walking, found no one at the Arthurs', realised there'd been no traffic, thought "Maybe I'm the only person left on the planet", went round a corner and found a wrecked car with three dead people in it. They'd hit a tree, but that hadn't killed them – they'd been shot up badly. Well, bad enough to kill them. You can imagine, I freaked out, and started running towards town. Around the next corner was the next shock – Uncle Al's house, which had been blown up. It was just a pile of smoking rubble. I saw a couple of vehicles coming, and instead of jumping on the road and flagging them down, which I would have done if they'd come along earlier, I hid and watched. They were military trucks, full of soldiers, and they weren't ours. So I thought "Either I've been using some very strange and heavy stuff or else this is not a typical day in the life of Wirrawee". It's been pretty weird ever since. Waking up in the middle of the night and seeing a BMW floating in the middle of the dam was just another part of it.'

Chris kept us entertained for a good half-hour by the time he'd told us what had happened to him and we'd told him our story. And more importantly, he kept us awake. But long before we got to my place Homer and Robyn were heavily asleep. Chris and Lee and I were the only ones still conscious. I don't know about the other two but it was a terrible struggle for me. I resorted to things like dabbing my eyelids with spit, which might sound strange, but it did help a bit. It was with deep relief that I saw the first soft light from the east reflecting off the galvanised iron roof of home. Only then did I realise I'd spent all that time driving the most elegant car I was ever likely to have, and I hadn't thought about it once. What a wasted opportunity. I was quite cross with myself.

Chapter Twelve

There'd been a few visitors in the short time we'd been away. Looters had come, and like at Chris's they had taken jewellery and a few other bits and pieces. My watch, some silver photo frames, my Swiss Army knife. They hadn't done much damage. I felt sick about it but was too tired to feel the full impact. Corrie and Kevin and Fi had come too – all the stuff on our list had been removed, and they'd left a message on the fridge: 'Gone where the bad people go. See you there!' I laughed and then rubbed at it till it was completely removed. I was getting really security conscious.

Homer and Robyn had Lee's dressing off and were inspecting his wound, Robyn with her new-found fascination for blood. I peered over their shoulders. I'd never seen a bullet wound in a human before. It didn't look too bad though. Mr Clement had done a good job, for a dentist. There were only a few stitches, but there was heavy bruising all around it, lots of interesting blue and black and purple colours. Some fresh blood had seeped out from the bottom of the row of stitches; that was obviously the blood I'd seen on his bandage.

'It looks swollen,' I said.

'You should have seen it yesterday,' Lee said. 'It's improved a lot.'

'Must have been the physio I gave it in the shovel.'

'What's it feel like to get shot?' Chris asked.

Lee put his head on one side, and thought for a moment. 'Like someone's stabbed a big hot piece of barbed wire through your leg. But I didn't realise it was a bullet. I thought something in the shop had fallen and hit me.'

'Did it hurt?' I asked.

'Not at first. But suddenly I couldn't walk on it. That's when Robyn grabbed me. It didn't hurt till we got inside the restaurant and I lay down. Then it felt like it was on fire. Really killed me.'

Homer had washed the whole wound site down with Dettol and now started putting the bandage back on. Robyn inspected my face and found a gash above my hairline that she Band-aided. Seemed like they were our only wounds. When she finished I went looking for the Landrover, and found it, neatly packed and hidden where we'd agreed, about half a k from the house, in the old orchard where my grandparents had built their first home on this land.

We had the whole day to waste before we went on up into the mountains to join the others. Sleep was everybody's first priority, except for Chris, who'd had quite a lot of it compared to us. He got dumped with the first sentry duty. And the second, third and fourth. It was too dangerous to sleep in the house, so we got blankets and set up in the oldest, furthest away haystack. I made everyone nervous by going and getting the firearms from the Landrover, but always in my thoughts now was what had happened at Corrie's and how Homer said we had to learn from that; we had to learn new ways.

Then we slept and slept and slept.

They say teenagers can sleep all day. I often used to look at dogs and be amazed by the way they seemed happy to sleep for twenty hours a day. But I envied them too. It was the kind of lifestyle I could relate to.

We didn't sleep for twenty hours, but we gave it our best shot. I stirred a couple of times during the morning, turned over, had a look at Lee, who seemed restless, glanced at Robyn beside me, who was sleeping like an angel, and dropped back into my heavy sleep. For once, I can recall my dreams vividly. I didn't dream of gunshots and smashing into vehicles, and people screaming and dying, although I know I've dreamt of those things often enough since. That morning I dreamt of Dad barbecuing for a whole lot of visitors, at home. I couldn't see what he was cooking, but he was working away busily with his fork, pricking sausages or something. It seemed like all the town was there, wandering through the house and garden. I said hello to Father Cronin, who was standing by the barbecue, but he didn't answer. I went into the kitchen but it was too crowded with people. Then Corrie was there, asking me to come and play, which was fine except that she was eight years old again. I followed her and we went down to a river and got in a boat. It turned out most of the townspeople were there, and Dad and Mum were captaining the boat, so as soon as Corrie and I were aboard they cast off and we sailed away. I don't know where we were going, but it was hot, everyone was sweating, people were taking off clothing. I looked back at the shore and there was Father Cronin waving goodbye – or was he shaking his fist angrily because we were all stripping off? And I didn't know now if we were stripping because we were hot, or for other reasons. Corrie was there still, but we weren't eight-year-olds any more, and then she had to go somewhere, with someone, and in her place Lee was standing. He was undressing too, very seriously, as though it were some holy ritual. We lay down together, still being very serious, and began touching each other, gently and lovingly. We were still doing that when I woke up, sweating, and found that I was now in full sun. The day was getting really hot. I turned and looked at the others, and the first person I saw was Lee, watching me with his dark eyes. I was so embarrassed after the dream that I blushed and began talking quickly.

'Oh, it's gone up about ten degrees. I'm baking away here. I'll have to move. I must have been asleep longer than I thought.' I picked up my blanket and moved to the other side of Lee, but about the same distance away. I kept gabbling. 'Do you want anything? Can I get you anything? Did you sleep much? Is your leg hurting a lot?'

'I'm fine,' he said.

I calmed down a bit now that I was out of the sun. From my new position I could see right across the paddocks to the bush, and on up into the mountains. 'It's beautiful, isn't it?' I said. 'Living here all my life, some days I don't even notice how beautiful it is. I still can't believe we might be about to lose it. But it's made me notice it all now. I notice every tree, every rock, every paddock, every sheep. I want to photograph it in my memory, in case... well, in case.'

'It is beautiful,' Lee said. 'You're lucky. There's nothing beautiful about the restaurant. And yet, I feel the same way about it as you do about your property. I think it's because we did it all ourselves. If someone smashes a window they're smashing glass that Dad cut, glass that I polished a thousand times, and they're tearing curtains that Mum made. You get an attachment to the place, and it becomes special to you. I guess maybe it does take on a kind of beauty.'

I wriggled a bit closer to him. 'Did you feel awful when you found it all wrecked?'

'There was so much to feel awful about I didn't know where to start. I don't think it's hit me even yet.'

'No, me neither. When we got here this morning and I found they'd been here . . . I don't know. I'd expected it, but I still felt awful, but I didn't feel awful enough. Then I felt guilty about not feeling worse. I think it's like you said, too many things. Too much has happened.'

'Yes.' Only one word, but I'll always remember the way he said it, like he was really involved with everything I'd been saying. I rolled around a bit so I was even closer to him, and kept talking.

'And then I think about Corrie and how it must be terrible for her, much worse than for me. For all you guys with little brothers and sisters. That must be terrible. And imagine how Chris's parents would feel, being overseas, probably not being able to get back into the country, not having a clue what's happened to Chris.'

'We don't know how widespread this thing is. It could involve a lot of countries. Remember that joke we made, up in Hell, about World War Three? We could have been right onto it.'

He put his arm around me and we lay there looking up at the old wooden rafters of the hayshed.

'I dreamed about you,' I said presently.

160

'When?'

'Just now, this morning, here on the haystack.'

'Did you? What did you dream?'

'Oh… that we were doing something like what we're doing now.'

'Really? I'm glad it came true.'

'So am I.'

I was too, but I was confused between my feelings for him and my feelings for Homer. Last night I'd been holding hands with Homer, and feeling so warm and good about it, and now here I was with Lee. He kissed me lightly on my nose, then less lightly on the mouth, then several more times, and passionately. I was kissing him back, but then I stopped. I didn't have any plans to become the local slut and I didn't think it was a good idea to get involved with two guys at once. I sighed and shrugged myself free.

'I'd better go and see how Chris is getting on.'

Chris was getting on all too well. He was asleep, and I was furious. I shouted, screamed, and then kicked him, hard. Even while I was doing it I was shocked at myself. Even now, as I think about it, I'm shocked at myself. The thing that scared me most was the thought that maybe all the violent things I'd been doing, with the ride-on mower and the truck, had transformed me in the space of a couple of nights into a raging monster. But on the other hand, it was unforgivable for Chris to have gone to sleep. He'd risked the lives of all of us by being so slack. I remember on our Outward Bound camp, talking one lunchtime, someone had said that in the Army the penalty for going to sleep on guard duty was death. We'd all been so shocked. We could see the logic in it, but maybe that was the shocking part, that it was so utterly logical. Cold-blooded, merciless, logical. You don't expect real life to be like that, not to that extreme. But I really felt for a moment like I could have killed Chris. He certainly looked scared of me when he rolled away and stood up.

'Geez Ellie, take it easy,' he mumbled.

'Take it easy?' I yelled into his face. 'Yeah, that's what you were doing all right. If we take it easy any more, we're dead. Don't you understand how it's all changed Chris? Don't you understand that? If you don't, you might as well get a rifle and finish us all off now. Because you're as good as doing that by taking it easy.'

Chris walked off, red-faced and muttering under his breath. I sat down in his spot. After a minute or two I think I did go into some sort of delayed shock. I'd blocked off all my emotional reactions because there hadn't been the time or the opportunity for those luxuries. But it's like they say, 'emotion denied is emotion deferred'. I'd done so much deferring, and now the bank had called in the loan. Most of that afternoon is a blank to me. Homer told me much later that I'd spent hours wrapped in blankets, sitting in a corner of the haystack, shivering and telling everyone to be careful. I guess I went down the same path as Corrie had, just in a slightly different way. I have a clear memory of refusing all food and becoming very hungry, but not eating because I was sure I'd be sick if I did. Homer said I was ravenous and I ate so much that they thought I would be sick and they refused to give me any more. Weird.

I was very upset when they wouldn't let me drive the Landrover, because I'd promised Dad so faithfully that I wouldn't let anyone else behind the wheel.

162

Suddenly though I got tired of arguing, crawled in beside Lee in the crowded back section, and went to sleep. Homer drove it up to Tailor's Stitch. If I'd known that I wouldn't have given up the argument so suddenly and so completely.

Somehow I walked into Hell late that night, crawled into a tent beside Corrie, who was hysterical with joy to see us, and slept for three days, waking only for occasional meals, toilet trips, and brief mumbled conversations. I do remember consoling Chris, who was sure that he'd been the cause of my having a nervous breakdown. I didn't think to ask how Lee had got in to Hell, but when I gradually got my wits back I found that they'd made a bush stretcher and carried him in; Robyn and Homer taking turns at one end of the stretcher and the lightly built Chris carrying the other, all the way down in the dark.

So I guess he atoned.

During my three days I had the nightmares I hadn't had that morning on the haystack. Demonic figures ran screaming from me, I felt skulls crush under my feet. Burning bodies stretched out their hands, begging for mercy. I killed everyone, even the people I loved most. I was careless with gas bottles and caused an explosion which blew up the house, with my parents in it. I set fire to a haystack where my friends were sleeping. I backed a car over my cousin and couldn't rescue my dog when he got caught in a flood. And although I ran around everywhere begging for help, screaming to people to call an ambulance, no one responded. They seemed uninterested. They weren't cruel, just too busy or uncaring. I was a devil of death, and there were no angels left in the world, no one to make me better than myself or to save me from the harm I was doing.

Then I woke up. It was early in the morning, very early. It was going to be a beautiful day. I lay in the sleeping bag looking at the sky and the trees. Why did the English language have so few words for green? Every leaf and every tree had its own shade of green. Another example of how far Nature was still ahead of humans. Something flitted from branch to branch in the top of one of the trees – a small dark-red and black bird with long wings, inspecting each strip of bark. Higher still a couple of white cockatoos floated across the sky. From the cries I could tell that there was a larger flock out of my sight, and the two birds were merely outriders, strays. I sat up to see if I could glimpse the rest of the flock by leaning forward, but they were still out of sight. So I shuffled out of the tent, clutching my sleeping bag to me like some kind of insect half-emerged from a chrysalis. The cockatoos were scattered across the heavens like raucous angels. They drifted on, too many to count, until they were out of sight, but I could still hear their friendly croaks.

I shed the sleeping bag and walked down to the creek. Robyn was there, washing her hair. 'Hello,' she said.

'Hi.'

'How are you feeling?'

'Good.'

'Hungry?'

'Yes, I am a bit.'

'I'm not surprised. You haven't had anything since teatime the day before yesterday.'

'Oh. Haven't I?'

'Come on. I'll fix you something. You like eggs?'

I had cold boiled eggs – we couldn't have a fire during the day – with biscuits and jam, and a bowl of muesli with powdered milk. I don't know if it was the cockatoos or Robyn or the muesli, but by the time I'd finished breakfast I felt I could maybe start to cope again.

Chapter Thirteen

One of the small rituals that developed each day was Corrie's Testing the Trannie. This was a solemn ceremony that took place whenever Corrie got the urge. She'd get up, look at the tent, give a little murmur like 'I think I might give the trannie another burl', and walk over to the tent. A moment later she'd emerge with the precious object in her hands and go to the highest point in the clearing and, holding the transistor to her ear, carefully turn the dial. She wouldn't let anyone else touch it, because it was her father's radio and no one but her could possibly be trusted with it. It was the only thing of his that she had. Although we laughed at her a little there was always some tension when she did it, but days passed with no result and Corrie reported that the batteries were gradually getting flatter.

One evening I happened to be sitting near her when she went through another fruitless search of the dial. As usual there was nothing but static. She turned it off with a sigh. We were chatting about nothing in particular, when she casually said, 'What are all these other things for?'

'What other things?'

'All these other settings.'

'How do you mean?'

She embarked on a long explanation about how the few times her father had lent her the radio he'd told that her stations would be on PO or FM.

'PO and FM? What are you talking about? Let's have a look.'

She handed it over a little reluctantly. I realised from the writing on it that it was a French one. I started translating for her. ' "Recepteur Mondial a dix bandes", that's "world reception to ten bands". FM's FM, obviously. PO's probably AM. "OC Etendue", well, "etendue", that's extended or expanded or something.' The implications of all this slowly began to dawn on me. 'This is no ordinary transistor, Corrie. This is a short wave.'

'What's that mean?'

'It means you can pick up stations from all around the world. Corrie, do you mean you've only been trying the local stations?'

'Well, yes, PO and FM. That's what Dad told me. I didn't know about all that other stuff, and I didn't want to flatten the batteries, mucking around with it. They're nearly dead now, and we don't have any more.'

I felt wildly excited and called to the others, 'Come here you guys, quick!'

They came quickly, drawn by the urgency in my voice.

'Corrie's radio can pick up short wave but she didn't realise it. You want to listen in? The batteries have nearly had it, but you never know your luck.' I selected 'OC Etendue 1' and handed the little black transistor back to Corrie. 'Give it the gun, Corrie. Just spin the dial the same way you did before.'

We crowded round as Corrie, tongue sticking out of the side of her mouth, slowly began to rotate the knob. And a moment later we heard the first rational adult voice most of us had heard in a long time. It was a female, speaking very fast among the static, but in a language we didn't understand.

'Keep going,' Homer breathed.

We heard some exotic music, an American voice saying 'You welcome Him into your heart and only then can you know perfect love', two more foreign language stations – 'That's Taiwanese,' said Fi, surprisingly, of one of them – then, as the radio started to die, a faint voice speaking in English. It was a male voice, and all we could hear was this:

'...warned America not to get involved. The General said that America would find herself in the longest, costliest and bloodiest war in her history if she tried to intervene. He said his forces have occupied several major coastal cities. Much of the inland has been taken already, and losses have been below expectations. Many civilian and military prisoners have been captured and are being held in humanitarian conditions. Red Cross teams will be permitted to inspect them when the situation stabilises.

'The General repeated his claim that the invasion was aimed at "reducing imbalances within the region". As international outrage continues to mount, FCA reports sporadic fighting in many country areas and at least two major land battles...'

And that was about it. The voice faded quickly. We heard a few scattered words, 'United Nations', 'New

Zealand', 'twenty to twenty-five aircraft', then it was gone. We looked at each other.

'Let's everyone get pens and paper and write down what we think we heard,' Homer said calmly. 'Then we can compare notes.'

We met again ten minutes later. It was amazing how different the versions were, but we agreed on the important details. What we could infer was as important as what the man had said. 'For one thing,' said Homer, sitting back on his heels, 'we can tell it's not World War Three. Not yet, anyway. It sounds like it's just us.'

'The part about the prisoners was good,' Corrie said. Everyone nodded. It sounded genuine somehow. It had helped all of us, a little, though awful fears still kept leaping up and attacking our minds.

'He's trying to remind the Americans of Vietnam,' Fi said. 'It's meant to have been their national nightmare or something.'

'Bigger nightmare for the Vietnamese,' Chris commented.

I glanced at Lee, whose face was impassive.

'The Americans don't like getting involved with other countries.' I remembered something we'd done in Twentieth Century History. 'Woodrow Wilson and isolationism, isn't that one of the topics we're meant to be preparing, over the holidays?'

'Mmm, remind me to do some work on it tonight.' That was Kevin.

'"International outrage" sounds promising,' Robyn said.

'That's probably our biggest hope. But I can't imagine too many other countries rushing in to spill their blood for us,' I said.

'But don't we have treaties and stuff?' Kevin asked. 'I thought the politicians were meant to organise all this. Otherwise, why've we been paying their salaries all these years?'

No one knew what to answer. Maybe they were thinking the same thing I was, that we should have taken an interest in all these things a long time ago, before it was too late.

'What does it mean "reducing imbalances within the region"?' Kevin asked.

'I guess he's talking about sharing things more equally,' Robyn said. 'We've got all this land and all these resources, and yet there's countries a crow's spit away that have people packed in like battery hens. You can't blame them for resenting it, and we haven't done much to reduce any imbalances, just sat on our fat backsides, enjoyed our money and felt smug.'

'Well, that's the way the cookie crumbles,' Kevin said uncomfortably.

'And now they've taken the cookie and crumbled it in a whole new way,' Robyn said. 'In fact it looks like they're taking the whole packet.'

'I don't understand you,' Kevin said. 'You sound like you don't mind. You think it's fair enough, do you? Let them walk in and take everything they want, everything your parents have worked for. Help yourself guys, don't mind us. Is that what you get out of the Bible? Do unto others, or whatever it is? Remind me not to go to your church.'

'Not much chance of that,' Corrie said, smiling and putting her hand on Kevin's knee, trying to calm him down. But Robyn wasn't put off.

'Of course I mind,' Robyn said. 'If I was a saint

maybe I wouldn't mind, but I'm not a saint so I mind rather a lot. And it's as not as though they're acting in a very religious way. I don't know any religion that tells people to go in and steal and kill to get what they want. I can understand why they're doing it but understanding isn't the same as supporting. But if you'd lived your whole life in a slum, starving, unemployed, always ill, and you saw the people across the road sunbaking and eating ice cream every day, then after a while you'd convince yourself that taking their wealth and sharing it around your neighbours isn't such a terrible thing to do. A few people would suffer, but a lot of people would be better off.'

'It's just not right,' said Kevin stubbornly.

'Maybe not. But neither's your way of looking at it. There doesn't have to be a right side and a wrong side. Both sides can be right, or both sides can be wrong. I think both countries are in the wrong this time.'

'So does that mean you're not going to fight them?' Kevin asked, still looking for a fight himself.

Robyn sighed. 'I don't know. I already have, haven't I? I was right there with Ellie when we smashed our way through Wirrawee. I guess I'll keep fighting them, for the sake of my family. But after the war, if there is such a time as after the war, I'll work damn hard to change things. I don't care if I spend the rest of my life doing it.'

'You were the one who thought we were taking too big a risk going to look for Robyn and Lee,' I said to Kevin. 'You didn't seem so fired up then.'

He looked uncomfortable. 'I didn't mean that,' was all he would say.

Homer spoke up. 'Maybe it's time to decide what we're all going to do. We've had a chance to rest up, get our breath back, think about things. Now we should decide if we're going to stay here in hiding till the war sorts itself out, or if we should get out there and do something about it.' He paused, and when no one spoke he continued. 'I know we're meant to be schoolkids, too young to do much more than clean a whiteboard for a teacher, but some of those soldiers I saw the other night weren't any older than us.'

'I saw two who looked a lot younger than us,' said Robyn.

Homer nodded. No one else spoke. The tension was heavy, like a humid night. Here in this secret basin we'd been insulated for a little while from the fear and sweat and bleeding of the outside world. People were keeping each other prisoner, hurting each other, killing each other, but we'd retreated to the paradise of Hell.

It was a bit irrelevant to what Homer was saying, but I spoke anyway. 'I can understand why the Hermit chose to live down here, away from it all.'

'Away from the human race,' Chris murmured.

'It's our own families,' said Corrie. 'That's what everyone's worried about, isn't it? I guess I'd fight for my country but I'm going mad wondering what's happened to my family. We don't know if they're alive or dead. We're thinking and hoping that they're at the Showground, and we're thinking and hoping that they're being well treated, but we don't know any of that. We've only got Mr Clement's word to go on.'

'Seeing Mr Coles at the Showground helped,' I said. 'He looked healthy. He didn't look too terrified or injured. That made a big difference to me.'

Fi spoke up. 'I think we should try to find out more about the Showground. If we know that everyone's there, that they're unhurt, that they're being fed properly and all that sort of thing, it'd make such a difference.' Homer was about to interrupt but she went on. 'I've been thinking about what Robyn and Kevin were arguing about. If I could get my family and friends back, healthy, I'd let these people have the stupid houses and cars and things. I'd go and live with my parents in a cardboard box at the tip and be happy.'

I tried to imagine Fi, with her beautiful skin and soft polished voice, living at the tip.

'It sounds like we should try to find out more about the Showground then,' Homer said. 'But it won't be easy.' He added modestly, 'Do you realise that every group that's gone into town has been spotted, except Fi and me?'

'Were you striped?' I asked, and got the groan I deserved.

Lee was lying on my left, against a rock that was still warm. It seemed to be his turn to speak. 'I don't think they'll be into tortures and mass executions. The world's changing, and any country that does that stuff knows there's going to be a stink about it. I mean, I know it still happens, but not as much as it used to. Nowadays they seem to do things unobtrusively, over a long period of time. These guys are obviously trigger-happy, but there's a big difference between shooting in hot blood and shooting in cold blood. We know that they're firing off endless bullets in hot blood – they're wild that way, and I've got the hole in my leg to prove it. But that's sort of normal in a war, and a lot of it's self-defence. It doesn't mean they're into concentration camps. The two things don't automatically go together.'

'I hate them,' said Kevin. 'I don't know why you're

all being so understanding. I just hate them and I want to kill them all and if I had a nuclear bomb I'd drop it right down their throats.'

He was really upset, and he'd stopped the conversation as though he had nuked it. But after a few moments of awkward silence Homer started in again.

'Well,' he said, 'do we want to check out the Showground more thoroughly? Can we do it with the stealth and finesse that Fi and I showed, or are we going to march in like a heavy metal band at a bowling club?'

'We could tunnel in,' I suggested.

'Yeah, or pole-vault over the fence. Anyone got a serious suggestion? And how badly do we want to do it anyway?'

'Badly,' I said.

'I won't pretend the thought doesn't scare the skin off me,' Corrie said softly. 'But it's what we have to do. We'll never sleep again at nights if we don't.'

'We'll never sleep again at nights if we're dead,' Chris said. 'Look, with my parents overseas, I'm not quite as involved as you guys. But I'll have a go, I suppose.'

'I know what our parents would say,' Fi said. 'They'd say that the most important thing to them is our safety. They wouldn't want us dead in exchange for them living. In a way we're what gives their lives their meaning. But we can't be bound by that. We have to do what's right for us. We have to find meanings for our own lives, and this might be one of the ways we do it. I'm with Corrie; scared out of my skin, but I'll do it because I can't imagine the rest of my life if I don't.'

'I agree,' Robyn said.

'All day and all night,' said Lee, 'I pray for my leg to get better so I can go and find my family.'

'I'm with the majority,' Kevin said.

We looked at Homer. 'I never thought I'd have to hurt other people just so I could live my own life,' he said. 'But my grandfather did it, in the Civil War. If I have to do it, I hope I'll have the strength, like Ellie did. Whatever we do, I hope we can do it without hurting anyone. But if it happens... well, it happens.'

'You're getting soft,' Kevin said.

Homer ignored him. He continued, briskly. 'I keep thinking of that quote Corrie mentioned the other day, "Time spent in reconnaissance is seldom wasted",' he said. 'The stupidest thing for us to do would be to charge in like Rambos with our little .22's popping away. Fi's right, our families don't want us stretched out cold on a slab in the morgue. If we take a few extra days, well, that's the way it has to be. The only reason we should take big risks is if we found that something terrible was about to happen to them. Of course it could have already happened, and if it has, well, we can't do anything about it.

'So, what I'm thinking is, we need some kind of observation place, somewhere hidden and safe, where we can watch the Showground. The more we know, the better our decisions will be and the more effective we can be. Judging from the radio, the whole country hasn't been a pushover, and there's a lot of action still going on. We ought to talk to anyone we can find in town, like Mr Clement, and even try to link up with the Army, or whoever's still fighting in other districts. We should set ourselves up as a real guerilla outfit, living off the land as much as possible, mobile and fast and tough. We might have to survive like this for months, years even.

'For example – you mightn't like this, so say so if you don't – suppose we sent two or three people into Wirrawee for forty-eight hours. Their job would be to get information, nothing more. If they're really careful they honestly shouldn't get seen. They've just got to become totally nocturnal and triple-check every move they make. The rest of us can start organising things more efficiently here. We'll never get a better base camp, but we should get more supplies in and make it a proper headquarters. It's frightening how quickly we're going through the food. We should start organising rations. And I'd like to set up other little hideaways through the mountains. Stock them with food and stuff, in case we get cut off from this place. Like I said, we've got to get more mobile.

'And living off the land, we've got to get serious about that. So the people back here should figure out some possibilities. Where are all the springs in these mountains? Can we trap rabbits or roos, or even possums? Ellie and I, our families have always killed our own meat, so we can do a bit of rough butchering.'

'Same for me,' Kevin said.

'I can do a nice sweet and sour possum,' Lee said. 'Or catch me a feral cat and I'll make dim sims.'

There was a groan of disgust. Lee leaned back and grinned at me.

'We could bring animals in here,' Corrie said. 'Chooks, a few lambs maybe. Goats.'

'Good,' said Homer. 'That's the kind of thing we need to look at, and think about.'

Kevin looked gloomy at the mention of goats. I knew what he was thinking. We'd been brought up as sheep cockies, and the first thing we learned was to despise goats. Sheep good, goats bad. It didn't mean anything, just went with the territory. But we'd have to unlearn a lot of the old ways.

'You're thinking in the long term,' I said to Homer.

'Yes,' he agreed. 'The really long term.'

We talked on for a couple of hours. Corrie's radio had had the last laugh. It spurred us out of our shock, our misery. By the time we stopped, exhausted, we'd come to a few decisions. Two pairs would go into town the next evening, Robyn and Chris, and Kevin and Corrie. They would operate independently, but stay in close contact. They'd stay there the next full night, most of the night after, and return by dawn the following day. So they'd be away about sixty hours. Kevin and Corrie would concentrate on the Showground. Robyn and Chris would cruise around town, looking for people in hiding, for useful information, for equipment even. 'We'll start to reclaim Wirrawee,' as Robyn put it. We worked out a lot of complicated details, like where they'd have their base (Robyn's music teacher's house), where they'd leave notes for each other (under the dog kennel), how long they'd wait on Wednesday morning if the other pair was missing (no time), and their cover story to protect us and Hell if they got caught ('Since the invasion we've been hiding under the Masonic Lodge and only coming out at nights'). We figured that was a place that wouldn't incriminate anyone else, and a place that the patrols wouldn't have checked. Robyn and Chris agreed to set up a fake camp in there, to give the cover story credibility.

The rest of us, back in Hell, would do pretty much what Homer had suggested – smuggle in more supplies, establish Hell as a proper base, organise food rationing, and suss out new hiding places.

Strangely enough I was quite elated at the thought of the next couple of days. It was partly that I was scared of going back into town, so it was a relief to get a reprieve from that. It was partly too that Kevin would be away for a few days, as he was getting on my nerves a bit. But mainly it was the interesting combinations that were possible among the people who were left. There were Homer and Lee, both of whom I had strong and strange feelings for, but made more complicated by Homer's obvious attraction to Fi. It was an attraction he still seemed too shy to do much about, although he was more confident with her now. There was Fi, who lately had lost her cool and become nervous and tongue-tied when she was near Homer, despite the fact that it was still hard to believe she could like him – well, like him in that kind of way. There was Lee, who kept looking at me with his possum eyes, as though his wounded leg was the only thing stopping him from leaping up and grabbing me. I was a little afraid of the depth of feeling in those beautiful eyes.

I felt guilty even thinking about love while our world was in such chaos, and especially when my parents were going through this terrible thing. It was the steers at the abattoirs all over again. But my heart was making its own rules and refusing to be controlled by my conscience. I let it run wild, thinking of all the fascinating possibilities.

Chapter Fourteen

Monday morning a dark river of aircraft flowed overhead for an hour or more. Not ours unfortunately. I'd never seen so many aircraft. They looked like big fat transport planes and they weren't being molested by anyone, though a half-hour later six of our Air Force jets whistled past on the same route. We waved to them, optimistically.

We'd been back to my place, very early, and brought up another load: more food, tools, clothing, toiletries, bedding, and a few odds and ends that we'd forgotten before, like barbecue tools, Tupperware, a clock and, I'm embarrassed to say, hot-water bottles. Robyn had asked for a Bible. I knew we had one somewhere and I found it eventually, dusted it off and added it to the collection.

It was tricky, because we couldn't take so much stuff that it would be obvious to patrols that someone was on the loose. So we went on to the Grubers, about a k away, and helped ourselves to a lot more food. I also picked up a collection of seeds and seedlings from Mr Gruber's potting shed. I was starting to think like Homer and plan for the long term.

The last things we got were half a dozen chooks – our best layers – some pellets, fencing wire and star pickets. As dawn broke we rattled on up the track, the chooks murmuring curiously to each other in the back. I'd let Homer drive this time, figuring he needed the practice. To amuse Fi I closed my eyes, picked up the Bible, opened it at random, pointed to a spot, opened my eyes and read the verse, saying at the same time, 'Through my psychic finger I will find a sentence that applies to us'. The one I'd picked was this: 'I hate them with perfect hatred; I count them my enemies.'

'Golly,' said Fi. 'I thought the Bible was meant to be full of love and forgiveness and all that stuff.'

I kept reading. ' "Deliver me, O Lord, from evil men; preserve me from violent men, who plan evil things in their heart, and stir up wars continually".'

The others were really impressed. So was I, but I wasn't going to let on to them. 'See, I told you,' I said. 'I do have a psychic finger.'

'Try another one,' Homer said. But I wasn't going to throw my reputation away that easily.

'No, you've heard the words of wisdom,' I said. 'That's all for today.'

Fi grabbed the Bible and tried the same ritual. The first time she got a blank section of page at the end of one of the chapters. The second time she read, ' "Then the king promoted Shadrach, Meshach and Abednego in the province of Babylon".'

'It's no good,' I said. 'You've got to have the psychic finger.'

'Maybe the one you read would make Robyn feel better about gunning soldiers down,' Homer said to me.

'Mmm, I've marked the page. I'll show her when they get back.' No one mentioned the possibility that they might not get back. That's the way people always are I think. They figure if they say something bad they might magically make it happen. I don't think words are that powerful.

We reached the top, hid the Landie, and took the chooks and whatever else we could carry into Hell. We'd have to wait until dark to get the other stuff. It was too dangerous being up on Tailor's Stitch with daylight coming on, and so many aircraft around. And it was shaping up to be a scorcher. Even down in Hell, where it was normally cool, the air was getting furnace hot. But to my surprise we found Lee leaning against a tree at the opposite end of the clearing to where we'd left him. 'Hooley dooley!' I said. 'You've risen from the dead.'

'I should have chosen a cooler morning,' he said, grinning. 'But I got sick of sitting there. Thought it was time for some exercise, now that I've recovered from that truck ride.' He was grinning, very pleased with himself, but sweating. I rinsed a towel in the creek and wiped his face.

'Are you sure you should be doing this?' I asked.

He shrugged. 'It felt right.'

I remembered how quite often when our animals got sick or injured they'd get themselves into a hole somewhere – under the shearing shed was a popular place for the dogs – and they'd stay there for days and days, until they either died or came out fresh and cured and wagging their tails. Maybe Lee was the same. He'd kept pretty still since he'd been shot, lying among the rocks, thinking his quiet thoughts. He wasn't yet wagging his tail, but the energy was returning to his face.

'The day you can sprint from one end of this clearing to the other,' I said, 'we'll chop off a chook's head and have a chicken dinner.'

'Robyn can cut the stitches out when she gets back from Wirrawee,' he said. 'They've been in long enough.' I helped him to a shady place near the creek, where we could sit together in a damp dark basin of rock, probably the coolest spot in Hell that day.

'Ellie,' he said. He cleared his throat nervously. 'There's something I've been meaning to ask you. That day back at your place, in the haystack, when you came over to where I was lying, and you laid down and we...'

'All right, all right,' I interrupted. 'I know what we did.'

'I thought you might have forgotten.'

'What, do you think I do that kind of stuff so often I can't remember? It wasn't exactly an everyday event for me you know.'

'Well you haven't looked at me once since then. You've hardly even spoken to me.'

'I was pretty out of it for a few days. I just slept and slept.'

'Yes, but since then.'

'Since then?' I sighed. 'Since then I've been confused. I don't know what I think.'

'Will you ever know what you think?'

'If I could answer that I'd probably know everything.'

'Have I said something to upset you? Or done something?'

'No, no. It's just me. I don't know what I'm doing half the time, so I do things and I don't always mean what I think I mean. Do you know what I mean?' I asked, hopefully, because I wasn't sure myself.

'So you're saying it didn't mean anything?'

'I don't know. It meant something, at the time, and it means something now, but I don't know if it means what you seem to want it to mean. Why don't we just say I was being a slut, and leave it at that.'

He looked really hurt and I was sorry I'd said that. I hadn't even meant it.

'It's a bit difficult sitting down here,' he said. 'If you want to get rid of me, you're the one who'll have to go.'

'Oh Lee, I don't want to get rid of you. I don't want to get rid of anyone. We all have to get on, living in this place the way we are, for God knows how long.'

'Yes,' he said. 'This place, Hell. It seems like Hell sometimes. Now for instance.'

I don't know why I was talking the way I was. It was all happening too unexpectedly. It was a conversation I wasn't ready for. I guess I like to be in control of things, and Lee had forced this on me at a time and a place that he'd chosen. I wished Corrie were there, so I could go and talk to her about it. Lee was so intense he scared me, but at the same time I felt something strong when he was around – I just didn't know what it was. I was always very conscious when I was near him. My skin felt hotter, I'd be watching him out of the corner of my eye, directing my comments at him, noticing his reactions, listening more for his words than for anyone else's. If he expressed an opinion I'd think about it more carefully, give it more weight than I would, say, Kevin's or Chris's. I used to think about him a lot in my sleeping bag at nights, and because I'd be thinking about him as I drifted into sleep I tended to dream about him. It got so that – this sounds stupid but it's true – I associated him with my

183

sleeping bag. When I looked at one I'd think of the other. That doesn't necessarily mean I wanted him in my sleeping bag, but they had started to go together in my mind. I nearly smiled as I sat there, thinking about that, and wondering how he'd look if he could suddenly read my thoughts.

'Do you still think about Steve a lot?' he asked.

'No, not Steve. Oh I mean I think about him in the same way I think about a lot of people, wondering if they're all right and hoping they are, but I don't think about him in the way you mean.'

'Well if I haven't offended you and you're not with Steve any more, then where does that leave me?' he asked, getting exasperated. 'Do you just dislike me as a person?'

'No,' I said, horrified at that idea but getting a bit annoyed too, at the way he was trying to bully me into a relationship. Guys do that all the time. They want definite answers – as long as they're the right answers – and they think if they keep at you long enough they'll get them.

'Look,' I said, 'sorry I can't give you a list of my feelings about you, in point form and alphabetical order. But I just can't. I'm all confused. That day in the haystack was no accident. It meant something. I'm still trying to figure out what.'

'You say you don't dislike me,' he said slowly, like he was trying to figure it out. He was looking away from me and he was very nervous, but he was obviously leading up to an important question. 'So that does mean you like me?'

'Yes Lee, I like you very much. But right now you're driving me crazy.' It was funny how often I'd thought of us having this conversation, but now that we were having it I didn't know if I was saying what I wanted to say.

'I've noticed you looking at Homer kind of ... special since we've been up here. Have you got a thing for him?'

'It'd be my business if I did.'

'Cos I don't think he's right for you.'

'Oh Lee, you're so annoying today! Maybe you shouldn't have tried walking on that leg. I honestly think it's weakened your brain. Let's blame it on that, or the weather or something, because you don't own me and you don't have any right to decide who's right or wrong for me, and don't you forget it.' I stormed off in a hot passion to the other side of the clearing where Fi and Homer had been making a yard for the chooks. The chooks were in it, looking shocked, maybe because they'd heard me chucking my tantrum; more likely because they were wondering what the hell they were doing there.

Oh. 'What the hell.' I just made a joke.

I watched the chooks for a while, then cut across the clearing again to where the creek wandered back into thick bush and lost itself in a dark tunnel of undergrowth. I'd been thinking for a few days I might try to explore down there a bit, impossible and impassable though it seemed. This might be the time to do it. I could work off some anger and get my mind onto something else. Besides, it looked cool in there. I took my boots and socks off, stuffed the socks in the boots, and tied the boots round my neck. Then I bent over and tried to pretend I was a wombat, a water wombat. I'm the right shape for that, and it was the only way to get under all the vegetation. I was using the creek as a path, but there was a definite sensation of

185

going along a tunnel. The greenery arched so low that it scraped my back even when I was almost kissing the water. It was cool – I doubt if the sun had penetrated the creepers for years – and I hoped I wouldn't meet too many snakes.

The creek was narrower through here than it was in our clearing, about a metre and a half wide and as much as sixty centimetres deep. The bottom was all stones, but smooth and old ones, not too many with cutting edges, and anyway my feet were getting tough these days. There were quite a few dark still pools that looked very deep, so I avoided them. The creek just chattered on, minding its own business, not disturbed by my creeping progress. It had been flowing here for a long time.

I followed it for about a hundred metres, through many twists and turns. The beginning of the journey had been sweet, like most new journeys I suppose, and there was the hope that the ending might be sweet also, but the middle part was getting tedious. My back was aching and I'd been scratched quite sharply on the arms. I was starting to feel hot again. But the canopy of undergrowth seemed to be getting higher, and lighter – here and there glints of sunlight bounced off the water, and the secret coolness of the tunnel was giving way to the more ordinary dry heat that we'd had back in the clearing. I straightened up a little. There was a place well ahead where the creek seemed to widen for ten metres before it turned to the right and disappeared into undergrowth again. It spread out into a wider channel, because the banks were no longer vertical there. They angled gently back, and I could see black soil, red rocks, and patches of moss, in a little shadowy

186

space not much bigger than our sitting room at home. I kept wading towards it, still bent-backed. There were little blue wildflowers scattered along the bank. As I got closer I could see a mass of pink wildflowers deeper in the bush, back from the creek. I looked again and realised that they were roses. My heart suddenly beat wildly. Roses! Here, in the middle of Hell! Impossible!

I splashed along the last few metres to the point where the banks began to open out, and sploshed out of the creek onto the mossy rock. Peering into the wild of the vegetation I struggled to distinguish between the shadows and the solid. The only certainty was the rosebush, its flowers catching enough sunlight through the brambles to glow like pieces of soft jewellery. But gradually I started to make sense of what I was seeing. Across there was a long horizontal of rotting black wood, here a pole serving as an upright, that dark space a doorway. I was looking at the overgrown shell of a hut.

I went forward slowly, on tiptoe. It was a quiet place and I had some sort of reverential feeling, like I did in my Stratton grandmother's drawing room, with its heavy old furniture and curtains always closed. The two places couldn't have been more different, the derelict bush hut and the solemn old sandstone house, but they both seemed a long way removed from living, from life. My grandmother wouldn't have liked being compared to a murderer, but she and the man who lived here had both withdrawn from the world, had created islands for themselves. It was as though they'd gone beyond the grave, even while they were still on Earth.

At the doorway of the hut I had to pull away a lot

of creeper and some tall berry canes. I wasn't too sure if I wanted to go in there. It was a bit like entering a grave. What if the hermit was still there? What if his body was lying on the floor? Or his spirit waiting to feed on the first living human to come through the door? There was a brooding atmosphere about the hut, about the whole place, that was not peaceful or pleasant. Only the roses seemed to bring any warmth into the clearing. But my curiosity was strong; it was unthinkable that I could come this far and not go further. I stepped into the dark interior and looked around, trying to define the black shapes I could see, just as a few minutes earlier I'd had to define the shape of the hut itself, from its wild surroundings. There was a bed, a table, a chair. Gradually the smaller, less obvious objects became clearer too. There was a set of shelves on a wall, a rough cupboard beside it, a fireplace with a kettle still hanging in it. In the corner was a dark shape, which gave me palpitations for a minute. It looked like a sleeping beast of some kind. I took a few steps and peered at it. It seemed to be a metal trunk, painted black originally but now flaking with rust. Everything was like the chest, in decay. The earth floor on which I stood was covered with twigs and clods of clay from the walls, and litter from possums and birds. The kettle was rusty, the bottom shelf hung askew, and the ceiling was festooned with cobwebs. But even the cobwebs looked old and dead, hanging like Miss Havisham's hair.

My eyes had adjusted to the murky light by then. There was no body on the bed, I was relieved to see, but there were the rotten remnants of grey blankets. The bed itself was made of lengths of timber nailed together, and still looked fairly sound. On the shelves were just a few old saucepans. I turned again to look at the chest and hit my head on a meat safe hanging from a rafter. It struck me right on the temple with its corner. 'Hell,' I said, rubbing my head hard. It had really hurt.

I knelt, to look into the chest. There seemed nothing else in the hut which would offer more than it had already shown me. Only the inside of the chest was still concealed. I tried to lift the lid. It was reluctant, jammed by dirt and rust, and I had to pull then shake it to get it a few centimetres open. Metal ground against metal as I slowly forced it up, warping it so much that it was never going to close neatly again.

My first reaction when I peered inside was disappointment. There was very little there, just a pathetic pile of tattered odds and ends at the bottom of the chest. Mostly bits of paper. I pulled everything out and took them back outside into better light. There was a belt made of plaited leather, a broken knife, a fork and a few chess pieces: two pawns and a broken knight. The papers were mainly old newspapers, but sheets of writing paper too, and half of a hardbound book called *Heart of Darkness*, by Joseph Conrad. A large black beetle came crawling out of the book as I opened it. It fell open to a beautiful colour plate of a boat penetrating the jungle. It was actually two books in one; there was a second story, called 'Youth'. But the other papers were too tattered and dirty and faded to be of any interest. It seemed that the Hermit's life was going to remain a mystery, even now, so many years after his disappearance.

I poked around for another ten minutes or so,

inside and out, without finding much. There had been other attempts to grow flowers: as well as the roses there was an apple tree, a sweetly scented white daisy, and a big wild patch of mint. I tried to imagine a murderer carefully planting and cultivating these beautiful plants; tried, and failed. Still, I supposed even murderers must have things they liked, and they must do something with their spare time. They couldn't just sit around all day for the rest of their lives and think about their murders.

After a time I picked up the belt and the book and waded back into the creek, for the hunchbacked shuffle through the tunnel to our camp. It was a relief to emerge back into sunshine from that gloomy place. I'd forgotten how hot the day was, out in the sunlight, but I almost welcomed its fierce glare.

As soon as I appeared Homer came striding over. 'Where have you been?' he said. 'We've been getting worried.' He was quite angry. He sounded like my father. It seemed I'd been away for longer than I'd thought.

'I've been having a close encounter with the Hermit from Hell,' I answered. 'A guided tour will leave soon; well, as soon as I've found the Iced Vo-Vo's. I'm starving.'

Chapter Fifteen

After our inspection of the Hermit's hut we kept working on into the evening. Lee, being less mobile, got to do the paperwork, in particular a system of food rationing that would preserve our supplies for close to two months, if we had the self-control to stick to it. Homer and Fi and I made a few little vegie gardens, and when the long day at last cooled we put in some seeds: lettuce, silverbeet, cauliflower, broccoli, peas and broad beans. We didn't much fancy eating those all the rest of our lives, but 'we need our greens', as Fi said firmly, and with Lee's cooking skills, broccoli could be turned into chocolate chip ice cream, and cauliflower into a fairy coach.

It had been a long day, a hot one, and a hard and tiring one. We'd started so early. My talk with Lee hadn't made it easier either. There was a bit of a strain between us now, which I hated, and there was a general strain caused by everyone snapping at each other in the final few hours of daylight. The only exception was Homer, who hadn't snapped at Fi. He'd had a go at me, about the amount of water I was putting on the vegetable seeds, and at Lee, over whether soccer was a better sport than footy, but Fi was immune. He wasn't immune from her though. When he broke off a big piece of fruit cake (Mrs Gruber's) and ate it, she burned his ears with a string of words like 'greedy' and 'selfish' and 'pig'. Homer was so used to being told off in his life that you might as well have told a rock off for being sedimentary, but when Fi went for him he stood there like a little kid, red in the face and wordless. He ate the rest of his slice of cake, but I don't think he enjoyed it. I was so glad she hadn't seen me with the Iced Vo-Vo biscuits.

Yes, finding the hut had been the only highlight of the afternoon.

Fi had moved into my tent while Corrie was away, and that night, as we lay in bed, she said to me, 'Ellie, what am I going to do about Homer?'

'You mean the way he likes you?'

'Yes!'

'Mmm, it's a problem.'

'I wish I knew what to do.'

This was my specialty, sorting out my friends' love lives. When I left school I was going to take it up as a career; open a business where people could come in off the streets and tell me all their boyfriend and girlfriend problems. It was just a shame I couldn't figure out my own.

So I rolled over to where I could see Fi's small face in the darkness. Her big eyes were wide open with worry.

'Do you like him?' We had to start somewhere.

'Yes! Of course!'

'But I mean...'

'I know what you mean! Yes, I think I do. Yes I do. I didn't at school, but honestly, he was such a moron there. If anyone had said to me then that I'd end up liking him, well, I'd have paid their taxi fare to the psychiatrist. He was so immature.'

'Yes, remember that water fight at the Hallowe'en social?'

'Oh, don't remind me.'

'So if you like him now, what's stopping you?'

'I don't know. That's the hard part. I don't know if I like him as much as he likes me, that's one thing. I'd hate to get into a relationship with him where he assumed I felt as strongly as he does. I don't think I ever could like him that much. He's so...' She couldn't think of a word to end the sentence, so I supplied one. 'Greek?'

'Yes! I mean, I know he was born out here, but he's still Greek when it comes to girls.'

'Do you mind that he's Greek, or part Greek, or whatever you call it?'

'No! I love it. Greek is sexy.'

'Sexy' sounded funny coming from Fi. She was so well brought up she didn't normally use words like that.

'So is that the only thing stopping you, that you don't feel as strongly as he does?'

'Sort of. I feel like I have to keep him at arm's length or he'll just take over. It's like, you build a dam upstream to stop the village being washed away. I'm the village, and I build a dam by being cool and casual with him.'

'That might just make him more passionate.'

'Oh, do you think so? I never thought of that. Oh, it's so complicated.' She yawned. 'What would you do if you were in my position?'

That was a tough question, because I was half in

193

her position anyway. It was my feelings for Homer that were stopping me from taking the plunge with Lee. It would have been just my luck to be a castaway on a desert island with two guys and to like both of them. But Fi's saying 'sexy' had made me realise that with Homer it was pretty physical. I didn't want to spend hours with him talking about life; I wanted to spend hours with him making animal noises, like sighs and grunts and 'Press harder', or 'Touch me there again'. With Lee it was something else. I was fascinated by his ideas, the way he thought about things. I felt I would see life differently, the more I talked to Lee. It was like I could learn from him. I didn't know much about his life, but when I looked at his face and eyes it was like looking into the Atlantic Ocean. I wanted to know what I could find in there, what interesting secrets he knew.

So in answer to Fi's question I just said, 'Don't string him along forever. Homer likes excitement. He likes to get on with it. He's not the world's most patient guy.'

She said sleepily, 'So you think I should try it?'

' "Better to have loved and lost than never to have loved at all." If you go for it and it doesn't work, well, what have you lost? But if he loses interest, so you never have anything with him, then you'll spend the rest of your life wondering what might have been.'

Fi drifted off to sleep, but I lay awake listening to the night sounds, the breeze in the hot trees, the howls of feral dogs in the distance, the occasional throaty call of a bird. I wondered how I'd feel if Fi got off with Homer. I still couldn't quite believe that I suddenly liked Homer so much. He'd been a neighbour, a brother, for so long. I tried to think back to the way he'd been a month ago, a year ago, five years ago when he was just a kid. I wanted to work out when he'd become attractive, or why I hadn't noticed it before, but I couldn't feel anything much for the way he'd been in those days. It was like he'd metamorphosed. Overnight he'd become sexy and interesting.

A dog howled again and I started wondering about the Hermit. Maybe that howl was the Hermit coming back to his violated house, coming to look for the people who'd trespassed into his secret sanctuary. I wriggled closer to Fi, feeling quite spooked. It had been strange, finding that little hut, so skilfully concealed. He must have really hated people to go to so much trouble. I'd half expected the place to feel full of evil, satanic powers, as though he'd huddled there for years holding black masses. What sort of man could do what he'd done? How could he have gone on with his life? But the hut hadn't felt all that evil. There had been an atmosphere there, but one that was hard to define. It was a sad, brooding place, but not evil.

As sleep crept up on me I turned my mind to my evening ritual, that I performed now, no matter how tired I was. It was a sort of movie that I ran in my head every night. In the movie I watched my parents going about their normal lives. I made sure to see their faces as often as possible, and I pictured them in all kinds of everyday situations: Dad dropping bales of hay off to sheep, waiting at the wheel while I opened a gate, swearing as he tightened the belts on the tractor, in his moleskins at the field days. Mum in the kitchen – she was a real kitchen person, Mum; feminism had made her more outspoken maybe but it hadn't changed her activities much. I pictured her looking for her library books, digging up spuds, talking on the phone, swearing as she lit the fuel stove, swearing that she'd change it for an electric one tomorrow. She never did. She claimed she was keeping the Aga because when we started taking tourists for farm stays they'd think it was picturesque. That made me smile.

I didn't know if I was making myself feel bad by trying to make myself feel good, thinking about my parents, but it was my way of keeping them alive and in my thoughts. I was scared of what might happen if I stopped doing that, if I let them start drifting away, the way I was drifting away now, into sleep. Normally I'd be thinking about Lee, too, at about this time, hugging him to me and imagining his smooth brown skin and firm lips, but tonight I was too tired, and I'd already thought about him enough today. I fell asleep and dreamt about him instead.

The couple of days with Homer and Fi and Lee had promised to be interesting and that's the way they were turning out. In fact they were almost too interesting – it was getting to be a strain on my emotions. We were all edgy anyway, wondering how the other four were getting on. But Tuesday started cooler and proved to be cooler in most ways. It was an intriguing day; a day I won't forget.

We'd agreed to get up early again. I'd noticed that the longer we stayed in Hell, the more we fell into natural rhythms, going to bed when it was dark and getting up at dawn. That wasn't the routine we had at home, no way. But here we gradually started doing it without noticing. It wasn't quite that simple. We often stayed up after dark to light a fire, to do some cooking for the next day or even just to have a cup of tea –

quite a few of us missed our cups of tea during the day – but before long people would be yawning and standing and stretching and throwing out the dregs in the mug, then wandering away to their tents.

So, when it was still cold and damp on that Tuesday morning we gathered at the dead fire, talking occasionally, and listening to the soft voices of the magpies and the startled muttering of the chooks. We had our usual cold breakfast. Most nights now I soaked dried fruit in water, in a tightly covered billy so the possums couldn't get at it. By morning the fruit was juicy and tasty, and we had it with muesli or other cereal. Fi usually had powdered milk, which we also reconstituted the night before, to have it ready for the morning. We'd scrounged a few more tubes of condensed milk on our trip to the Grubers', but again they hadn't lasted long: all we diabetics-in-training sucked them dry within twenty-four hours.

Our major job that morning was to get firewood. We wanted to build up a big pile, then camouflage it. It sounds crazy with all the bush around us, but firewood was quite hard to get, because the bush was so dense. There were lots of little jobs needed doing too – chopping wood, digging drainage trenches around the tents, digging a new dunny (we'd filled our first one), making up tightly sealed packs of food that we could store around the mountains, as Homer had suggested. Because Lee was still not very mobile he got the last job, as well as the dishwashing, and cleaning the rifles.

The plan was to work hard most of the morning, have a break after lunch, then go out that night to bring more loads in from the Landie. And we did get a lot done before the day warmed up enough to slow us down. We got a stack of firewood that was about a metre high and three metres wide, plus a separate pile of kindling. We dug our trenches and dunny, then put up a better shelter for the chooks. It was amazing how much work four people could get through, compared with what Dad and I could achieve. But it did worry me that we were still so heavily dependent on supplies brought up in the four-wheel drives. That was a short-term solution. Even with our own vegetables, even with the hens, we were a long way off being self-sufficient. Suppose we were here for three months... or six... or two years. It was unthinkable – but it was very possible.

Over lunch, when the other two were busy for a minute, Lee said to me, in a low voice, 'Would you be able to show me the Hermit's hut this afternoon?'

I was startled. 'But yesterday, when the other two came... you said your leg...'

'Yes, I know. But I've used it quite a bit today. It feels quite good. Anyway, I was in a bad mood with you yesterday.'

I grinned. 'OK, I'll take you. And I'll do a Robyn and carry you back if you need it.'

There must have been something in the air, because when I told the other two that if Lee's leg was good enough we'd be away for an hour or two, Homer gave Fi a swift wink. I think Fi must have given Homer some encouragement during the morning, because it wasn't the 'Ohhh, Lee and Ellie' type wink; it was the 'Good, we'll get some time together' wink. It was very sneaky of them. I'm sure if we hadn't given them the opportunity they would have come up with some lie to get away on their own. It made me feel jealous though, and I wished I could cancel our paddle so I could stay back and chaperone. Deep down in my heart I really didn't want Homer and Fi to be together.

There was nothing I could do though. I'd been neatly trapped. So, at around two o'clock, I set off towards the creek with Lee limping beside me. The journey was surprisingly quick this time, because I knew how to do it now and went there more deliberately and confidently, and because Lee was moving more freely than I'd expected. The water gurgled along, refreshingly cold, and we just went with the flow.

'It's the perfect path in,' Lee commented, 'because we don't leave any tracks.'

'Mmm. You know, on the other side of Hell is the Holloway River and Risdon. There must be a way through from here. It'd be interesting to try to find it, by following this creek maybe.'

We got to the hut but Lee's first priority was to talk. He sat down on a rather damp log by the edge of the creek.

'I'll just give my leg a rest,' he said.

'Is it hurting?'

'A little. Only an ache from being used again. I think exercise is probably the best thing for it.' He paused. 'You know, Ellie, I didn't ever thank you properly for coming to get me that night, from the restaurant. You guys were heroes. You really put it on the line for me. I'm not too good at big emotional speeches, but I won't forget that, for the rest of my life.'

'That's OK,' I said uncomfortably. 'You did thank me once already. And you'd have done the same for us.'

199

'And I'm sorry about yesterday.'

'What's to be sorry about? You said what you wanted to say. You said what you thought. Which is more than I did.'

'Well, say it now.'

I grinned. 'Maybe I should. Although I wasn't planning to say any more.' I thought for a minute, and decided to take the plunge. I was nervous, but it was exciting. 'All right, I'll say what I think I think, but just remember, it's not necessarily what I really think, because I don't know what I think.'

He groaned. 'Oh Ellie, you're so frustrating. You haven't even started and already you're getting me churned up. This is the same as yesterday.'

'Well do you want me to be honest or don't you?'

'All right, go on, and I'll try to keep control of my blood pressure.'

'OK.' Having said that I wasn't even sure of where to start. 'Lee, I do like you, very much. I think you're interesting, funny, smart, and you've got my favourite eyes in Wirrawee. I'm just not sure that I like you in that way, you know what I mean. That day in the hayshed, my feelings got the better of me. But there's something about you, I don't know what it is, but you make me nervous a little. I've never met anyone quite like you. And one thing I wonder is, suppose we started going round together, and it didn't work out? Here we are, the seven of us, no, eight now, living in this out-of-the-way place in these really strange times, with the whole world turned upside down, yet we get on pretty well together – most of the time. I'd hate to spoil that by us two suddenly having a falling out and deciding we didn't want to see each other, or we were embarrassed to be together. That'd be awful.

It'd be like Adam and Eve having a fight in the Garden of Eden. I mean, who would they talk to then? The apple tree? The snake?'

'Oh Ellie,' Lee said. 'Why do you have to reason everything through all the time? The future is the future. It has to take care of itself. You can sit here all day and make guesses about it, and at the end of the day, what have you got? A lot of dead guesses, that's what. And in the meantime you haven't done anything, you haven't lived, because you've been so busy reasoning it all out.'

'That's not true,' I said, getting annoyed. 'The way we got the truck and rescued you, that was all done with reason. If we hadn't figured out all the possibilities first, it never would have worked.'

'But a lot of it you were just making up as you went along,' he said. 'I remember how you told me you changed the plan about something, the route you took I think it was. And there were lots of things, like slamming the brakes on to catch the car behind: that was you going with your gut feelings.'

'So you think I should live life from the gut, not from the head?'

He laughed. 'Not when you put it like that. I guess there's a place for both. I'll tell you what it's like. It's like my music.' Lee was brilliant, Grade 6 piano already, the best for his age in Wirrawee. 'When I'm learning a piece, or when I'm playing, I've got to have my heart and my mind involved. My mind is thinking about technique and my heart is feeling the passion of the music. So I suppose it's the same as life. You've got to have both.'

'And you think I'm all head and no heart?'

'No! Stop twisting what I'm saying. But remember

the guy who lived here. His heart must have gradually dried up, till it was like a little dried apricot, and all he had left was his reason. I hope it was a big consolation to him.'

'So you do think I'm all head and no heart! You think I'll end up in this little hut, the Hermitess from Hell, no friends, no one to love me. Excuse me, I'm going down the garden to eat worms.'

'No, I just think that for some things, for example liking someone, for example liking me, you're being too careful and calculating. You should just go with the feelings.'

'But my feelings are that I'm confused,' I said miserably.

'That's probably because your feelings are being confused by your mind. Your feelings might be coming through loud and clear, but before they get to the surface your brain gets in the way and muddles them around.'

'So I'm a sort of TV that's been put too close to a computer? I'm getting interference with my picture?' I wasn't sure if I believed all this or if it was just Lee spinning a line. Guys will say anything.

'Yes!' Lee said. 'The question is, what programme's showing on the TV? A debate on the meaning of life, or a passionate love story?'

'I know what you'd like it to be,' I said. 'A porno starring us.'

He grinned. 'How can I say I love you for your mind, after everything I've just said? But I do.'

It was the first time he'd used the word love, and it sobered me, a bit. This relationship could easily get serious. The trouble was, I was avoiding mentioning Homer, and one reason Lee couldn't understand me was because he didn't understand about Homer – although he'd had a guess, the day before. I think he'd have been less confused if I'd been more honest with him. But I knew about Homer, and I was still confused. I sighed, and got up.

'Come on cripple, let's go and look at the hut.'

This was my third trip to the hut, so it was losing interest for me a little. But Lee poked around for quite a while. There was more light in there this time; it probably all depended on the time of day, but there was some filtered sunlight that relieved the darkness along the back wall. Lee went to the hut's only window, a glassless square in the back wall. He put his head through it and had a look at the mint outside, then investigated the rotting window frame.

'Beautifully made,' he said. 'Look at these joints. Wait, there's some metal here.'

'How do you mean?' I came up beside him as he started wrestling with the window sill. I could see then what he meant – the sill was rotting through, and between the decayed splinters a dull black metal surface was visible. Suddenly Lee lifted the sill straight off. It was clearly made to do that, for underneath was a geometrically neat cavity, not much bigger than a shoe box. And fitting neatly into it was a grey metal cashbox, about shoebox size.

'Wow!' I was astonished and excited. 'Unreal! It's probably full of gold.'

Lee, eyes staring, lifted it out.

'It's pretty light,' he said. 'Too light for gold.'

The box was showing the early signs of rust, with some red lines starting to creep along it, but it was in good condition. It was unlocked, and opened easily. Craning over Lee's arm, I saw nothing but papers and photographs. It was disappointing, although as I realised later gold wasn't much use to us, living our guerilla life up in the mountains. Lee lifted out the papers and the photos. Underneath them was a small blue case, like a wallet, but made of stiffer material and fastened with a small gold clasp. He opened that, carefully. Inside, wrapped in tissue paper and resting on white linen cloth, was a brightly coloured short wide ribbon, attached to a heavy bronze medal.

'Fantastic,' I breathed. 'He was a war hero.'

Lee took it out. On the front was a relief of a king – I'm not sure which one – and the words 'He who would valiant be'. Lee turned it over. On the back was engraved: 'Bertram Christie, for gallantry, Battle of Marana', and a date which was too blurred to read. The ribbon was coloured red, yellow and blue. We handled it, felt it, wondered over it, then wrapped it back up carefully and replaced it in its box before turning our attention to the papers.

There were a few of these: a notebook, a letter or two, some newspaper clippings and a couple of official looking documents. There were three photographs: one of a stern looking young couple on their wedding day, one of the woman alone, standing in front of a bare wooden house, and one of the woman with a toddler. The woman was young, but looked sad; she had long dark hair and a slim smooth face. She might have been Spanish. I looked at the photos intently.

'These must be the ones he murdered,' I whispered.

'Funny that he kept their photos if he murdered them,' Lee said.

I looked at the face of the man in the wedding

photo. He looked young, younger than the woman maybe. He gazed steadily at the camera, clear strong eyes and a firm clean-shaven chin. I could see nothing of the murderer in his face and nothing of the victim in his wife's or child's.

Lee started opening the documents. The first seemed to be a newspaper account of a sermon. I only read the first paragraph. The sermon was based on a verse from the Bible, 'A fool's mouth is his ruin, and his lips are a snare to himself'. It looked long and boring, so I didn't read any more. The other newspaper clipping was a short article that was headlined 'Victims of Mt Tumbler Tragedy Laid to Rest'. It read:

A small group of mourners were in attendance at the Mt Tumbler Church of England on Monday last, where Revd Horace Green conducted a service for Burial of the Dead. Laid to rest were Imogen Mary Christie, of Mt Tumbler, and her infant child Alfred Bertram Christie, aged three.

The Christie family were not well known, being newly arrived, living a goodly distance from town, and being apparently of reclusive disposition, but the tragedy has aroused considerable sentiment in the district, which was touched on most feelingly by Revd Green in his address, which had for its text 'Man that is born of woman hath but a short time to live and is full of misery; he cometh up and is cut down like a flower'.

The deceased were then interred in the Mt Tumbler cemetery.

A public meeting will be held in the Mt Tumbler School of Arts on Monday next, under the chairmanship of Mr Donald McDonald, JP, to canvass again the possibility of obtaining the services of a medical practitioner for the Mt Tumbler district. The Christie tragedy has led to fresh agitation for the provision of medical services for the area.

An inquest into the deaths of Mrs Christie and her child will take place at the next visit of the magistrate to the district, on April 15. In the meantime Constable Whykes has cautioned against idle tongues making loose speculation upon the facts of the case; a sentiment most earnestly shared by this correspondent.

That was all. I read it over Lee's shoulder. 'It seems to raise more questions than it answers,' I said.

'Doesn't mention the husband at all,' Lee said.

The next item was a stiff formal card of cream paper, though yellowed now. It seemed to be the citation to accompany the medal. In ornate flowing writing it described the actions of Private Bertram Christie in running forward under enemy fire to rescue a wounded and unconscious 'corporal of another regiment'. 'In conveying his fellow-soldier safely back to his own lines Private Christie endangered his own life and displayed conspicuous gallantry, for which His Majesty is pleased to honour Private Bertram Christie with the award of the St George Medal.'

'Curiouser and curiouser,' Lee said.

'Sounds like you and Robyn,' I said. 'I reckon she should get a medal.'

There were a few odds and ends then: birth certificates for all three Christies, the marriage certificate of Bertram and Imogen, a postcard addressed to Bertram from his wife, and saying merely 'We will be on the 4.15 train. Mother sends her kind regards. Your devoted wife, Imogen.' There were some bank documents and a notebook containing lots of accounts and figures. I pointed to one item that said, 'To a double bed, £4/10/6'.

'How much is that?' Lee asked.

'About eight dollars I think. Don't you double the number of pounds? I don't know what you do with the shillings and pence.'

Then we came to the last of the formal documents, a long sheet of paper with a red seal on top. It was typed and signed at the bottom with a black flourish of ink. We settled down to read it, and found in the dry language of the coroner the story of the man who had killed his wife and child:

Be it known by all persons having business with His Majesty's Courts that I, HAROLD AMORY DOUGLAS BATTY, being duly appointed Magistrate and Coroner in the District of Mt Tumbler, make the following findings and recommendations with respect to the deaths of IMOGEN MARY CHRISTIE, aged twenty-four, married woman of this parish, and ALFRED BERTRAM CHRISTIE, aged three, infant of this parish, both residing at Block 16A on the Aberfoyle track, forty-four miles to the southwest of Pink Mountain:

1. That both deceased met their deaths on or about December 24 last, at the hands of BERTRAM HUBERT SEXTON CHRISTIE, as a result of bullet wounds to the head.

2. That both deceased lived with BERTRAM HUBERT SEXTON CHRISTIE, farmer, in the relationships respectively of wife and son to the said

BERTRAM HUBERT SEXTON CHRISTIE, in a wooden cottage at the above address, this being a particularly remote part of the Mt Tumbler district.

3. That there is no evidence of marital disharmony between BERTRAM HUBERT SEXTON CHRISTIE and IMOGEN MARY CHRISTIE, and that on the contrary BERTRAM HUBERT SEXTON CHRISTIE was a loving husband and father, IMOGEN MARY CHRISTIE a dutiful and even-tempered wife, and the child ALFRED BERTRAM CHRISTIE a sweet child of good disposition, and that is the testimony of WILSON HUBERT GEORGE, farmer, and neighbour to the deceased, and MURIEL EDNA MAYBERRY, married woman and neighbour to the deceased.

4. That the nearest medical practitioner or nursing sister to the Christies was at Dunstan Lake, being a day and a half's ride away, and further

5. That severe bushfires were burning on and around the Aberfoyle track, the Mt Tumbler–Mt Octopus Road, Wild Goat Track and to the south of Pink Mountain, which had the effect of isolating the Christie property, and that this information was known to BERTRAM HUBERT SEXTON CHRISTIE.

6. That both deceased met their deaths EITHER as a result of bushfire consuming the Christie residence, during which both were terribly burnt, and that BERTRAM HUBERT SEXTON CHRISTIE, believing their injuries to be mortal and unable to bear their suffering, and knowing also that medical aid was beyond immediate reach, killed both deceased with single shots to the head from a rifle owned by BERTRAM HUBERT SEXTON CHRISTIE; and that

is the testimony of BERTRAM HUBERT SEXTON CHRISTIE

OR that both deceased were wilfully and feloniously murdered by BERTRAM HUBERT SEXTON CHRISTIE with the aforesaid rifle, and the bodies deliberately burned in an attempt to conceal the facts of the case.

7. That medical science cannot say as to which came first, the bullets or the burning, and that is the testimony of Dr JACKSON MUIRFIELD WATSON, medical practitioner and forensic scientist, of Stratton and District Hospital, Stratton.

8. That police inquiries have been unable to locate any other persons with evidence bearing upon the deaths of IMOGEN MARY CHRISTIE or ALFRED BERTRAM CHRISTIE, and that is the testimony of Constable FREDERICK JOHN WHYKES of the Police Station, Mt Tumbler.

10. That on the evidence before me I am unable to make any further findings as to the manner in which the deceased met their deaths.

RECOMMENDED:

1. That urgent consideration be given to the provision of medical services at Mt Tumbler.

2. That the Director of Public Prosecutions lays an information of WILFUL AND FELONIOUS MURDER against BERTRAM HUBERT SEXTON CHRISTIE.

Signed by the hand of me, HAROLD AMORY DOUGLAS BATTY, in the Mt Tumbler Magistrate's Court this day, the 18th of April.

Chapter Sixteen

There were two other documents in the box.

One was a letter from Imogen Christie's mother. She wrote:

Dear Mr Christie, (' "Mr Christie!" ' Lee commented; and I said, 'Well, they were very formal in those days.') I am in receipt of your letter of November 12. Indeed your position is a difficult one. As you know I have always stood by you and defended your account of the dreadful deaths of my dear daughter and my dear grandson, as being the only possible true one, and I have always believed and devoutly prayed it so to be. And I rejoiced, as you know, when the jury pronounced you innocent, for I believe you to have been a man unjustly accused, and if the Law does not know a case such as yours then more shame on the law I say, but the jury did the only thing possible, despite what the Judge said. And you know I have always held to the one point of view and have said so from one end of the district to the other. I cannot think that I could have done any more. No man, and no woman either, can still wagging tongues, and if they are as bad as you say and you will be forced to leave the district it is a shame but there is no stopping women once they begin to gossip, and I say it although I am a traitor to my sex, but there it is, that is the way of the world and no doubt always will be. And you know you will always be welcome under the roof of,

Imogen Emma Eakin

The last thing was a poem, a simple poem:

In this life of froth and bubble,
Two things stand like stone.
Kindness in another's trouble,
Courage in your own.

When we'd read that, Lee silently wrapped everything up again and replaced it in the tin. It didn't surprise me when he put the tin back in the cavity and dropped the windowsill on top of it. I knew that we weren't necessarily leaving it there forever, to decay into fragments and then dust, but at the moment there was too much to absorb, too much to think about. We left the hut silently, and we left it to its silence.

Half way back along the creek I turned to face Lee, who was splashing along behind me. It was about the only spot in the cool tunnel of green where we could stand. I put my hands around the back of his neck and kissed him hungrily. After a moment of shock, when his lips felt numb, he began kissing me back, pressing his mouth hard into mine. There we were, standing in the cold stream, exchanging hot kisses. I explored not just his lips but his smell, the feeling of his skin, the shape of his shoulder blades, the warmth of the back of his neck. After a while I broke off and laid my head against his shoulder, one arm still around him. I looked down at the cool steady-flowing water, moving along its ordained course.

'That coroner's report,' I said to Lee.

'Yes?'

'We were talking about reason and emotion.'

'Yes?'

'Have you ever known emotion dealt with so coldly as in that report?'

'No, I don't think I have.'

I turned more, so that I could nuzzle into his chest, and I whispered, 'I don't want to end up like a coroner's report'.

'No.' He stroked my hair, then felt up under it and squeezed the back of my neck softly, like a massage. After a few minutes more he said, 'Let's get out of this creek. I'm freezing by slow degrees. It's up to my knees and rising.'

I giggled. 'Let's go quickly then. I wouldn't like it to get any higher.'

Back in the clearing it was obvious that something had happened between Homer and Fi. Homer was sitting against a tree with Fi curled up against him. Homer was looking out across the clearing to where one of Satan's Steps loomed high in the distance. They weren't talking, and when we arrived they got up and wandered over, Homer a little self-consciously, Fi quite naturally. But as I watched them a little during the rest of the afternoon – not spying, just with curiosity to see what they were like – I felt that they were different to us. They seemed more nervous with each other, a bit like twelve-year-olds on their first date.

212

Fi explained it to me when we managed to sneak off on our own for a quick goss.

'He's so down on himself,' she complained. 'Everything I say about him he brushes off or puts himself down. Do you know,' she looked at me with her big innocent eyes, 'he's got some weird thing about my parents being solicitors, and living in that stupid big house. He always used to joke about it, especially when we went there the other night, but I don't think it's really a joke to him at all.'

'Oh Fi! How long did it take you to work that out?'

'Why? Has he said something to you?' She instantly became terribly worried, in her typical Fi way. I was a bit caught, because I wanted to protect Homer and I didn't want to break any confidences. So I tried to give a few hints.

'Well, your lifestyle's a lot different to his. And you know the kind of blokes he's always knocked around with at school. They'd be more at home hanging out at the milk bar than playing croquet with your parents.'

'My parents do not play croquet.'

'No, but you know what I mean.'

'Oh, I don't know what to do. He seems scared to say anything in case I laugh at him or look down my nose at him. As if I ever would. It seems so funny that he's like that with me when he's so confident with everyone else.'

I sighed. 'If I could understand Homer I'd understand all guys.'

It was getting dark and we had to start organising for a big night, starting with another hike up Satan's Steps. I was tired and not very keen to go, especially as Lee wouldn't be able to come. His leg was still stiff and sore. When the time came I trudged off behind Homer and Fi, too weak to complain – I thought I'd feel guilty if I did. But gradually the sweetness of the night air revived me. I began to breathe it in more deeply, and to notice the silent mountains standing gravely around. The place was beautiful, I was with my friends and they were good people, we were coping OK with tough circumstances. There were a lot of things to be unhappy about, but somehow the papers I'd read in the Hermit's hut, and the long beautiful kiss with Lee, had given me a better perspective on life. I knew it wouldn't last, but I tried to enjoy it while it did.

At the Landie we set about constructing a new hideaway for the vehicles, so that they'd be better concealed from anyone using the track. It wasn't easy to do, and in the end we had to be content with a spot behind some trees, nearly a k further down the hill. Its big advantage was that to drive in there you had to go over rocks, which meant no tracks would be left, as long as the tyres were dry. Its big disadvantage was that it gave us a longer walk to get into Hell, and it was a long enough walk already.

Fi and Homer were going to wait up there for the other four, whom we were expecting back from Wirrawee at about dawn, but I didn't want to leave Lee at the campsite on his own for the night. So, for that charitable reason, and no other, I filled a backpack to the brim, took a bag of clothes in my hand and, laden like a truck, put myself into four-wheel drive and trekked back into Hell on my own. It was about midnight when I left Fi and Homer. They said they were going to stretch out in the back of the Landrover for a few hours' sleep while they waited.

214

That's what they said they were going to do, anyway.

The moon was well up by the time I left. The rocks stood out quite brightly along the thin ridge of Tailor's Stitch. A small bird suddenly flew out of a low tree ahead of me, with a yowling cry and a clatter of wings. Bushes formed shapes like goblins and demons waiting to pounce. The path straggled between them: if a tailor had stitched it he must have been mad or possessed or both. White dead wood gleamed like bones ahead of me, and my feet scrunched the little stones and the gravel. Perhaps I should have been frightened, walking there alone in the dark. But I wasn't, I couldn't be. The cool night breeze kissed my face all over, all the time, and the smell of the wattle gave a faint sweetness to the air. This was my country; I felt like I had grown from its soil like the silent trees around me, like the springy, tiny-leafed plants that lined the track. I wanted to get back to Lee, to see his serious face again, and those brown eyes that charmed me when they were laughing and held me by the heart when they were grave. But I also wanted to stay here forever. If I stayed much longer I felt that I could become part of the landscape myself, a dark, twisted, fragrant tree.

I was walking very slowly, wanting to get to Lee but not too quickly. I was hardly conscious of the weight of the supplies I was carrying. I was remembering how a long time ago – it seemed like years – I'd been thinking about this place, Hell, and how only humans could have given it such a name. Only humans knew about Hell; they were the experts on it. I remembered wondering if humans were Hell. The Hermit for instance; whatever had happened that terrible Christmas Eve, whether he'd committed an act of great love, or an act of great evil... But that was the whole problem, that as a human being he could have done either and he could have done both. Other creatures didn't have this problem. They just did what they did. I didn't know if the Hermit was a saint or a devil, but once he'd fired those two shots it seemed that he and the people round him had sent him into Hell. They sent him there and he sent himself there. He didn't have to trek all the way across to these mountains into this wild basin of heat and rock and bush. He carried Hell with him, as we all did, like a little load on our backs that we hardly noticed most of the time, or like a huge great hump of suffering that bent us over with its weight.

I too had blood on my hands, like the Hermit, and just as I couldn't tell whether his actions were good or bad, so too I couldn't tell what mine were. Had I killed out of love of my friends, as part of a noble crusade to rescue friends and family and keep our land free? Or had I killed because I valued my life above that of others? Would it be OK for me to kill a dozen others to keep myself alive? A hundred? A thousand? At what point did I condemn myself to Hell, if I hadn't already done so? The Bible just said 'Thou shalt not kill', then told hundreds of stories of people killing each other and becoming heroes, like David with Goliath. That didn't help me much.

I didn't feel like a criminal, but I didn't feel like a hero either.

I was sitting on a rock on top of Mt Martin thinking about all this. The moon was so bright I could see forever. Trees and boulders and even the summits of other mountains cast giant black shadows across the ranges. But nothing could be seen of the tiny humans who crawled like bugs over the landscape, committing their monstrous and beautiful acts. I could only see my own shadow, thrown across the rock by the moon behind me. People, shadows, good, bad, Heaven, Hell: all of these were names, labels, that was all. Humans had created these opposites: Nature recognised no opposites. Even life and death weren't opposites in Nature: one was merely an extension of the other.

All I could think of to do was to trust to instinct. That was all I had really. Human laws, moral laws, religious laws, they seemed artificial and basic, almost childlike. I had a sense within me – often not much more than a striving – to find the right thing to do, and I had to have faith in that sense. Call it anything – instinct, conscience, imagination – but what it felt like was a constant testing of everything I did against some kind of boundaries within me; checking, checking, all the time. Perhaps war criminals and mass murderers did the same checking against the same boundaries and got the encouragement they needed to keep going down the path they had taken. How then could I know that I was different?

I got up and walked around slowly, around the top of Mt Martin. This was really hurting my head but I had to stay with it. I felt I was close to it, that if I kept my grip on it, didn't let go, I might just get it out, drag it out of my begrudging brain. And yes, I could think of one way in which I was different. It was confidence. The people I knew who thought brutal thoughts and acted in brutal ways – the racists, the sexists, the bigots – never seemed to doubt themselves. They were always so sure that they were right. Mrs Olsen, at school, who gave out more detentions than the rest of the staff put together and kept complaining about 'standards' in the school and the 'lack of discipline' among 'these kids'; Mr Rodd, down the road from us, who could never keep a worker for more than six weeks – he'd gone through fourteen in two years – because they were all 'lazy' or 'stupid' or 'insolent'; Mr and Mrs Nelson, who drove their son five kilometres from home every time he did something wrong and dropped him off and made him walk home again, then chucked him out for good when he was seventeen and they found the syringes in his bedroom – these were the ones I thought of as the ugly people. And they did seem to have the one thing in common – a perfect belief that they were right and the others wrong. I almost envied them the strength of their beliefs. It must have made life so much easier for them.

Perhaps my lack of confidence, my tortuous habit of questioning and doubting everything I said or did, was a gift, a good gift, something that made life painful in the short run but in the long run might lead to … what? The meaning of life?

At least it might give me some chance of working out what I should or shouldn't do.

All this thinking had tired me out more than the work hiking up and down the mountains. The moon was shining brighter than ever but I couldn't stay. I got up and went down the rocks to the gum tree and the start of the trail. When I got back to the campsite I was disgusted to find Lee sound asleep. I could hardly blame him, considering how late it was, but I'd been looking forward all evening to seeing him and talking to him again. After all, it had been his fault that I'd been going through this mental sweat-session. He'd started it, with his talk about my head and my heart. Now I had to console myself with crawling into his tent and sleeping next to him. The only consolation was that he would wake in the morning and find he had slept with me and not even known it. I think I was still smiling about that when I fell asleep.

Chapter Seventeen

Robyn and Kevin and Corrie and Chris were beaming. It wasn't hard to beam back. It was such a relief, such a joy, to see them again. I hugged them desperately, only then aware how frightened I'd been for them. But for once everything seemed to have gone well. It was wonderful.

They hadn't told Homer and Fi much, because they were tired, and because they didn't want to repeat themselves when they reached Lee and me. All they'd said was that they hadn't seen any of our families, but they'd been told they were safe and at the Showground. When I heard this, it was such a relief that I sat down quickly on the ground, as though I'd had the breath knocked out of me. Lee leant against a tree with his hands over his face. I don't think anything else mattered to us much. We did have lots of questions, but we could see how exhausted everyone was, so we were content to let them have their breakfasts before they told us any more. And with a good breakfast in them – even a few fresh eggs, cooked quickly and dangerously on a small fire, which we put out just as quickly – they settled down, full of food and adrenalin, to tell us the lot. Robyn did most of the talking. She'd already been their unofficial leader when they left, and it was interesting to see how much she was running the show now. Lee and I sat on a log holding hands, Fi sat against Homer in the V formed by his open legs, and Kevin lay on the ground with his head in Corrie's lap. It was like Perfect Partners, and although I still wondered if I might have liked to swap places with Fi, I was happy enough. It was just too bad that there was no chance of Chris and Robyn getting off together, then we really could have had Perfect Partners.

Chris had brought back a few packets of smokes and two bottles of port that he'd 'souvenired', as he called it. He sat on the log beside me, until he lit up and I politely asked him to move. I couldn't help wondering how far we could go with this 'souveniring' idea. It made me reflect on what I'd been thinking about the night before. If we were going to ignore the laws of the land, we had to work out our own standards instead. I had no problem with all the laws we'd broken already – so far we could have been charged with stealing, driving without a licence, wilful damage, assault, manslaughter, or murder maybe, going through a stop sign, driving without lights, breaking and entering, and I don't know how many other things. It seemed like we'd be committing under-age drinking soon too, not for the first time in my life, I have to admit. That didn't bother me either – I'd always thought the law on that was typical of the stupidity of most laws. I mean, the idea that at seventeen years, eleven months and twenty-nine days you were too immature to touch alcohol but a day later you could get wasted on a couple of slabs wasn't exactly bright. But I still didn't like the idea of Chris picking up grog and cigarettes whenever and wherever he felt like it. I suppose it was because they weren't as essential as the other things we'd knocked off. Admittedly I'd taken some chocolate from the Grubers', which wasn't much different, except that at Outward Bound they'd given us chocolate for energy, so there was at least something good you could say about chocolate. There wasn't an awful lot you could say for port or nicotine.

I wondered what would happen if Chris brought anything stronger into Hell, or if he tried to grow dope or something down here. But meanwhile Robyn was starting on the big speech, so I stopped thinking about morality and started concentrating on her.

'OK boys and girls,' she began. 'Everyone ready for story time? We've had a pretty interesting couple of days. Although,' she added, looking at Lee and me, and Homer and Fi, 'you guys seem to have had an interesting couple of days yourselves. It mightn't be safe to leave you here alone again.'

'OK Mum, get on with it,' Homer said.

'All right, but I'm watching you, remember. Well. Where do I start? The first thing, as we've said already, is that we haven't seen any of our families, but we've heard about them. The people we talked to swear they're all OK. In fact everyone in the Showground is meant to be in good nick. What we said jokingly a while back is quite true: they have got plenty of food. They've eaten the scones, the decorated cakes, the sponges, the home-made bread, the matched eggs, the novelty cakes... Have I left anything out?'

'The fruit cakes,' said Corrie, who was an expert on these subjects. 'The jams, preserves and pickles. The Best Assorted Biscuits.'

'OK, OK.' About three people spoke at once.

'And,' said Robyn, 'they're eating their way through the livestock. It's a shame really, because it's some of the best stock in the district. So they should be getting some top quality tucker. They bake bread in the CWA tearooms every morning – there's a couple of stoves in there. For a while they were running short of greens, once they'd eaten the Young Farmers' display, which I might add I helped set up, the day before we went on our hike.'

'You're not a Young Farmer,' I said.

'No, but Adam is,' she said, looking faintly embarrassed.

When our immature wolf whistles and animal noises had died down, she continued, undaunted.

'But there's been a few developments,' she said. 'They've now got work parties going out of the Showground each day. They go in groups of eight or ten, with three or four guards. They do jobs like cleaning the streets, burying people, getting food – including the greens – and helping in the Hospital.'

'So the Hospital is running? We thought it was.'

'Yes. Ellie's been keeping it busy.'

As soon as she said that, she looked like she wished she hadn't.

'What? Did you hear something?'

She shook her head. 'No, no, nothing.'

'Oh come on, don't do that Robyn. What did you hear?'

'It's nothing Ellie. There were some casualties. You know that.'

'So what did you hear?'

Robyn looked uncomfortable. I knew I'd be sorry but I'd gone too far to stop. 'Robyn! Stop treating me like a kid! Just tell me!'

She grimaced but told me. 'Those three soldiers hit by the ride-on mower, two of them died, they think. And two of the people we ran over.'

'Oh,' I said. She'd said it flatly and calmly, but the shock was still terrible. Sweat broke out on my face and I felt quite giddy. Lee gripped my hand hard, but I hardly felt it. Corrie came and sat on my other side, where Chris had been, and held me.

After a minute Chris said, 'It's different from the movies, isn't it?'

'Yes,' I said. 'I'm OK. Please, just go on Robyn.'

'Are you sure?'

'I'm sure.'

'Well, the Hospital's had a few other casualties. The first day or two there was a lot of fighting, and a lot of people got hurt or killed. Soldiers and civilians. Not at the Showground – the surprise was so complete that they took the whole place in ten minutes – but in town and around the district, with people who hadn't gone to the Show. And it's still going on – there's a few groups of guerillas, just ordinary people like us I guess, who are hanging around and attacking patrols when they get a chance. But the town itself is quiet. They seem to have flushed everyone out, and they're confident that they've got it under control.'

'Are they treating people well?'

'Mostly. For example, the people who were in hospital the day of the invasion have been kept there, and looked after. The people we've talked to say the soldiers are anxious to keep their noses clean. They know that sooner or later the United Nations and the Red Cross'll be wandering around, and they don't want to attract a lot of heat from them. They keep talking about a "clean" invasion. They figure that if there's no talk of concentration camps and torture and rape and stuff, there's less chance of countries like America getting involved.'

'That's pretty smart,' Homer said.

'Yes. But for all that, there's been about forty deaths just around Wirrawee alone. Mr Althaus, for one. The whole Francis family. Mr Underhill. Mrs Nasser. John Leung. And some people have been bashed for not obeying orders.'

There was a shocked silence. Mr Underhill was the only one of those I knew well. He was the jeweller in town. He was such a mild man that I couldn't imagine how he might have aggravated the soldiers. Perhaps he'd tried to stop them looting his store.

'So who have you been talking to?' Lee asked at last.

'Oh yes, I was getting to that. I'm telling this all out of order. OK, so this is what happened. We cruised into town the first night, no problems. We got to my music teacher's house about 1.30 am. The key was where she always left it. It is a good place to hide out, like I said, because there's so many doors and windows you can get out of. There's a good escape route out of an upstairs window, for example, where you can go across the roof, onto a big branch, and be next door in a couple of seconds. Also, the sentry has a great view of the street and the front drive, and there's no way anyone could get over the back fence without a tank. So that was cool. The first thing we did after we sussed out the house was to get some gear together and go and set up the fake camp under the Masonic Hall. That was quite fun – we put in a few magazines and photos and teddy bears to make it look authentic. Then Kevin took the first sentry duty and the rest of us went to bed.

'At about eleven in the morning I was on sentry duty and suddenly I saw some people in the street. There was a soldier and two of our people. One of them was Mr Keogh, who used to work at the Post Office.'

'You mean the old guy with no hair?'

'Yes. He retired last year I think. Well, I woke the others fast, as you can imagine, and we watched them working their way along the street. There were three soldiers altogether, and six people from town. They had a ute and a truck, and it seemed like they were clearing stuff out of each house. Two of them would go into a house while the soldiers lounged around outside. The people spent about ten minutes in each house, then they'd come out with green garbage bags full of stuff. They'd chuck some bags straight into the truck, but other bags were checked by the soldiers and put in the ute.

'So what we did was, when they got close to us we hid in different parts of the house and waited for them. I was in the kitchen, in a broom cupboard. I'd been there about twenty minutes when Mr Keogh came in. He opened the fridge door and starting clearing out all this smelly, foul stuff. It was the job we hadn't been able to bring ourselves to do on an empty stomach when we'd got there at 1.30.

'"Mr Keogh!" I whispered. "This is Robyn Mathers." You know, he didn't even blink. I thought, this guy is cool. Then I remembered that he's quite deaf. He hadn't even heard me. So I opened the door of the broom cupboard and snuck up behind him and tapped his shoulder. Well! I know Chris said a few minutes ago that war's not like the movies, but this sure was. He jumped like he'd touched a live wire in the fridge. I had to hold him down. I thought "Help, I hope he doesn't have a heart attack". But he calmed down. We talked pretty fast then. He had to keep working while we talked – he said if he took too long the soldiers would get suspicious and come in. He said his job was to make the houses habitable again, by cleaning out mouldy food, and dead pets, and to pick up valuables, like jewellery. He told me about our families, and all that other stuff. He said the work parties would be going out to the country too, starting any day now, to look after the stock and get the farms going again. He said they're going to colonise the whole country with their own people, and all the farms will be split up between them, and we'll just be allowed to do menial jobs, like cleaning lavatories I suppose. Then he had to go, but he told me they were doing West Street after Barrabool Avenue, and if I got into a house there we could talk some more. And off he went.

'Well, when the house was empty again we had a quick conference. Kevin had talked to a lady called Mrs Lee, who'd come into the bedroom where he was hiding, and he'd got more information from her. So we agreed to go to West Street and try again. We got there fairly easily, by going through people's gardens, and we tried a few different houses. The first two were locked still but the third one was open, so we spread ourselves around it. I got under the bed in the main bedroom. Chris kept watch and told us when they were getting close, which wasn't for nearly two hours. It was pretty boring. If you want to know how many cross-wires the people at 28 West Street have got on the underside of their bed, I can tell you. But finally someone came in. It was a lady I didn't know, but she had a green bag and she went to the dressing table and started scooping stuff out. I whispered "Excuse me, my name's Robyn Mathers", and without looking round she whispered "Oh good, Mr Keogh told me to watch out for you young ones". We talked for a few minutes, with me still under the bed, but sticking my head out. She said she hated having to do this work, but the soldiers occasionally checked a house after they came out, and they got punished if they'd left anything valuable behind. "Sometimes I'll hide something in the room if it looks like a family heirloom," she said, "but I don't know if it'll make any difference in the long run." She also told me that they were picking the least dangerous people for the work parties – old people and kids mainly – and they knew that if they tried to escape or do anything wrong, their families back at the Showgrounds would be punished. "So I don't want to talk to you for long dearie," she said. She was a nice old duck. The other thing she told me was that the highway from Cobbler's Bay is the key to everything. That's why they hit this district so hard and so early. They bring their supplies in to Cobbler's by ship and send it down the highway by truck.'

'Just like I said,' I interjected. I'd never thought of myself as a military genius, but I was pleased to find I'd got this right.

Robyn went on. 'Anyway there we were, chatting away like old mates. She even told me how she used to work as a cleaner at the chemist, part-time, and

228

how many grandchildren she had, and their names. She seemed to have forgotten what she'd said about having a short conversation. Another couple of minutes and I think she would have taken me into the kitchen and made a cup of tea, but I suddenly realised there were these soft little footsteps coming along the hall. I pulled my head back in like a turtle, but I tell you, I moved quicker than any turtle. And the next thing, there were these boots right next to the bed. Black boots, but very dirty and scuffed. It was a soldier, and he'd come sneaking along the corridor to try to catch her out. I thought "What am I going to do?" I tried to remember all the martial arts stuff that I'd ever heard of, but all I could think of was to go for the groin.'

'That's all she thinks of with any guy,' Kevin said.

Robyn ignored him. 'I was so scared, because I didn't want to cause any trouble for this nice old lady. I didn't even know her name. Still don't. And I didn't want to get myself killed either. I'm funny like that. But I was so paralysed I couldn't move. I heard the guy say, very suspiciously, something like "You talking". I knew I was in trouble then. I rolled across the floor to the other side of the bed and crawled out from under the bedspread. I was in this little gap between the bed and the wall, about a metre wide I guess. I heard the old lady laugh nervously and say "To myself. In the mirror." It sounded weak to me and I guess it did to him too. All I had going for me was my hearing, and my guesses. I knew he was going to search the room and I guessed he'd start by lifting the bedspread and looking under the bed. Then he'd come round the base of the bed and either go to the built-in, or look in the little gap where I was lying. There were no other places in the room where anyone could hide. It was a bare room, not very nice at all. So I listened for the little swish of his lifting the bedspread, and sure enough the room was so quiet I heard it. In fact the room was so quiet I thought I could hear the old lady's heart beating. I knew I could hear my own heart beating. I could hardly believe that the soldier couldn't hear it. Anyway, the trouble was I couldn't hear the second little swish that he should have made when he dropped the bedspread back down. I was in agony, wondering if he was still staring under the bed or if he was coming around to where I was lying. God, I was listening so hard I could feel my ears grow. I felt like I had two satellite dishes on the sides of my head.'

'You look like you do,' said Kevin, who never missed an opportunity.

'And I did hear something – the tiniest creak of what I thought was his boot, and it seemed to be coming round the base of the bed. I couldn't hear my heart any more – it had stopped. So I thought "Well, I can't lie here and wait to be shot. I've got to take the risk." And so I rolled back under the bed. And sure enough, about a second later I saw his boots in the gap that I'd just left. The fronds on the edge of the bedspread were just moving slightly from where I'd hit them, and I had this terrible time, lying there wondering if he'd notice them, thinking that he must notice them. They seemed so obvious to me, so conspicuous. He seemed to stand there forever. I don't know what he was looking at – there wasn't much to see, just a picture of a long bridge across a ravine, in Switzerland or somewhere I think. Then the boots turned and I could hear him more distinctly, going over to the cupboards and opening them and searching through them. Then he said to the lady "Come on, next house", and out they went. I lay there for so long – I thought it might have been a trap – but at last Kevin came and got me and told me they'd gone. I'd had a pretty bad time though – well, I don't need to tell you guys what it was like.

'Corrie talked to someone too, in the kitchen, didn't you?' she said, looking at Corrie, who gave a little nod. 'That's when you were told about the casualties from our two fights with them?'

'Yes,' Corrie said. 'I think they caused a bit of a sensation. I talked to a funny little man who looked about fifty. I don't know his name either. He didn't want to talk to me much. He was just so scared that we'd be caught. But he told me there was a bit of guerilla activity going on. He was the one who had this theory of the "clean" invasion, too.'

'So,' said Robyn, 'that was the end of our secret chats with the work parties. We made our way back to our hideout and stayed there till dark.' She looked at Homer while she said the next bit. It was like they felt a bit guilty, but they were defiant too about the way they'd done things. 'Now,' she said, 'I know we had all these carefully worked out plans about Kev and Corrie spying on the Showground and so on, but it's different when you get there. The whole time we were in Wirrawee we didn't want to lose sight of each other.'

'Young love,' I said. 'It's beautiful.'

Robyn continued without missing a beat. 'So that night we stayed together again. For a start we walked out to the highway, to see what was going on. And it is being heavily used. We stayed an hour and there were two convoys just in that time. One had forty vehicles and the other had twenty-nine. So it's doing big business, for a little old rural road. It hasn't seen that much excitement since the surf carnival. After that we came back into town and went over to the Showground. That was bloody scary too, I suppose because of what happened to you guys on your visit there. In fact I thought it was pretty gutsy of Corrie and Kev to go there again. And believe me, it is a dangerous place. See, they've got their headquarters and their barracks there, as well as our folks, so I guess that's why they guard it so heavily. They've cut down most of the trees in the carpark, so we couldn't find any approach to it that would provide any cover – I suppose that's why they cut them down. And they've put rolls of wire all the way around it, about fifty metres from the main fence. I didn't know there was that much wire in Wirrawee. And they've rigged up new lights, floodlights, which have got the entire surrounding area lit up like it's daytime. There's a lot of very confused birds flying round there. All we could do was peek from Racecourse Road, which we did for an hour or so. I guess we were too scared to go any closer, but honestly, I don't think there's much to see, just a lot of sentries and patrols wandering round. If anyone has any ideas of rolling up there in combat uniform and shooting their way in and rescuing everybody, I think they can go back to sleep. Fantasyland is for TV. This is real life.'

To be honest, which I swore I'd be, we'd all had those delusions at times. They were only daydreams, but they were powerful daydreams, to liberate our families, to fix everything, to be heroes. But in a secret, guilty way, of which I was ashamed, I felt relieved to have the daydream so firmly squashed. In reality the prospect of doing something like that was so horrifying and frightening that it made me ill to think of it. We would surely die if we tried it, die with our guts blown out and spread across the dirt of the Showground carpark, to have flies feed on us as we turned rotten in the sunlight. It was an image I couldn't get out of my head, probably born from all the dead sheep I'd seen over the years.

'We were quite glad to get out of there,' Robyn went on. 'We moved back into town and just flitted around like little bats, trying to make contact with dentists or anyone else. Which reminds me,' she said, smiling sweetly at Lee, 'it's time I took your stitches out.' Lee looked nervous. I was trying to imagine Kevin flitting. It was hard to picture. 'We didn't find anyone though,' Robyn said. 'Not a soul. There's probably still a few people around, but they're lying very low.' She grinned, and relaxed. 'And that concludes our report to the nation. Thank you and good night.'

'Hey, we could end up being the nation,' Kevin said. 'We could be the only ones left free, so we'd be the government and everything, wouldn't we? Bags being Prime Minister.'

'I'll be the Police Commissioner,' Chris said. We all chose jobs, or got given them. Homer was Minister for Defence, and Chief of the General Staff. Lee was Pensioner of the Year, because of his leg. Robyn wanted to be Minister for Health but got Archbishop instead. Corrie said, 'I'll be Minister for Kevin'. She really could be sickening at times. Fi was Attorney General, because of her parents. I got named as Poet Laureate, which I was quite pleased about.

Maybe it was that which first planted in Robyn's head the idea of my writing all this down.

'So anyway,' Chris said eventually, 'your turn. What have you guys been doing back here, apart from working on your tans?'

They'd already admired the chook yard, and they'd sampled the eggs. But we told them the rest, especially about the Hermit's hut, which we figured would make a great back-up base for us.

'I want to find a way out of the back of Hell, to the Holloway River,' I said. 'I'm sure that's where this creek must go. And if we had a back way out of here we'd be in an even safer position. Once we're in the Holloway we can get to that whole Risdon area.'

Lee and I didn't tell them about the metal box with the Hermit's papers. There was no particular reason. We hadn't even discussed not telling them. It just seemed too private.

'Listen, you know these chooks,' Kevin said, 'I've been thinking about other livestock we could have. I'm no vegetarian, and I want my meat. And I think I've got the answer.'

We all waited expectantly. He leaned forward and said one word, in a solemn, almost reverent tone.

'Ferrets.'

'Oh no,' Corrie squealed. 'Yuk! They're disgusting! I hate them.'

Kevin looked wounded at this disloyalty from the one person he could normally count on. 'They're not disgusting,' he said, sounding hurt. 'They're clean and they're intelligent and they're very friendly.'

'Yeah, so friendly they'll run up your trouser leg,' Homer said.

'What are they?' Fi asked. 'Do you eat them?'

'Yeah, between two slices of bread. And you don't kill them first. You eat them alive, as they squirm and squeal in the sandwich. They're the world's freshest food.' That was Kevin, being funny. He proceeded to give Fi a lesson on ferrets, during which it became obvious that he didn't know much about them either.

Homer said, 'It's true that some of those old blokes around Wirrawee, the retired miners, keep a few ferrets and live on the rabbits. They haven't got a quid to rub between them, so that's how they keep themselves in meat.'

'There, you see?' said Kevin, sitting back on his heels.

It was quite a smart idea. I didn't know much about them either, except that you needed nets which you put over all the holes and the rabbits ran into them and were caught. And although there wouldn't be many rabbits up here in the mountains, there was never any shortage of them around the district.

Then Chris threw a fly into the ointment. 'Wouldn't they all be dead?' he asked. 'The ferrets? If their owners are prisoners, or dead, there'd be no one to look after the ferrets and keep them alive.'

Kevin looked smug. 'Ordinarily, yes,' he said. 'But my uncle, the one out past the Stratton turn-off, lets them run free. He's got heaps of them and he's trained them to come in when he whistles. They're like dogs. They know they'll get food when they hear that signal. He loses a few of them that go feral, but he's got so many he doesn't care.'

We added ferrets to our list of things to get, do, or investigate.

'Let's grab some sleep,' Homer said then, standing and stretching and yawning. 'Maybe Ellie could run another guided tour to the Hermit's hut after lunch, for those wishing to partake of this unique and interesting historical experience. Then I vote we have a Council of War later this afternoon, to work out our next move.'

'Well, you're the Minister for Defence,' I said.

Chapter Eighteen

The Minister for Defence was sitting on a rock with his feet in the creek. Kevin actually lay in the cold water, letting it run over his big hairy body. Fi was perched above Homer's head on another rock, looking like a little goddess. She was so light I wouldn't have been surprised to see her suddenly grow rainbow-coloured wings and flutter away. Robyn was lying on her back on the bank, reading *My Brilliant Career*. Chris was a few metres from me, under a tree, his smokes beside him.

I don't know whether I should really call them his smokes though.

He was gazing at the big rocky cliffs that we could see through the trees, in the distance.

Corrie was sitting next to Robyn. She had her radio out again. They'd brought fresh batteries that they'd found in Wirrawee and she was trying them. One of the women they'd talked to had said that some pirate radio stations were on the air at times, giving news and advice. Corrie was checking the short wave bands too, but it would be hard to get them in daytime, and we weren't in an easy place for radio reception.

I was curled up into Lee, my head in his chest, burrowing into him like I was a baby. We'd spent most of the afternoon passionately holding and kissing and touching, till I felt I would fall apart; as though the fibres that held my body together were disappearing. It had been Homer whom I'd felt more physically attracted to. Originally what drew me to Lee was his mind, his intelligent, sensitive face, and the security that I felt with him. Homer didn't exactly radiate security. But beneath Lee's calm exterior I'd found someone deeply passionate. I was a virgin and I know Lee was; matter of fact I think we all were, except maybe Kevin. I'm pretty sure he and Sally Noack had done the dirty deed regularly when they'd had a long relationship last year. But if we'd had the privacy that hot afternoon in the clearing in Hell I think Lee and I might have lost our virginity simultaneously. I was clinging to him and pressing against him as though I wanted to get my whole body inside him, and I liked the way I could make him groan and gasp and sweat. I liked giving him pleasure, although it was hard to tell what was pleasure and what was pain. I was teasing him, touching him and saying 'Does that hurt? Does that? Does that?' and he was panting, saying 'Oh God... no, yes, no'. It made me feel powerful. But he got his revenge. I'm not sure who had the last laugh – or the last cry. Normally when I'm out of control, when I get swept off by the white water, whether it's the giggles or the blues or one of my famous tantrums, I can still stand outside myself and smile and think 'What a maniac'. Part of my mind stays detached, can watch what I'm doing, can think about it and be aware of it all. But that afternoon with Lee, no. I was lost somewhere in the rapids of my feelings. If life is a struggle against emotion, then I was losing. It was almost scary. I was actually relieved when Homer yelled that it was time to start our conference.

I said to Robyn, 'Good book?'

She said, 'Yeah, it's OK. We've got to read it for English.'

We still hadn't adjusted to the fact that the world had changed, that school wasn't going to start on the normal day. I suppose we should have been delighted at the thought of not going to school, but we weren't. I was starting to want to use my brain again; to wrestle with new ideas and difficult theories. I decided then that I'd follow Robyn's example and read some of the harder books we'd brought with us. There was one called *The Scarlet Letter* that looked like a good tough one.

'Well,' Homer began, 'we've got to make more decisions guys. I've been looking up at the sky every five minutes, waiting for the American troops to drop down in their big green choppers, but there's no sign of them yet. And Corrie hasn't heard any news flashes yet, to tell us that help is on its way. So we might just have to do it on our own for a bit longer.

'The way I see it, these are our choices, now that we know a bit more about the deal. One, we can sit tight and do nothing. And there's nothing chicken about that. It's got a lot to recommend it. We're not trained for this stuff, and it's important for ourselves, and for our families, and for that matter even our country, that we stay alive. Two, we can have a go at getting our families and maybe other people out of the Showground. That's a tough one, probably way beyond our reach. I mean, we've got rifles and shotguns but they'd

238

be popguns compared to what these turkeys are using. Three, we can do something else to help the good guys. That's us, I might add, in case anyone's confused.' He grinned at Robyn. 'We could involve ourselves in some way that would help us win this war and get our country back. There's other things we could do too of course, other options, like moving somewhere else, or surrendering, but they're so remote I don't think they're worth discussing, although we will if anyone wants to of course.

'So, that's the deal, that's for real, that's what I feel. Three choices, and I think it's time we made one and stuck to it.' He leaned back and crossed his arms and put his feet in the water again.

There was quite a silence, then Robyn took up the invitation.

'I'm still not sure what's right or wrong in this whole setup,' she said. 'But I don't think I could sit around here for months, not doing anything. It's just an emotional thing – I couldn't do it. I agree with Homer that the Showground's beyond our reach, but I feel we've got to get out and have a go at something. On the other hand I don't want us to go around killing a lot of people. I've read those Vietnam books like *Fallen Angels*, where the woman hid a mine in her own kid's clothes and gave it to a soldier to hold, then blew them both up. I still have nightmares about that. I'm already having nightmares about those people we ran down in the truck. But I guess my nightmares are small suffering compared to what some people have had. My nightmares are just the price I have to pay, I know that. Despite what these people say about a "clean" invasion, I think all wars are filthy and foul and rotten. There was nothing clean about them blowing up Corrie's house, or killing the Francis family. I know this might sound a bit different from what I said before, but I don't think it is. I can understand why these people have invaded but I don't like what they're doing and I don't think there's anything very moral about them. This war's been forced on us, and I haven't got the guts to be a conscientious objector. I just hope we can avoid doing too much that's filthy and foul and rotten.'

No one else had much to add for a while. Then Fi, who was looking white and miserable, said, 'I know logically we should do this and we should do that. But all I know is that the thought of doing anything makes my nose bleed. All I really want to do is to go down to the Hermit's hut and hide under his mouldy old bed till this is over. I'm really fighting myself to stop from doing that. I suppose when the time comes I'll probably do whatever I have to do, but the main reason I'll do it is because I feel the pressure of keeping up with you guys. I don't want to let you down. I'd feel so ashamed if I couldn't match you in whatever it is we decide to do. I don't think there's any way we can help our families right now, so not losing face with you all has become my biggest thing. And what worries me is that I can't guarantee I won't pack up under pressure. The trouble is, I'm so full of fear now, that anything could happen. I'm scared that I might just stand there and scream.'

'Peer group pressure,' said Lee, but with a sympathetic smile at Fi. He was using one of Mrs Gilchrist, our Principal's, favourite phrases.

'Well, of course you're the only one who feels that way,' Homer said. 'The rest of us don't know the word "fear". Kevin can't even spell it. We know no feelings.

240

We're androids, terminators, robocops. We're on a mission from God. We're Superman, Batman and Wonder Woman.' He went on more seriously. 'No, it's a big problem. None of us knows how we'll react when the fan gets hit. I know what it's been like for me so far, just doing little things, like waiting in that car in Three Pigs Lane. My teeth were chattering so bad I had to hold my mouth shut to keep them in. I don't know how I didn't vomit. I was absolutely convinced I was going to die.'

We kept talking on, over, under and around the topic. Apart from Fi, the ones who were least keen were Chris and, strangely enough, Kevin. I could understand it a bit with Chris. He just lived in his own world most of the time, his parents were overseas, he didn't have many friends. In fact I don't think he liked people all that much. He probably could have lived in the Hermit's hut quite happily, unlike Fi, who would have gone crazy in half a day. But I got the impression that, like Fi, Chris'd go along with whatever we decided; in his case because he didn't have the energy or initiative to stand out against the group. Kevin was more of a puzzle, changing his attitude from one day to the next. There were times when he seemed blood-thirsty and times when he seemed chicken. I wondered if it depended on how long it had been since he'd been close to danger. Maybe when he'd had some action recently he went a bit quiet, dived for cover. But when things had been safe for a while he started getting his aggression back.

As for me, I was a mess of different feelings. I wanted to be able to make calm, logical decisions, to put points for and against on opposite sides of a piece of paper, but I couldn't get my feelings out of the road

241

enough to do it. When I thought about those bullets, and the ride-on mower, and the truck ride, I shook and felt sick and wanted to scream. Just like Fi and Homer and everyone else. I didn't know how I'd handle it if and when it all happened again. Maybe it'd be easier. Maybe it'd be harder.

Nevertheless, I think we all felt that we should do something, if only because the idea of doing nothing seemed so appalling that we couldn't even contemplate it. So we started tossing a few ideas around. Gradually we found ourselves talking more and more about the road from Cobbler's Bay. It seemed like that was where the most important action was. We decided that when Homer and Fi and Lee and I went out, the following night, we'd concentrate our attentions there.

I walked away from our meeting, leaving everyone, even Lee, and went back up the track quite a way. I ended up sitting on one of Satan's Steps, in the last of the hot afternoon. I could hear the creek churning away over a pile of rocks below me. I'd been there about ten minutes when a dragonfly landed near my feet. By then I must have become part of the landscape, because he seemed to ignore me. When I looked at him I realised he had something in his mouth. Whatever it was, it was still wriggling and flitting its little wings. I bent forward slowly and looked more closely. The dragonfly kept ignoring me. I could see now that it was a mosquito that he had, and he was eating it alive. Bit by bit the mosquito, still struggling wildly, was munched up. I watched, fascinated, until it was completely gone. The dragonfly perched there for another minute or so, then suddenly flew away.

I sat back again, against the hot rock. So, that was Nature's way. The mosquito felt pain and panic but the dragonfly knew nothing of cruelty. He didn't have the imagination to put himself in the mosquito's place. He just enjoyed his meal. Humans would call it evil, the big dragonfly destroying the mosquito and ignoring the little insect's suffering. Yet humans hated mosquitos too, calling them vicious and blood-thirsty. All these words, words like 'evil' and 'vicious', they meant nothing to Nature. Yes, evil was a human invention.

Chapter Nineteen

It was dark, probably around midnight. We were lying in a culvert, looking out over the edge at the dry black highway. We'd just come within seconds of making a very big, very fatal mistake. The way Robyn and the others had described it, they'd bowled up to the road, sat there watching for an hour or so, then shoved off again. So we'd taken much the same approach. We were about fifty metres from the gravel edge. I was leading, then came Lee limping along, then Fi, and Homer bringing up the rear. It was just the slightest unnatural sound that caught my ear. I was going to ignore it and go on, but my instincts took over, and I stopped and looked to the right. And there they were, a dark solid mass coming slowly down the road.

Now my instincts betrayed me: they told me to freeze; they stopped me from going anywhere. I had to get rational again, and fast. I had to activate that determined voice in my brain: 'If you do nothing, you'll die. Move, but move slowly. Be controlled. Don't panic.' I started fading back, like a movie played backwards, and nearly stepped straight into Lee.

Luckily he didn't say anything; I felt his surprised hesitation, then he too started stepping backwards. By then the patrol was so close that it became dangerous to move any further. We stood still and pretended we were trees.

There were about ten soldiers and they were in double file, dark shapes against the skyline, higher than us because we were in the scrub off the shoulder of the highway. I didn't know where Fi and Homer were but I hoped they wouldn't suddenly come blundering out of the bushes. Then my heart seemed to stop at a sound away to the left, a startled rattle of movement. The soldiers reacted as though someone had pressed a button in their backs. They leapt around, spread out in a wide line and threw themselves to the ground. They came shuffling forward on their elbows, facing Lee and me, but with the nearest one just metres to our left. The whole thing was frighteningly efficient. It seemed like these were the professional soldiers Mr Clement had told us about.

A moment later a giant torch, its light burning a path through the night, began to search the bush. We followed its traverse as though we were already caught in its beam. Then the light hesitated, stopped, focused, and I saw what actually was caught in its beam. A rabbit, very young, crouched low to the ground, its little head searching to the left and right, sniffing at the white shining around him. There was laughter from the road. I could feel the relaxation. Men started standing. I heard a rifle being cocked, a few comments, then a violently loud explosion. The rabbit suddenly became little fragments of rabbit, spread over the ground and rocks, a bit of fur splattered on the trunk of a tree. No one came down the embankment. They were just bored soldiers, enjoying themselves. The light switched off, the patrol got back into its formation, and continued down the road like a dark crocodile.

Only when they were out of sight and hearing, and Fi and Homer had come forward, did I allow myself to get the shakes.

When we did go on into the culvert we travelled like snails rather than crocodiles or soldiers, crawling silently along. I don't know about the others but I could easily have left a glistening trail behind me, a trail of sweat.

We stayed there about an hour, and in that time we saw only one small convoy. There were two armoured cars in the lead, followed by half a dozen jeeps, half a dozen trucks, then two more armoured cars. We also saw a second patrol; a truck with a spotlight mounted on the roof of the cabin and a machine gun in the back. It wasn't a very smart arrangement, because we could see it from a long way off, the light combing the bush, backwards and forwards. We had time to slide back into the scrub and watch from behind trees. I wouldn't like to have been a soldier in that truck, because guerillas could have picked them off easily. Perhaps it showed that guerillas weren't so active around here. But as I waited behind the tree for the truck to pass I was surprised and a little alarmed to realise how much I was starting to think like a soldier. 'If we were up a tree with rifles,' I thought, 'and one person shot out the spotlight and the others went for the machine gunner... Better still have one person out the front shooting through the windscreen to get the people in the cabin...'

246

Satisfied with our 'time spent in reconnaissance' we withdrew further into the bush to talk. We agreed that it was dangerous and probably pointless to stay there any longer. We looked at Homer, for ideas on what to do next.

'Can we just go up to the Heron?' he asked. 'I want to have a look at something.'

The Heron was the local river, not named after the birds but after Arthur Chesterfield Heron, who'd been the first person to settle in the district. Half of Wirrawee, including the High School, was named after him. The river flooded occasionally, so that the bed was wide and sandy, and the water itself meandered across its bed in a pretty casual way. A long old wooden bridge – almost a kilometre long – crossed the Heron just outside Wirrawee. The bridge was too narrow and rickety for the highway, and about every twelve months there'd be a big ruckus about the need for a new one, but nothing ever seemed to get done. To close it for any time would have been a big inconvenience, as the detour into town was a long and awkward one. In the meantime the bridge was quite a tourist attraction – there wasn't a big demand for postcards in Wirrawee but the few that you could buy showed either the bridge or the War Memorial or the new Sports Centre.

Under the bridge, along the banks of the river, were the picnic grounds and the scenic drive. 'Scenic' was a joke; it was just a road that went past the rotunda and the barbecues and the swimming pool, and on into the flower gardens. But that's where Homer wanted to take us, and that's where we went. Three of us, anyway. Lee had done enough. His leg was hurting and he was sweating. I realised how exhausted he was when we parked him under a tree and told him to wait, and he hardly complained at all. He just closed his eyes and sat there. I kissed him on the forehead and left him, hoping we'd be able to find the tree again on the way back.

We got very cautious once we were close to the bridge, as we figured it might be heavily guarded. It was obviously the weakest link of the highway, which I guessed was why Homer was so anxious to see it. We came at it from a sideways direction, across country, through the Kristicevics' market gardens. I wondered how my mate Natalie Kristicevic was doing, as I munched on her snowpeas. It was good to have some fresh greens, even if Fi got nervous at the noise I made crunching them.

From among the sweet corn we had a good view of the bridge and the picnic grounds. We could see the dark silhouettes of soldiers walking along the bridge. There seemed to be six of them, four standing at one end while the other two prowled around on a regular beat. Another convoy came through, and the sentries gathered at the end of the bridge, watching it. One held a clipboard and made notes, checking the number of vehicles maybe. One talked to the drivers; the others seemed to search under the trucks. It took quite a while. The bigger trucks then crawled across the bridge with wide gaps between them. They obviously didn't have a lot of faith in Wirrawee's mighty bridge.

At about 4 am we picked Lee up and retreated to our hide-out, which was a tourist cabin on the Fleets' property; a little place that they rented to people from the city. It was quite isolated and unobtrusive, so we figured it was safe. Fi volunteered to be first sentry;

248

the rest of us fell gratefully into the beds and slept and slept.

It was midafternoon before we had the energy to talk tactics. It was obvious that Homer had spent a good bit of time thinking about the bridge, because he went straight to the point.

'Let's blow it up,' he said, his eyes shining.

The last time I'd seen his eyes shine like that was at school, when he told me he'd taken all the screws out of the Principal's lectern in the Assembly Hall. If blowing up the bridge was going to be as big a disaster as that day turned out to be, I didn't want to be a part of it.

'OK,' I said, humouring him. 'How are we going to do that?'

With his eyes going to high beam, he told us.

'What Ellie did with the ride-on mower gave me the idea,' he said. 'Petrol's our easiest and best way of making explosions. So I tried to think of how we could repeat what Ellie did, but on a bigger scale. And of course the biggest version of a ride-on mower is a petrol tanker. What we've got to do is get a petrol tanker, park it under the bridge, on the scenic drive, then blow it up. Should be quite a bang.'

There was a deadly silence. I wanted to ask a lot of questions, but couldn't get enough breath to do it. For a start, I knew who'd be driving the petrol tanker.

'Where would we get the tanker?' Fi asked.

'Curr's.'

Curr's was the local distributor for Blue Star petrol. They came round to our place once a month to fill our tank. It was a big business and he had quite a fleet of tankers. That part was certainly possible. In fact it might be the easiest part of the whole insane scheme.

Homer was asking me something, interrupting my thoughts.

'What?'

'I was asking, can you drive an articulated vehicle?'

'Well, I guess. I think it'd be the same as driving the truck at home when we've got the trailer on. The question is, how the hell am I going to drive it under a bridge, get out and blow it up while the soldiers on the bridge just watch, wave and take photographs?'

'No problems.'

'No problems?'

'None.'

'Oh good,' I said. 'Now that's settled I'll just relax.'

'Listen,' said Homer, 'while you guys were walking towards Wirrawee last night with your eyes shut, I was noticing a few things. For example, what's around the corner from the bridge, going towards Cobbler's Bay?'

Homer was fast becoming like the teachers he'd always despised.

'I don't know sir, you tell us,' I said helpfully.

'Kristicevics' place,' said Fi, a little more helpfully.

'And on the other side?'

'Just paddocks,' said Fi. We were all looking at Homer, waiting for him to pull the rabbit out of the hat.

'Not just paddocks,' said Homer, offended. 'That's the trouble with you townies. One of the most famous studs in the district, and you call it "just paddocks".'

'Mmm,' I said, remembering. 'That's Roxburghs' place. Gowan Brae Poll Hereford Stud.'

'Yes,' said Homer, emphatically. I was still struggling to make connections.

'So what do we do? Train the cattle to tow the tanker into position? Or use methane for the explosion? If we find a cow that's been dead long enough to bloat, we can put a hole in his side and light the gas. I've seen that done.'

'Listen,' Homer said. 'I'll tell you what I noticed. That paddock right on the highway, Mr Roxburgh's got a lot of cattle in there, all in good nick too. It's heavily stocked, but it's a good paddock and it can take it. Now suppose you're a young soldier in a foreign country and you're guarding a long narrow bridge and it's late at night and you're struggling to stay awake and alert. And suddenly you hear a noise and you turn around and there's a hundred or so prime head of Hereford charging towards you, flat chat. About fifty tonnes of beef travelling at 60 or 70 k's, looming out of the darkness straight at you. What do you do?'

'You run,' said Lee promptly.

'No you don't,' Homer said.

'No you don't,' I agreed, thoughtfully. 'There's too many of them, and they're coming too fast for that.'

'So what do you do?' Homer asked again.

'You run to the sides. And then you probably climb up the sides. Which happens to be pretty easy on that old wooden thing.'

'And which way do you look?' Homer asked.

'At the cattle,' I said, more slowly still.

'Exactly,' Homer said. 'I rest my case.' He sat back and folded his arms.

We gazed at him, three people thinking three different collections of thoughts.

'How do you make the cattle do what you want?' Fi asked.

'How do you get away afterwards?' Lee asked. 'I can't run far on this.' He gestured at his bandaged leg.

I didn't have any questions. I knew the details could be worked out. It was a high risk plan, but it was a brilliant one.

Homer answered Lee's question first though. 'Motorbikes,' he said. 'I've been thinking for some time that if we wanted to be effective guerillas we'd get ourselves ag bikes and use cross-country travel instead of roads. We could become very mobile and very slippery. Now, I'll get the cattle going by using my superior mustering skills to get them into the road. I've mustered before at night. It works well – in fact it's better in some ways. They're not so suspicious then. If it's a bright enough night, which it should be, you don't even use lights, cos it stirs them up too much. So I'll get them out and then Lee and I'll fire them up, if Lee's fit enough. We can use an electric prod, for example, and maybe an aerosol can and a box of matches. I got into so much trouble for making a flamethrower from them at school, but I knew it would come in handy one day. A blast of that on their backsides and they'll keep running till dawn. Once we've got them blitzing down the road we'll fade off into the darkness to the motorbikes and make our getaway.'

He turned to Fi and me. 'I always seem to get out of things with the least dangerous jobs,' he apologised. 'But it has to be this way, I think. Ellie's our best driver, so we need her for the tanker. And Lee's too lame to run, which is hopeless for the passenger, because they'll both have to be quick on their feet. And I'm the one who's had the most experience with cattle.'

252

Homer was being modest. He was a natural with stock. But he was still talking, 'So, that's how it seems to work out. What I thought was, if you steal a tanker and bring it down to the bridge by slow degrees, with Fi walking to each corner, checking the coast is clear, then signalling you on. You hide it round that corner near the bowling greens, nice and close to the bridge. We'll wait for a convoy to go through, which seems to get the soldiers up to the right end of the bridge, and also gives us a good chance of a clear interval before the next convoy. Then we'll move the cattle out into the road and stampede them. As the cattle hit the bridge at one end you bring the tanker down under it at the other – you might even be able to coast down with the engine off. There's a good slope there. Jump out, run a trail of petrol away to a safe distance – one of you do it, so if she gets any on her clothes she can get clear before the other one lights it. Then light it and go like stink to a couple of motorbikes that we'll hide around the next corner. And you're out of there. How's that? Simple, eh? Just call me Genius.'

We talked and talked for hours, trying to find the flaws, trying to improve the arrangements. There were endless ways it could go wrong of course. The cattle mightn't move, another vehicle might come along the road at the wrong moment, the tankers might be guarded or empty – they mightn't even be there. I thought the most dangerous part might be when Fi and I were getting from the tanker to the motorbikes. We'd be quite exposed then, for thirty seconds or so. If the sentries saw us we'd be in real trouble. But Homer was confident that they'd be occupied by the cattle.

Yes, it was a good plan. It was very clever. And

maybe the thing I liked most about it was the effect it had on Lee. He was determined to do it. He lifted his head more and more as we talked; he became outspoken, he started smiling and laughing. He'd been depressed a lot of the time since he copped the bullet, but now he actually said to me, 'If we do this, if we succeed, I'll be able to feel pride again'.

I hadn't realised how ashamed he'd been of not being able to help his family.

We made a list of all the things we needed, just a little list: four motorbikes, two walkie-talkies, two pairs of wirecutters, bolt cutters, torches, aerosol cans, matches, cattle-prods, rope, and a petrol tanker. Just a few odds and ends like that. We started our search on the Fleets' place, and then moved onto the neighbouring farm, collecting as we went. The motorbikes were the biggest problem. Most rurals don't take much care of their bikes. Half the ones we found were held together with fencing wire and masking tape. We had to have fast, reliable bikes, that would start first time. Then they had to be fuelled up, have their oil and headlights and brakes checked, and brought together in a central spot, which happened to be Fleets' garage. We worked pretty hard that afternoon.

Chapter Twenty

Curr's Blue Star Fuel and Oil Distributors was in Back Street, about six blocks from the bridge. Fi and I found it with no trouble but with much relief. We'd agreed between the two of us that we could have a rest when we got there, and we sure needed one. We'd wheeled those bloody great bikes about four k's, stopping and hiding a dozen times when one or both of us imagined we'd heard a noise or seen a movement. We were pretty twitchy just doing that; I hated to think what we'd be like when the real action started.

I was a bit nervous being paired with Fi, I must admit. There was no way I was ever going to be a hero, but at least I was used to doing outdoors, practical things, and I suppose that gives you a bit of confidence. I mean just the little things at home that I took for granted, chopping wood, using a chain saw, driving, riding the horses (Dad still liked using horses for stockwork), being a rouseabout, marking lambs and drenching sheep – these were the commonplace routines of my life, that I'd never valued a lot. But without my noticing it they'd given me the habit of doing things without looking over my shoulder every sixty seconds to see if an adult was nodding or shaking his head. Fi had improved heaps in that respect, but she was still kind of hesitant. I admired her courage in taking on the job Homer had given her, because I guess true courage is when you're really scared but you still do it. I was really scared, but Fi was really really scared. I did just hope that when the chips were down she wouldn't stand there frozen with fear. We didn't want frozen chips. Ha ha.

Once we'd hidden the bikes we set off for Curr's. I tried to put into practice the lessons I'd learned from computer games. My favourite game was Catacomb and I'd found the only way I could get to level ten was to keep my head. When I got angry or overconfident or adventurous I got wiped out, even by the most simple and obvious little monsters. To get the best scores I had to stay smart, think, be alert and go cautiously. So we crept along, block by block, checking round every corner as we came to it. The only time we spoke was when I said to Fi, 'This is the way we'll have to do it on the way back with the tanker'. She just nodded. The only time my concentration wavered was when I caught myself wondering if I'd ever get to play computer games again.

As far as we could see it was all quiet on the Curr's front. There were big wire gates, locked with a chain and padlock, and a high wire fence all the way around the depot, but we were prepared for that with the wirecutters. We'd brought bolt cutters as well but they were no match for the gate: the chain was just too big. Plan B was to use the truck to break through the gate.

We took a smoko for twenty minutes. We sat behind a tree opposite the depot, getting our breath back, while Fi tried to call up Homer and Lee on the walkie-talkie. Just as we were about to abandon the attempt and go for the tanker we heard Homer's hoarse whisper coming from the receiver.

'Yes, we can hear you Fi. Over.'

It was somehow vastly exciting, and a wild relief, to hear his voice. Fi's eyes glistened.

'How's Lee?'

'Fine.'

'Where are you? Over.'

'Where we said we'd be. How about you? Over.'

'Yes, the same. We're about to try to get in. It looks OK. They've got plenty of what we want. Over.'

'OK, good. Call us back when you're in business. Over.'

'Bye,' Fi whispered. 'Love you.'

There was a pause, then the answer. 'Yeah, I love you too Fi.'

For Homer to say that to anyone was pretty good; for him to say it with Lee and me listening was amazing. We switched the walkie-talkie off and moved cautiously over to the fence of the depot. There were big security lights along the wire fence, but the power seemed to be switched off to this part of town. I hoped that meant that any burglar alarms would be inoperative too. I took a deep breath and made the first cut. No bells rang, no lights flashed, no sirens howled. I cut again, and kept cutting until I'd made a hole about big enough for a hare.

'We'll never get through that,' Fi muttered. As she was the size of a rabbit and I'm the size of a Shetland, it was obvious who she meant by 'we'.

257

'We'll have to,' I said. 'It makes me nervous standing here. It's too exposed. Come on.'

Fi put one leg through, then gracefully twisted her body after it and followed with her other leg. All those ballet lessons were good for something, I thought enviously. It was obvious that the hole had to be bigger, so I cut some more, but even when I did get through I ripped my T-shirt and scratched my leg.

We scurried across the yard to where the trucks were parked. I tried the doors of a couple but they were locked. We went over to the office and peered through the grimy window. On the opposite wall was a board hung with keys.

'That's our target,' I said. I turned and found a rock, picked it up and came back to the window.

'Wait,' Fi said.

'What?'

'Can I do it? I've always wanted to break a window.'

'You should have joined Homer's Greek Roulette gang,' I said, but I handed over the rock. She giggled and drew back her arm and smashed the rock hard into the window, then jumped back as glass showered over us both. It took us a few moments to shake it out of our clothes and hair. Then I leaned in and opened the door from the inside.

The keys were neatly marked with the registration numbers of the trucks, so we took a handful and went back to the yard. I chose the oldest, dirtiest semi-trailer, because the newer smarter ones seemed to shine too much in the moonlight. It was a flat-fronted International Acco. The first thing we did was to go to the back of the trailer and climb up the thin steel ladder to the top, walking along the curved surface to

258

inspect the storage compartments. It turned out that there were four lids, spaced at equal intervals along the top. I twisted one of the lids and took it off. It was much like the lids of the milk cans that we still had in our old dairy. It came away easily, even though it was quite heavy. I tried to see if there was any petrol inside but it was impossible to tell. I searched my memory. When the truck came to our place each month, what was it the driver did? 'Hold this,' I whispered urgently to Fi, giving her the lid, then shinnying down the ladder. Sure enough I found what I was looking for – the dipstick on a bracket on the base of the trailer. I pulled it off, and hurried back up the ladder. I dipped the tank that we'd opened. It was too dark to get a reading but the glint of wetness in the moonlight showed there was plenty of fuel in it.

We replaced the lid and checked the other three. Two of them were full; we didn't need to dip them. The last one was nearly empty, but it didn't matter. We had enough to cause a bigger explosion than Krakatoa. We screwed the lids back on and hurried down the ladder.

I went round to the driver's door, unlocked it, got in, and opened the passenger door for Fi, then began inspecting the controls. It looked OK but when I switched on the ignition a continuous beep began sounding, and a red warning brake light started flashing. I waited for it to go off, but it didn't.

'There's something wrong with the brakes,' I said to Fi. 'We'd better try another one.'

We spent ten minutes going along the row of trucks, trying each one, but always with the same result. I began to regret the time spent on our rest break. We might end up getting to the bridge too late.

259

'It's no good,' I said at last. 'We'll just have to take the first one and risk it with no brakes. I'll use the gears as much as I can.'

We jumped back into the Acco, and started the engine, which throbbed into immediate life. To my astonishment the warning beep and the flashing light stopped within seconds.

'Air brakes,' I said to Fi, annoyed with myself for not having thought of it earlier. 'They have to build up pressure or something. I've never driven anything with air brakes before.'

I had more trouble finding first, having to pump the clutch a few times to get it. I was sweating heavily and Fi was trembling. The engine sounded so loud in the quiet night air. Then I eased the clutch out. The prime mover jerked, took up the strain of the trailer, and crept forward. I brought it well out into the yard, clear of the other vehicles, so I had plenty of room to make my turn. Then I swung it round and aimed at the gates.

It's really quite frightening to crash a vehicle directly and deliberately into something. At the last moment my nerve failed me and I slowed right down, bumping too gently into the gate to do any damage. I was really annoyed with myself. With my typical arrogance I'd been worried about Fi's nerves, but I should have been more worried about my own. I cursed, nearly destroyed the gearbox trying to find reverse, found it, and was startled by the loud warning beeps that immediately began at the back of the vehicle. Seemed like this truck beeped at any excuse. In my impatience I then backed up too fast. The trailer slewed and hit a stanchion, nearly jackknifing. Fi went white and grabbed the back of the seat.

'Ellie!' she said. 'It's petrol in the back, not water!'

'I know,' I said. 'Sorry.'

This time I rolled it smoothly and firmly into the gates, which strained for a moment, then sprang open like a bursting dam. I gave Fi a quick grin, and made another wide turn to get into the street without hitting anything. The trailer followed beautifully. To keep the noise down I put the gearstick into neutral and coasted down to a clump of trees, parking under them. Fi was already trying to call the boys on the walkie-talkie, but there was too much interference from the truck engine.

'I'll go down to the corner and check that it's clear,' she said, 'and call them from there.'

'OK.'

She slipped out of the cab and set off for the corner. I watched her through the windscreen. I always admired so much about Fi, but now it was her courage I was admiring, instead of her grace and beauty. She looked like a breeze would blow her over, but here she was going alone through the deserted streets of a town in a war zone. Not many people would do it; still fewer people who'd had the sheltered life she'd had. I saw her get to the corner, take a long careful look in each direction, give me a thumbs up and then start talking into her transmitter. After a few minutes she waved me forward; I hit reverse again, but then found first, and rolled the truck down to pick her up.

'Did you get through?'

'Yes. They're fine. A couple of patrols have been past, but no convoys. Oh Ellie,' she said, turning suddenly to me, 'do you really think we can do this?'

I tried to give her a confident grin. 'I don't know, Fi. I think maybe we can. I hope we can.'

261

She nodded and faced forward again. We drove towards the next corner. 'I'll walk from here on,' she said, 'and call you from each corner. It'll be just as quick. Turn the engine off while you're waiting each time though, do you think? It's pretty noisy.'

'OK.'

We made two blocks that way, but at the next I saw her take one look down the street to the right then draw back and come sprinting towards me. I jumped down from the truck and ran to meet her. She gasped just one word: 'Patrol', and together we went over a low fence into someone's front garden. There was a huge old gum tree right in front of us. I was so nervous that it seemed to be the only thing I could see. My eyes and mind focused entirely on it; nothing else existed for me at that moment. I climbed it like a possum, scratching my hands but not feeling any pain. Fi followed. I got about three metres up before I heard voices from the corner, which slowed me down, made me quieter, more cautious. I inched out along a branch to take a look. I didn't know if getting up here had been a mistake or not. I remembered Dad, one day when he'd put a big ugly patch on a hole in the eaves that possums had made, saying 'The human eye doesn't look above its own height'. At this moment in my life I sure hoped he was right. The trouble was that if they did see us we'd be, not like possums up a tree, but like rats up a drainpipe. There was no escape from here.

We waited and watched. The voices continued for a while, then we heard them grow in volume as they turned towards us. I felt intense disappointment. This marked the end of our Grand Plan. It could mark the end of us, too, because once they saw the tanker their first reaction would be to seal off the area and search it. I was surprised they hadn't seen it already. They'd stopped talking now, but I could hear the scuffle of their boots. My mind was racing; too many thoughts going through it too quickly. I tried to grab one of them to see if it might be any use in suggesting a way out of here, but I was panicking too much to get a grip on it, on anything except the tree. Fi, I slowly realised from the steady pain in my left leg, was gripping onto me as though she were a possum on an insecure branch. She had her talons dug in so hard that I was sure I'd end up with bruises. I saw a movement now, through the foliage, and a couple of moments later the soldiers slowly came into view. There were five of them, three men and two women. One of the men was quite old, at least forty, but the other two looked about sixteen. The women were maybe twenty. They were dawdling along, two on the footpath and three on the road itself. They'd stopped talking to each other and were just gazing around as they walked, or looking down at the ground. They didn't look very military. I guessed they were conscripts. The tanker was on the other side of the road, about fifty metres from them. I couldn't believe they hadn't seen it yet, and braced myself for the sudden cry of discovery. Fi's fingers had now cut off the circulation in my leg; it was only a matter of time before my whole limb, from the shin down, dropped off into the garden below. I wondered how the soldiers would react if they heard it drop, and almost let out an hysterical giggle. The patrol kept walking.

And they kept walking. They went right on past the truck as though it didn't exist. It wasn't until they were a hundred metres past and Fi and I were out of our tree and peering at their distant dark backs that we allowed ourselves to believe that we were safe. We looked at each other in surprise and relief. I was so happy that I didn't even mention the bruises on my leg. I shook my head.

'They must have just thought it was another parked vehicle,' I said.

'I guess if they hadn't been along this particular street before...' Fi said. 'I'd better call Homer.'

She did so, and I heard his soft reply quite quickly.

'We've been held up for a bit,' Fi said. 'Ellie wanted to climb a tree. We'll get under way again in about five minutes. We're three blocks away. Over.'

There was a snort from the receiver, not of static either, before she signed off.

We waited nearly ten minutes, to be safe, then I turned the key, and heard the shrill beep of the brake warning before the engine rumbled into life again. We made two more blocks; when Fi signalled me from the last corner I switched the engine off and tried coasting silently downhill towards her. This was a big mistake. The brake warning began beeping and flashing redly at me again and I realised I wouldn't have any brakes. A moment later the steering wheel gave a shudder and locked itself into position, so I didn't have any steering either. I tried for a gear, to clutch start it, but missed the one I wanted and got only a crunching sound that set my teeth on edge. The truck lurched over the gutter and began to veer further and further left, aiming for a row of fences. I remembered Fi's warning: 'That's petrol in the back, not water', and felt very sick. I grabbed at the ignition key, turned it, and got nothing, turned it again and, with the fences now just metres away, got the beautiful sound of the beautiful engine. I swung the wheel. 'Not too hard, you'll jack-knife.' That was my voice. The trailer sideswiped something, a row of somethings, fences or small trees or both, nearly sideswiped Fi, then juddered to a halt just a metre from the corner. I switched off the ignition, then pulled on the handbrake, wondering what would have happened if I'd thought of doing that before. I leaned back in the seat panting, my mouth open to get air into my tight aching throat.

Fi jumped into the cabin. 'Gosh, what happened?' she asked.

I shook my head. 'I think I just failed my driving test.'

Our plan had been to park further across, behind some trees in the picnic area. I didn't know whether to do that, which meant taking the noisy risk of starting the engine again, or to stay where we were, out on the open side of the street. Finally we decided to move. Fi slipped across to where she had a view of the bridge and watched until all the sentries were at the far end. It was twenty minutes before that happened. Then she signalled to me and I moved the truck into the dark shadows of the trees.

We contacted the boys by radio, and made our preparations. We climbed the ladder to the top of the tanker again and loosened the lids of the four tanks. Then we fed the rope into one tank until it was submerged, all but the end of it, which we tied to a safety handle beside the lid. We climbed down again.

Now there was nothing to do but to wait.

Chapter Twenty-one

Oh, how we waited. We talked softly for a little while. We were well away from the truck, for safety's sake, sitting up among the trees looking out over the gas barbecues. It was very quiet. We talked about the boys mostly. I wanted to hear as much about Homer as I could, and I certainly wanted to talk about Lee.

Fi had become totally infatuated with Homer. It amazed me how she felt. If anyone had told me a year ago, or even a month ago, that this would happen, I would have asked for their Medicare card. They would have been headed for a long stay in a private ward. But here she was, elegant, Vogue, designer label, big house on the hill Fi, completely in love with rough as guts, King Gee, one of the boys, graffiti king Homer. On the surface it looked impossible. Except that it was no secret now that there was more to both of them than I'd ever realised. Fi seemed delicate and timid, and she even claimed herself that she was, but she had a determination I hadn't recognised before. There was a spirit to her, a fire burning inside her somewhere. One of those Avgas fires maybe, that burn invisibly. And Homer, well, Homer was the surprise of my life. He even seemed better looking these days, probably because his head was up and he walked more confidently and carried himself differently. He had such imagination and sense that I could hardly believe it. If we ever did get back to school I'd nominate him for School Captain – then hand out smelling salts to the teachers.

'He's like two people,' Fi said. 'He's shy with me but confident when he's in a group. But he kissed me on Monday and I think that broke the ice a bit. I thought he'd never do it.'

Right, sure, I thought. I was embarrassed at how far Lee and I had progressed beyond our first kiss already.

'You know,' Fi continued, 'he told me he had a crush on me in Year 8. And I never knew. Maybe it's better I didn't though. I thought he was such a reptile then. And those kids he used to hang round with!'

'He still does,' I said. 'Or at least he did before all this happened.'

'Yes,' said Fi, 'but I don't think he wants to have much to do with them any more. He's changed so much, don't you think?'

'God yeah.'

'I want to learn all I can about farming,' Fi said, 'so when we're married I can help him heaps and heaps.'

Oh my God! I thought. You know they're beyond help when they talk like that. Not that I hadn't had nice little fantasies of Lee and me travelling the world together, the perfect married couple.

But it occurred to me as I listened to Fi, that the real reason I felt attracted to Homer lately, attracted in powerful and puzzling ways, was that I was jealous of losing him. He was my brother. As I didn't have a brother and he didn't have a sister, we'd sort of adopted each other. We'd grown up together. I could say things to Homer that no one else could get away with. There had been times, when he was acting really crazily, that I'd been the only person he would listen to. I didn't want to lose that relationship, especially now, when we'd temporarily or permanently lost so many other relationships in our lives. My parents seemed so far away; the further away they got, the closer I wanted to bind Homer to me. I was quite shocked to have such an insight to my feelings, as though there was an Ellie lurking inside me that I didn't have much knowledge or awareness of. Just like there'd been Homers and Fiona's lurking away inside them. I wondered what other surprises the secret Ellie might have for me, and resolved then and there to try to keep better track of her in future.

Fi asked me about Lee then and I said simply 'I love him'. She didn't comment, and I found myself going on. 'He's so different to anyone I've ever known. It's like he's coming out of my dreams sometimes. He seems so much more mature than most of those guys at school. I don't know how he stands them. I guess that's why he keeps to himself so much. But you know, I get the feeling that he'll do something great in life; I don't know what, be famous or be Prime Minister or something. I can't see him staying in Wirrawee all his life. I just think there's so much to him.'

'The way he took that bullet wound was incredible,' Fi said. 'He was so calm about it. If that had happened to me I'd still be in shock. But you know, Ellie, I'd never have picked you and Lee as a likely couple. I think it's amazing. But you go so well together.'

'Well how about you and Homer!'

We both laughed and settled down to watch the bridge. The hours ground slowly on. Fi even slept for twenty minutes or so. I could hardly believe it, although when I challenged her she denied furiously that she'd even closed her eyes. For me the tension grew as the time passed. I just wanted to get it over with, this mad reckless thing that we'd talked ourselves into doing.

The trouble was that there was no convoy. Homer and Lee had wanted to come in behind a convoy to guarantee themselves a period of grace before the next lot of traffic came along. But as the time got close to 4 am the road stayed frustratingly empty.

Then suddenly there was a change in the pattern of activity on the bridge. The sentries were all down the Cobbler's Bay end but even from our distance I could see them become more alert, more awake. They gathered in the centre of the bridge and stood looking down the road, in the opposite direction to us. I nudged Fi.

'Something's going on,' I said. 'Might be a convoy.' We stood and looked, straining our eyes to peer down the dark highway. But it was the behaviour of the sentries that again told us what was happening. They started backing away, then their little group broke up and they split, half going to one side of the bridge, half to the other. One ran in little circles for a moment, then started running down the road towards Wirrawee, then changed his mind, and he too fled to the side.

'It's the cattle,' I said. 'It's got to be.'

We sprinted for the tanker, leaving the silent, useless walkie-talkie behind. There was no time to wonder about a patrol coming down the street. We leapt into the truck and started the engine. I put it in gear and looked up, and although speed was now vital to us, I couldn't help but lose a second as I caught the wonderful view on the bridge. A hundred or more head of beef, prime Hereford cattle, beautiful big red beasts, were steaming onto the old wooden structure like a mighty train of meat. And they were steaming. Even at this distance I could hear the thunder of the hooves on the timber. They were going like wound-up locomotives.

'Wow,' I breathed.

'Go!' screamed Fi.

I pressed the accelerator and the tanker lumbered forward. We had about five hundred metres to go and I was pumping adrenalin so hard I felt immune to danger, to bullets, to anything. 'Go!' cried Fi again. As we came in under the bridge I slid the tanker as far across to the left as I could get it, so that it was nestled under the lowest section of the superstructure. The trick was to do it without sideswiping the pylon and causing sparks, which might have finished Fi and me off quickly and horribly. But we got in there nice and close, leaving less than two metres clearance between the top of the tanker and the bridge. That was the first time any of us had thought of the possibility of the tanker not fitting under the bridge at all; it was a little too late by then to consider that problem. We'd been lucky. Fi couldn't get her door open because she was so close to the pylon, so she started sliding across to my side. I half leapt, half fell out of the cab. Above my head the bridge shook and thundered as the first of the stampeding cattle reached our end. I was going up the ladder to the top of the tanker as Fi came out of the truck and without looking at me sprinted for the motorbikes. This run, which I too would have to do in a moment, was our greatest risk. It was across clear ground for about two hundred metres, to where we'd hidden the bikes in the bushes. There was no cover, no protection from any angry bullets that might come buzzing after us. I shook my head to clear the frightening thoughts, and ran along the walkway on top of the trailer, crouched over to avoid hitting the bottom of the bridge. When I reached the rope I glanced up. Fi had disappeared and I had to hope she'd made the bushes safely. I started pulling out the rope, coil after sopping coil, throwing it to the roadway below. The fumes were terrible in that confined space. They made me giddy and gave me an instant headache. Another thing we should have thought of, I realised: a sinker to tie to the end of the rope that had to stay in the tank, to stop it being pulled out when I ran off with the other end. Too late for that now. All I could do was jam the lid down as tightly as possible and hope that would hold it in.

I scrambled back down the ladder. It seemed to have taken forever to get the rope out. All that time I'd been oblivious of the thunder just centimetres above my head, but now I noticed that it was starting to lessen. I could make out individual hooves. I broke out in an instant sweat, found the loose end of the rope, grabbed it and ran. I had petrol all over me, had been breathing petrol, and felt very odd as a result, as though I was floating across the grass. But it wasn't a pleasant float, more the sort of floating that made me seasick.

I was about a hundred metres from the bushes when I heard two sounds at once; one that was welcome, one that was not. The welcome sound was the throbbing of the motorbikes. The unwelcome one was a shout from the bridge.

There are sounds the throat produces which may not be in English, but which have an unmistakable meaning. When I was little I'd had a dog called Rufus, who was a border-collie springer-spaniel cross. He was just a natural rabbiter, and I used to take him out most afternoons for the joy of seeing him at full stretch after a fleeing rabbit. Whenever he was in hot pursuit he uttered a peculiar high-pitched yelp, that he never used at any other time. It didn't matter where I was or what I was doing, when I heard that sound I knew Rufus was chasing a rabbit.

The shout from the bridge, although not in my language, was unmistakable too. It was a shout of 'Alarm! Come quickly!' Although I had a hundred metres to go it suddenly looked forever. I felt that I would never reach my target, that I could never cover so much ground, that I could run for the rest of my life and not get to safety. That was a terrible moment, when I came very close to death. I entered a strange state when I felt as though I was now in the territory of death, even though no bullet had struck me. I don't know if a bullet had even been fired. But if a bullet had struck me then I don't think I would have felt it. Only living people can feel pain, and I was floating away from the world that living people inhabit.

Then Fi appeared and screamed, 'Oh Ellie, please!' She was standing in the bushes but she seemed right in front of me, and her face looked huge. It was the word 'please' that reached me I think: it made me feel that she needed me, that I was important to her. Our friendship, love, whatever you want to call it, reached

272

across the bare ground and reeled me in. I became aware that there were bullets stinging through the air, that I was pounding hard across the ground, that I was gasping for breath and that my chest hurt, and then I was in the safety of the trees and stumbling towards the motorbikes, dropping the end of the rope for Fi to gather it. I would have liked to hug Fi, but I was rational enough to know that I was a petrol-soaked leper, and a hug from me would have been a death sentence for Fi.

I grabbed the furthest bike and kicked it off its stand, then swung it round to face Fi. As I did there was a whoosh, and a string of fire began to speed across the grass. Fi came running back. To my surprise her face was alight, not with flame but from within. She was utterly elated. I began to wonder if there was a secret pyromaniac lurking inside her somewhere. She grabbed her bike; we wheeled them around and spun the back wheels doing takeoffs that dug gouges in the well-tended grass of the Wirrawee picnic grounds. Fi led the way, with wild war whoops. And yes, I admit now that we were the ones who did the wheelies on the seventh green of the golf course. I'm sorry. It was very immature of us.

Chapter Twenty-two

When we met Homer and Lee, up in a gully behind the Fleets' house, there was a babble of noise for about ten minutes, with everyone trying to talk at once. Relief, excitement, explanations, apologies.

'Everybody shut up!' Lee finally yelled, using Homer's tactic, and in the sudden silence said, 'There, that's better. Now Fi, you go first.' We told our stories, then the boys told theirs. Feeling safer on their side of the river, they had stayed to watch the explosion; the earthquake that we had only heard and felt.

'Oh Ellie,' Homer said, 'it was the greatest thing I've ever seen.' I began to fear that we'd turned him into a pyromaniac too.

'Yeah,' said Lee, 'It was a real blast.'

'Tell us everything,' I said. 'Take your time. We've got all day.' The morning had begun and we were breakfasting on cans from the Fleets' pantry. I had baked beans and tuna. I was feeling pretty good; I'd had a predawn swim in the dam and was glad to have washed the last of the petrol from my skin. I was in the mood to be treated gently, and was looking forward to snuggling into Lee for most of the day. But in the meantime I was happy to lie back and close my eyes and hear a bedtime story.

'Well,' Homer said. 'It went so well at first. We got to the stud with no hassles, although pushing those bikes for the last few k's was hard work.' Homer had done it twice; taking his bike to the hiding place, then going back for Lee's. 'As you know,' he went on, 'our plan was for me to do the mustering and get them out to the road nice and quietly. Then Lee was going to hide on the road and jump out at them with the flash, while I used the prod to stampede them.'

We'd only been able to find one prod and we'd ruled out the aerosol can as too dangerous, but we'd found a battery-operated flash attachment for a camera, and Homer was confident that the quick, blinding flashes of light would do the trick.

'So there we were,' Homer continued. 'Nicely set up, just lying back in the paddock, watching the stars and dreaming of huge fresh T-bone steaks. We had a few chats to you, as you know, and we were happy to wait for a convoy to roll through. Then we hit our two big problems. One was that no convoy came. That wouldn't have been so bad maybe, if we could at least have called you and told you we were going ahead anyway. Although there was still the big danger that we'd suddenly find a convoy up our backsides. But the other problem was that the bloody walkie-talkie packed it in. We couldn't believe it. We tried everything – in the end Lee just about took it to bits – but it was as dead as the dinosaurs.

'Well, we were pretty desperate. We knew you'd be sitting there, in a lot of danger, waiting for a signal that wasn't going to come. We got close to panic at that point, I guess. We had two choices – to go ahead

275

with the cattle and hope you'd be able to react in time, or to call it off. But we couldn't call it off without telling you – that would have left you in an impossible situation. That was a weakness in our planning – we relied too much on the walkie-talkies. That's one thing I've learnt – don't put too much trust in machines.'

'So we only had one choice really. It was getting so late we couldn't wait any longer for a convoy. Lee went out in the road to do his flashing, and I got the cattle moving.'

'How?' Fi asked.

'Eh?'

'How? How do you get a big mob of cattle to do what you want, in the middle of the night?'

I remembered she'd wanted an answer to this question before. She was serious about becoming a rural.

'Well,' said Homer, looking a bit silly. 'You hiss.'

'You what?'

'You hiss. Old cattleman's trick. Old Miss Bamford taught me. They don't like hissing, so you walk around behind them making like a snake.'

I half expected to see Fi take out a notebook and earnestly write it down. Having given away one of his professional secrets, Homer went on.

'Our big ambition was to hold them in the road until the sentries were at the right end of the bridge, but it was hopeless. The cattle were too restless and we were scared that a convoy or a patrol would turn up. So we got the prod and the flash and away we went.'

'It was fun,' Lee said reflectively. 'Except for the first few seconds, when I thought they were going to charge me.'

'But the guards were at the right end of the bridge,' I said. 'They were in the perfect spot.'

'Were they? Well, that's the best bit of luck we had in the whole business then. That was totally unplanned. We just worked the cattle up to a frenzy, till they were outrunning us, then we raced back and got the bikes. Next thing we saw was when we stopped the bikes along the riverbank to have a look. And I tell you what, I wished we'd brought the camera as well as the flash. It was unbelievable. The last cattle were rumbling off the bridge, and the soldiers were still hanging off the sides of it, but they were firing at you Ellie, like it was the duck season. Ellie, to the end of my days I'll never understand how those bullets didn't hit you. The air must have been just full of them. We were screaming: "Go Ellie, go, go!" You were still holding the rope, that was the amazing thing. We could see the tanker sitting patiently under the bridge, waiting to be blown up. Then you disappeared into the bushes. Tell the truth, you seemed to float into them, like an angel. I had this bizarre idea that you'd been hit and you were dead and I was watching your spirit.'

I just laughed and didn't say a word.

'Then,' Homer said, 'a second later along came this flame. I don't think the soldiers could work it out. They just stood there, pointing at it and calling to each other. They couldn't see the tanker, cos it was tucked very nicely in under the bridge. But then they all suddenly decided that they were in danger. They turned around and went belting off the bridge. They were just in time. You'll be glad to know,' he said, looking at me, 'that I don't think any of them were hurt.'

I nodded a thank-you to him. It meant a lot to me, but not everything. If I knowingly did things like blowing up bridges, then the fact that by sheer good luck no one was hurt didn't let me off the hook. Once I'd made my decision to go with the tanker I'd been ready to live with the consequences, whatever they were.

'There was a pause of another second,' Homer went on. 'And then she blew. I tell you, I've never seen anything like it. The bridge lifted about five metres at the tanker end. It actually hung in the air for a few seconds, before it fell back. But when it fell back everything seemed just slightly out of alignment. Then suddenly there was a second explosion and bits flew everywhere. This massive fireball went straight up, then there were two more explosions, and all we could see was fire. There were spot fires everywhere, as well as the main fire. The whole park seemed to be burning, let alone the bridge. Like Lee said, it was a real blast.'

'Well, Wirrawee's been wanting a new bridge for a long time,' Lee said. 'Looks like they'll have to get one now.'

Homer's bedtime story had been exciting, and I'd enjoyed it, even though I was almost scared by the power of what we'd done, and what we were able to do. The only thing Homer had left out was the way he'd wept when he'd found us both safe. I saw the sweetness of Homer then, that he'd had as a little guy, but which some people probably though he'd lost as a teenager.

We went off to some shady spots in among the rocks. Lee had first sentry duty. I wanted to sit up with him, to keep him company, but suddenly a wave of fatigue hit me, so powerfully that I really did buckle at the knees. I crawled into a cool gap between some boulders, and with a purloined pillow made myself comfortable. I went into a sleep so deep that it was more like unconsciousness. Lee told me later that he'd tried to get me up to do a sentry turn, but he couldn't wake me, so he did my shift for me. I didn't wake till 4 o'clock.

It was nearly dark before any of us showed much life or energy. The only thing that got us going was a desire to get home, to see the other four again. We decided it was safe to use the bikes – we worked out a route that would both take us back to my place, where we'd left the Landrover, and a leapfrog pattern of travelling that should protect us from unwelcome patrols.

It's funny, when I look back on that trip, I wonder why I didn't feel any premonition. We were all too tired I suppose, and we felt that the worst was over and we'd done our job and now we deserved a rest. You're sort of brought up to believe that that's the way life should be.

So, at about ten o'clock we set off. We were careful, we travelled slowly, we were as quiet as possible. It was about midnight when we rode up my familiar driveway, bypassing the house and going straight to the garage. The Landrover was hidden in the bush, but I wanted some more tools from the shed. I switched the bike off and put it on its stand then turned the corner into the big machinery shed.

What I saw there was like one of those Christmas tableaus at church, with Joseph and Mary and the shepherds and stuff, standing in their positions, life-like but frozen. The tableau in our shed was lit by a

279

dim torch, its batteries starting to weaken. Kevin was sitting against an old woolpress that was up against the wall. Crouched beside him was Robyn, with one hand on his shoulder. Chris was standing on his other side, looking down at Corrie. Corrie was lying across Kevin's lap. Her eyes were closed and her head was back and there was no colour in her face. As I stood there Kevin and Chris and Robyn all turned their faces towards me, but Corrie still didn't open her eyes. I couldn't move. It was as though I too had joined the tableau.

Then Kevin said, 'She's been shot Ellie'.

His voice broke the spell. I ran forward and knelt beside Corrie. I heard the exclamations from Homer and the others as they came into the shed, but I had eyes only for Corrie. There was a little blood coming out of her mouth, tiny bright bubbles of pink blood.

'Where was she hit?' I asked them.

'In the back,' Chris answered. He seemed almost unnaturally calm. Robyn was sobbing soundlessly; Kevin was shaking.

'What are we going to do?' Fi asked, coming forward. I glanced up at her. Her huge eyes seemed to fill her face with shock and horror.

'We'll have to take her into town,' Homer said. 'We know the Hospital's still functioning. We'll have to trust them to look after her. There's no other choice.'

He was right. There wasn't.

'I'll get the Landie,' I said, standing up.

'No,' Homer said swiftly. 'The Merc's still here. It's closer and it'll give her a better ride.'

I ran to get it. I backed it into the shed and jumped out to help lift Corrie in. But they didn't need me for that; they moved her carefully and slowly into the back seat. Then we stuffed the footspace with hessian sacks, and jammed cushions all around her, so she couldn't roll or move. I choked on my sobs as I watched her lying there, her chest slowly rising and falling with each gurgling breath. This was my dear Corrie, my lifelong friend. If Homer was my brother, Corrie was my sister. Her face looked so calm, but I felt that there was a terrible war being waged inside her body, a fight to the death. I straightened up and turned to the others. Homer was speaking.

'This is going to sound cruel,' he said, 'but the only thing to do is to take her to the gate of the Hospital, abandon the car with Corrie in it, ring the bell, and run like hell. We've got to try to think rationally about it. Seven people are better than six. If we lose not just Corrie but someone else too, well, it weakens us badly. Not to mention the unpleasant questions that person would have to face.'

Kevin stood. 'No,' he said. 'No. I don't give a stuff what's rational and what's logical. Corrie's my mate and I'm not going to dump her and run. It has to be me or Ellie because we're the only drivers, and Ellie, if you don't mind, I want to do it.'

I didn't say anything, didn't move. I couldn't.

Kevin walked around to the driver's seat and got in. Fi leaned through the window and kissed him. He held her arm briefly then let it go.

'Good luck Kevin,' Lee said.

'Yes,' Homer echoed, as the car started to reverse. 'Luck Kevin.'

Chris patted the bonnet of the car. Robyn was crying too much to speak. I ran around the front of the car and leaned in Kevin's window, walking with the car as it continued to back.

'Kevin,' I said. 'Give my love to Corrie.'

'Sure will,' he answered.

'And to you Kevin.'

'Thanks Ellie.'

The car was out in the open and making its turn. He put it in first and turned on the lights and drove away. I could see the concentration in his face as he avoided the bumps in the driveway. I knew Corrie was in good hands, and I understood the lights too. I stood watching until the red tailspots had disappeared in the distance.

'Let's go home,' Homer said, 'to Hell.'

Epilogue

It's hard to work out where stories begin – I seem to remember saying that at the start of this one. And it's hard to work out where they end, too. Our story hasn't ended yet. We've been holed up here for a week since Kevin drove away with Corrie in the back seat. I've been writing frantically all that time, but the others have been up on Tailor's Stitch a lot, checking around. There's no sign of any patrols yet, so we think Kevin's been able to fake them out with some story about where he and Corrie were hiding. That camping stuff was still under the Masonic Hall, so maybe he remembered that and made good use of it.

We don't talk about the other possibilities, that Kevin didn't even get as far as the Hospital, for example. We just don't know what's happened, but I pray my guts out a dozen times a day for them. If I go an hour without thinking about them, I feel guilty.

I'm glad I got this up to date. Guess I'll have to show it to the others now. Hope they like it. It's a big thing to leave a record, to be remembered. I keep thinking about the Hermit's tin box. Without that we'd have known nothing about him, except the rumours, which really told us so little.

I don't know how long we'll be here. Maybe as long as the Hermit. We've got the chooks, and we've planted vegetables, and we still hope to get ferrets and nets. That's where Kevin and Corrie went that night, to Kevin's uncle's, to get some. They didn't even see the soldiers who shot them. Suddenly there were bullets flying, and Corrie got hit. Kevin ran back, picked her up, and carried her all the way to my place.

Loyalty, courage, goodness. I wonder if they're human inventions too, or if they just are.

I look around me. There's Homer, making lists and drawing plans. God knows what he's got in mind for us. Robyn's reading the Bible. She prays quietly every night. I like Robyn and I like how strong she is in her beliefs. Chris is writing too, probably a poem. I don't understand any of the ones he's shown me so far – I don't know if he understands them himself – but I try to make intelligent comments about them. Fi's putting in some posts for a bigger chookyard. Lee's sitting next to me, trying to make a rabbit trap. It doesn't look as if it'd catch any rabbit with an IQ of more than 10, but who knows? Maybe rabbits have IQs in single figures. Anyway I like the way Lee stops every few minutes to stroke my leg with his lean brown fingers.

We've got to stick together, that's all I know. We all drive each other crazy at times, but I don't want to end up here alone, like the Hermit. Then this really would be Hell. Humans do such terrible things to each other that sometimes my brain tells me they must be evil. But my heart still isn't convinced.

I just hope we can survive.

Author's Note

The settings in this book are based on real places. Hell is a reasonably accurate description of Terrible Hollow, in the Australian Alps, near Mt Howitt in Victoria. Small cliffs, like steps, descend into the hollow, and are known as the Devil's Staircase. Tailor's Stitch is the Crosscut Saw, a long ridge of rock which runs for miles from Mt Howitt to Mt Speculation, through Big Hill and Mt Buggery. It is a particularly beautiful route for bushwalkers, and gives good views into the Terrible Hollow.

It is generally accepted by locals that a hermit did live in or around Mt Howitt and the Terrible Hollow for many years. There were eyewitness sightings, particularly in the late 1970s. In 1986 a hiker, Scott Vickers-Willis, found a beautifully carved handmade walking stick concealed in a bush on the edge of the Terrible Hollow. I have seen this stick, which is still in Mr Vickers-Willis' possession; its discovery, in such a remote and wild part of the world, lends startling support to the hermit theory.

Other locations used in *Tomorrow, When the War Began*, include China Walls, a rugged mountainous area on private farmland near Khancoban in NSW, and the long wooden bridge across the Murrumbidgee River at Gundagai in NSW. Generally though the settings used in this book could be found in any Australian State.

John Marsden
The Dead of the Night

There was a crashing sound from the bushes. I spun round, wondering if this was my death, the last movement I would ever make, the last sight I would see . . .

It's tough surviving in Hell. But sometimes Hell can be a haven.

Their country has been invaded. Their homes have been occupied by strangers. Their families are facing death at the hands of a merciless enemy. Only one group of teenagers – fugitives in a remote valley – will never give in.

But courage can demand too high a price . . .

The electrifying sequel to *Tomorrow When the War Began*.

John Marsden
A Killing Frost

The bloke read a lot of stuff. It was about how I'd destroyed property, committed acts of terrorism, murdered people; and I'd been sentenced to death. Sentence to be carried out next Monday at 11 a.m.

They are a handful of teenagers against a brutal invading army. An encmy that has stolen their land, seized their homes and wrecked their future.

The time has come to fight back. To damage the invaders in a way they will never forget.

The plan is insanely bold. The ultimate test of courage. But will it require the ultimate sacrifice?

The stunningly powerful sequel to *Tomorrow When the War Began* and *The Dead of the Night*.

John Marsden
Darkness, Be My Friend

That's what war does to you. Either kills you in one go or destroys you bit by bit. One way or the other, it gets you.

Unless you go back and face the nightmare. Unless you go back and stand up for your dreams.

In an enemy-occupied land, five teenagers return to fight – for their country, their families and their future. But most of all, for their self-respect.

The fourth book in an electrifying series about lives changed for ever in a world at war.

John Marsden
Letters from the Inside

Dear Tracey
I don't know why I'm answering your ad, to be honest. It's not like I'm into pen pals, but it's a boring Sunday here, wet, everyone's out, and I thought it'd be something different . . .

Dear Mandy
Thanks for writing. You write so well, much better than me. I put the ad in for a joke, like a dare, and yours was the only good answer . . .

Two teenage girls. An innocent beginning to friendship. Two complete strangers who get to know each other a little better each time a letter is written and answered.

Mandy has a dog with no name, an older sister, a creepy brother, and some boy problems. Tracey has a horse, two dogs and a cat, an older sister and a great boyfriend. They both have hopes and fears . . . and secrets.

'John Marsden's *Letters from the Inside* is, in a word, unforgettable. But this epistolary novel deserves more than one word. It is absolutely shattering as it brings to vivid life two teenage girls and then strangles your heart over what happens to their relationship . . . John Marsden is a major writer who deserves world-wide acclaim.'
Robert Cormier